# A Child of the Revolution

by

## Baroness Orczy

# Contents

This is the story which Sir Percy Blakeney, Bart., told to His Royal highness that evening in the Assembly Rooms at Bath.

The talk was of the recent events in France, the astounding fall of Robespierre: the change in the whole aspect of the unfortunate country: and His Royal Highness expressed his opinion that among all those men who had made and fostered the Revolution, there was not one who was anything but a scoundrel, a reprobate, a murderer, and worker of iniquity.

Sir Percy then remarked: "I would not say that, sir. I have known men–"

"You, Blakeney?" His Royal Highness broke in, with an incredulous laugh.

"Even I, sir. May I tell you of one, at least, whose career I happened to follow with great interest?"

And that is how the story came to be told.

# Book I

## Chapter I

"In Heaven's name, what has happened to the child?"

This exclaimed Marianne Vallon when, turning from her washtub, she suddenly caught sight of André at the narrow garden gate.

"In Heaven's name!" she reiterated, but only to herself, for Marianne was not one to give vent to her feelings before anyone, not even before her own son.

She raised her apron and wiped her large, ruddy face first and then her big, capable hands, all dripping with soapsuds; after which she stumped across the yard to the gate: her sabots clacked loudly against the stones, for Marianne Vallon was a good weight and a fair bulk; her footsteps were heavy, and her movements slow.

No wonder that the good soul was, inwardly, invoking the name of Heaven, for never in all his turbulent life had André come home looking such a terrible object. His shirt and his breeches were hanging in strips; his feet, his legs, the whole of his body, and even his face, were plastered with mud and blood. Yes, blood! Right across his forehead, just missing his right eye, fortunately, there was a deep gash from which the blood was still oozing and dripping down his nose. His lip was cut and his mouth swollen out of all recognition.

"In Heaven's name!" she reiterated once more, and aloud this time, "thou little good-for-nothing, what mischief hast thou been in now?"

Marianne waited for no explanation; obviously the boy was not in a fit state to give her any. She just seized him by the wrist and dragged him to her washtub. It was not much Marianne Vallon knew of nursing or dressing of wounds, but her instinct of cleanliness probably saved

André life this day, as it had done many a time before. Despite his protests, she stripped him to the skin; then she started scrubbing.

Soap and water stung horribly, and André yelled as much with impatience as with pain; he fought like a young demon, but his mother, puffing like a fat pug dog, imperturbable and energetic, scrubbed away until she was satisfied that no mud or dirt threatened the festering of wounds. She ended by holding the tousled young head under the pump, swilling it and the lithe, muscular body down with plenty of cold water.

"Now dry thyself over there in the sun," she commanded finally, satisfied that in his present state of dripping nudity he couldn't very well get into mischief again. Then, apparently quite unruffled by the incident, she went back to her washtub. This sort of thing happened often enough; sometimes with less, once or twice with even more disastrous results. Marianne Vallon never asked questions, knowing well enough that the boy would blurt out the whole story all in good time: she didn't even glance round at him as he law stretched out full length, arms and legs outspread, as perfect a specimen of the young male as had ever stirred a mother's pride, the warm July sun baking his skin to a deeper shade of brown and glinting on the ruddy gold of the curls which clustered above his forehead and all around his ears.

"What a beautiful boy!" strangers had been heard to exclaim when they happened to pass down the road and caught sight of André Vallon bending to some hard task in garden or field.

"What a beautiful boy!" more than one mother in the village had sighed before now, half in tenderness, half in envy. And "André Vallon is so handsome!" tall girls not yet out of their teens would whisper, giggling, to one another. If Marianne Vallon's heart swelled with pride when she overheard some of this praise, she never showed it. No one really knew what went on behind that large red face of hers, which some wag in the village had once compared to a bladder of lard. People called her hard and unfeeling because she was not wont to indulge in those "Mon Dieu!'s" and "Sainte Vierge!'s" when she passed the time of day with her neighbours, or in any of the "Mon chou's" and "Mon pigeon's" when she spoke to her André.

She just went about her business in and around her cottage, or at the château when she wanted up there to do the washing, uncomplaining, untiring, making the most of the meagre pittance which was all that was left to her now of a once substantial fortune. Her husband had died a comparatively rich man—measured by village standards, of course. He had left his widow a roomy cottage, with its bit of garden and a few hectares of land whereon she could plant her cabbages, cultivate her vines, keep a few chickens and graze a cow. But, bit by bit, the land had to be sold in order to meet the ever growing burden of taxes, of seignorial dues, to be paid by those who had so little to others who seemed to have so much, of tithes and rents and rights, all falling on the shoulders of the poor toilers of the land, while the seigneurs were exempt from all taxation. Then came two lean years—drought lasting seven months in each case, resulting in a total failure of the crops and poor quality of the wine. André was ten when the last piece of land was sold, which his father had acquired and his mother tended with the sweat of her brow; he was twelve when first he saw his mother stooping over her own washtub. Hitherto, Annette from down the village had come daily to do the rough work of the household; then one day she didn't come. André took no notice. It was nothing to him that at dinner time it was his mother who brought in the soup tureen, that it was she who carried away the plates and the knives, and that she disappeared into the kitchen after dinner instead of sitting in the old wing chair sipping her glass of wine, the one luxury she had indulged in of late. Annette or Maman, what cared he who brought him his dinner? He was just a child.

But when he saw his mother at the washtub with a huge coarse apron round her portly person, her sleeves tucked up above those powerful arms, the weight of which he had so often felt on the rear part of his person when he had been a naughty boy, then he began to ask questions.

And Marianne told him. He was only twelve at the time, and she did not mince matters. The sooner he knew, the better. The sooner he spared her those direct questions and those inquiring looks out of his great dark eyes, the sooner, she thought, would he become a fine man. So she told him that the patrimony which his father had left in trust for him had all dwindled away, bit by bit, because the tax collector's visits were getting more and more frequent, the sums demanded more and more beyond her capacity to pay. There were the imposts due to the seigneur, and the tallage levied by the King; there were the rates due to the commune, and the tithes due to the Church.

Pay! Pay! Pay! It was that all the time. And two years' drought, during which, the small revenues from the diminished land had shrunk only too palpably. Pay! Pay! Pay! And there were the seignorial rights. No corn or wine or live stock allowed to be sold in the market until Monseigneur's wine and corn and live stock, which he wished to sell, had all been disposed of. No wine press or mill to be used, except those set up by Monseigneur and administered by his bailiffs, who charged usurious prices for their use. Pay! Pay! Pay! It was best that André should know. He was twelve—almost a man. It was time that he knew.

And André had listened while Maman talked on that cold December afternoon three years ago, when the fire no longer blazed in the wide-open hearth because wood was scarce and no one was allowed to purchase any until Monseigneur's requirements were satisfied. André had listened, with those great inquiring eyes fixed upon his mother, his fingers buried in the forest of his chestnut curls, and his brows closely knit in the great endeavour to take it all in. He wanted to understand; to understand poverty as his mother explained it to him: the want of flour with which to make bread, the want of wood wherewith to make a fire, even the want of a bit of thread or a needle, simple tools with which his breeches and shirts—which were forever torn—could, as heretofore, be mended.

Poor? Yes, he was beginning to understand that he and Maman were now poor as Annette and her father down in the village were poor, so that Annette had to go and scrub floors in other people's houses and wash other people's soiled linen so as to bring a few sous home every day wherewith to buy salt and bread. Not that this primitive idea of poverty worried the young brain overmuch. It was not like a sudden descent from affluence to indigence. It was some time now since his favourite dishes had been put upon the table and since he had last wore a pair of shoes. The descent into the present slough of want had been very gradual, and, childlike, he had not noticed it.

Nor did his mother's lengthened homily make a very deep impression upon his mind. From a race of children of the soil he had inherited a sound measure of philosophy and a passionate love of the countryside. While he could run about in the meadows, or watch the rabbits at evening scurrying away across the fields, while he could pick black berries in the hedgerows and gather the windfalls in the neighbouring orchards, while he could scramble up the old walnut trees and furtively touch the warm smooth eggs in the nests among the branches, he was perfectly happy.

What he didn't like was when Marianne set him to do the tasks, which used to devolve on Annette. He didn't like scrubbing the kitchen floor, and he hated wringing out the linen and hanging it up to dry. But it never as much entered his dead to disobey. Mother was not one of those whom anyone had ever though of disobeying, André least of all. She was large and fat and comfortable, and—especially in the olden days—she loved a good joke and would laugh heartily till the tears rolled down her fat cheeks, but she knew how to use the flat of her hand, as André had often learned to his cost. She was not one of those who believed in sparing the rod, and many a time had André gone to sleep on his narrow plank bed lying on his side because it hurt him to lie on his back.

But the fear of his mother's heavy hand did not really keep him out of mischief. As he grew older the desire for mischief grew up with him. A vague sense of injustice would, moreover, inflame that desire until it led him to acts which caused not only Mother's hand to descend upon him, but, also, of a certain hard stick, which was very painful indeed. That time when he chased Lucile Godart, the miller's daughter, all down the road and then kissed her in sigh of Hector Talon, her fiancé, who was short, fat, and bandy-legged, and was too slow in his movements to come to her rescue, was a memorable occasion, for, though Hector had not felt sufficiently valiant to administer punishment to the young rascal, Godart, the miller, had no such qualms. And André got his punishment twice over, Mother's being by far the more severe. But he said that it was worth it. To kiss a girl, he declared, when she is placid and willing was well enough, but when she was a little spitfire like Lucile and fought and scratched like a wildcat, then to hold her down, kiss her throat and shoulder and, finally, her mouth, that was as great a lark as ever came a man's way—and well worth a whipping, or even two. What Lucile thought about it he neither knew or cared.

# Chapter II

The incident with Lucile Godart had occurred two years ago. André was thirteen then, and already the girls were wont to blush when their eyes met his, so dark and bold.

Since the Lucile had married her Hector, who was now an assistant bailiff on Monseigneur's estate and lived with his young wife in a stone house on the edge of the wood. At the side of the house there was a field, which at eventide was alive with rabbits. That field exercised an irresistible fascination over André Vallon. He would cower behind the hedge and for hours watch the little cottontails bobbing in and out of the scrub. More than once, he had been warned off by Hector Talon; once he had actually been caught unawares and driven off with some hard kicks.

But today a tragedy had occurred.

Lying on his back at this moment on the hard stones not far from his mother's washtub, and in the state in which God first made him, he was perhaps wondering whether in this instance the game was going to be worth the candle. He was too old now to get a whipping from Mother, and he did not think that what he had done was punishable by law. Still, Hector Talon was a spiteful beast, and Lucile... Well, the little she-devil would get her deserts one day, on the faith of André Vallon.

While the hot July sun was baking his skin and staunching the blood of his wounds, his brain was working away on the possible consequences of today's adventure. He wondered what his mother thought about it. For the moment she appeared to be immersed, both with hands and with mind, in her washtub. Her broad back was turned towards him, and André thought that it looked uncompromising. Still, Mother would have to know sooner or later, so better now, perhaps, while she was busy with other things. And before he knew that he had begun to think aloud, words were pouring out of him a kind of passionate outburst of resentment.

"Rabbits! Rabbits! Why! There are thousands and thousands of them in that field," he went on with childish sense of exaggeration. "M. Talon himself is obliged to put fencing round his kitchen garden to keep them away. And I didn't put up any snare or trap—I swear I didn't. There was nobody about, and I just got over the fence to see.... Well, I don't know. I just did get over the fence, and there in the long grass was the tiniest wee rabbit you ever saw! He was all crouching together till he looked like a ball of brown fur, and his round eyes were wide open, looking—I suppose he was horribly frightened—so frightened that he couldn't move. Anyway, I just stooped to pick him up. The house was all quiet, there didn't seem to be any one at home, and that brute of a dog of theirs was on the chain."

André paused a moment; his hand had gone mechanically up to his forehead, to his lips, his shoulder, all of which were smarting horribly. Perhaps, he thought, it was time Mother said something, but she just went on with her washing, and all that André saw of her was that large, uncompromising back.

"How could I guess?" the boy went on; and suddenly he sat up, his brown arms encircling his knees, his chest striped with the red of the blood oozing from his shoulder. "How could I guess that that little vixen Lucile was spying from the window? I had got the young beggar by the ears, and I remember just thinking at the moment what luscious strew he was going to make. Of course, I had no intention of putting him down again, and I was trying to tuck him out of sight inside my shirt. And then, all of a sudden, I heard Lucile's voice calling to that dog of hers: 'Hue! César! hue!' What a devil! My god! What a devil! That great brute César! He was on me before I could drop the rabbit and take to my heels. He was on me and got me on the shoulder. Then I did drop the rabbit, and it scooted away. I wanted both my hands to defend myself. I knew it would be no use trying to run, and César would have had me by the throat if I hadn't got him. And there was that little devil Lucile, running down the field and shouting, 'Hue! Hue!' all the time."

André was warming to his story. He was fighting his battle with César over again. His nostrils quivered; perspiration glistened on his forehead; his eyes, wide open and dilated, were as dark as the blackberries in the hedgerows.

"I got César by the throat," he went on in a shaky, hoarse voice, his words coming out jerkily, interspersed with gasps that were half laughter and half tears. "I squeezed and I squeezed, and all the while his horrid hot breath made me feel so sick that I thought I should have to let go. Once he got me on the forehead, and once I felt his nasty slimy teeth right inside my mouth. That gave me the strength to squeeze tighter, for I thought that I didn't he would probably kill me. Then that little devil Lucile began to laugh, and I could hear bits of words that she said, 'That will teach you to insult honest girls. César also thinks it a lark to get a boy down and kiss him on the shoulder, what? And on the mouth. Hue, César! Hue!' Isn't she a troll, Mother, a witch, a vixen, a she-devil, nursing vengeance like this for two years—or is it three? —but I'll kiss her again. I will! And what's more, I will..."

Once more André paused. His mother's broad back was still turned towards him, but she had turned her head, and through the corner of her eye she was looking at him. That is why he did not complete the sentence or put into words the ugly thought that had taken root in his brain. He remained quite still and silent for a moment or two, then he said abruptly:

"I never let go of César's throat till I had squeezed the life out of him."

But at this bald statement of fact, Marianne Vallon's outward placidity gave way. "Jésus! Mon Dieu!" she exclaimed, and faced that naked young daredevil with horror and anxiety distorting her squab features. "Not content with poaching in M. Talon's field, thou hast killed his dog?"

"He would have killed me else. Wouldst rather César had killed me, Mother?" André retorted with an indifferent shrug of his lean shoulders.

"Don't be a fool, André!" Marianne Vallon went on once more, in her usual placid way. "M. Talon—dost not know it?—Has only to go before the magistrate and denounce thee—"

"Well, they can't hang me for killing a dog in self-defence, and I didn't poach the rabbit."

"No, but they can..."

It was the mother's turn to leave the phrase incomplete, which involuntarily had come to her lips. Just like André a moment ago, she did not wish to put into words the thoughts that had come tumbling into her brain and were filling her heart with the foreknowledge of a calamity which she knew she could not avert.

If she could she would have packed André off somewhere, to friends, relations, anywhere; away from the spite of Talon, who already had a grudge against the child and who would feel doubly vindictive now. But when Marianne Vallon first fell on evil days she lost touch with her former friends or relations, who, in their turn, were content to forget her. André must stop at home and face the calamity like a man.

It came soon enough.

Talon, who was a man of consideration in the commune, laud a complaint before M. le Substitut against André Vallon for poaching and savage assault on a valuable dog, resulting in the latter's death.

André, in consideration of his youth—he was only fifteen—was condemned to be publicly whipped. M. le Substitut told him that he could consider himself most fortunate in being let off with so mild a punishment.

# Chapter III

A blind unreasoning rage, an irresistible thirst for revenge; a black hatred of all those placed in authority; of all those who were rich, or independent, or influential, filled André Vallon's young soul to the exclusion of every other thought and every other aspiration.

He was only fifteen, and in his mind he measured the long years that lay before him in which he could find the means, the power, to be even with those who had inflicted that overwhelming shame upon him. It was not the blows he minded.... Heavens above! That lithe, young body of his was inured to every kind of hardship, to every kind of pain. It was not the blows, it was the shame. Talon, who was influential and who was egged on by his wife, had prevailed upon the magistrate to make an order that all the inhabitants of the commune who were not engaged in work were to be present in the market place to see justice done on the young reprobate. And these were still the days when no one dared go against an order, however absurd and however unjust, framed by M. le Substitut du Procureeur Général.

Monseigneur also came in his coach and brought friends to see the spectacle. There were two ladies among them who put up their lorgnettes and stared at the straight, sinewy young body, so like a statue of the Hermes with its slender, perfectly modelled limbs and narrow hips, and its broad shoulders and wide chest, smooth and dark as if cast in bronze.

"But the boy is an Adonis!" one of the ladies exclaimed in ecstasy.

"Quelle horreur!" she exclaimed a moment later when the stripes fell thick and fast on the smooth back she had admired. The days were not yet very far distant when ladies of high degree would crowed on balconies and windows to watch the execution of conspirators who perhaps had been their friends before then.

But for André Vallon, the bitter, humiliating shame!

His mother was waiting for him when he got home. She had prepared a little bit of hot supper for him, to which sympathisers in the village had also contributed: things he liked—a little hot soup, a baked potato, a bit of bread and salts. André ate because he was a young, healthy animal and was hungry, but he never said a word. Silent and sullen, he sat and ate. Not a tear came to those big dark eyes of his, in which there burned a fierce hatred and an overpowering humiliation.

Marianne, of course, said nothing. It was never her way to talk. She saw to it that André had his supper, and when he had finished she took him by the wrist and led him to his little room at the back. She undressed him and washed and dried his poor aching young body; then she wrapped him up in one of her wide gingham skirts which had become soft as silk after many washings, and laid him down on his narrow plank bed with his head resting on an old coat of his father's, which had survived the dispersal of most of the household goods. Before she had finished tucking him up in her wool shawl he was asleep.

She watched for a moment or two the beautiful young face, with the blue-veined lids veiling in sleep the sullen, glowering look of the eyes; stooped and softly touched the moist forehead with her lips. Two heavy tears found their way down her furrowed cheeks; a heavy sigh came though the firm obstinate lips, and slowly she came down on her knees. With clasped hands flung across the bed, she remained kneeling there for some time, praying for guidance, for strength to fight a brave fight with this turbulent young soul, and for power to guide it in the path of rectitude.

This was the year of grace 1782, and Marianne Vallon, in common with many men and women in the land these days, was not blind to the tempest which already was gathering force in every corner of France, framed by the ardour of young enthusiasts with a grievance like her André, or by the greed of profligate agitators, soon to burst in all its fury, sweeping before it all the old traditions, the old beliefs, the old righteousness of this country and its people, and inflicting wounds that it would take centuries to heal.

# Chapter IV

M. le Curé de Val-le-Roi, in the province of Burgundy, where they make such excellent wine, was a kindly and worthy man. He came of a good family—the Rosemondes of Nièvre, and though his intelligence was perhaps not of the highest order, his piety was sincere and his human understanding very real.

On the tragic day of André Vallon's public punishment he stood beside the whipping post the whole time that Marius Legendre—the local butcher employed by the Commune to administer punishment to juvenile offenders—was lamming into the boy. André, with teeth set and eyes resolutely closed, appeared not to hear the Curé's gentle words, exhorting him to patience and humility.

Patience and humility, forsooth! Never was there a vainer exhortation.

It was only when it was all over and he was freed from the post that André opened his eyes and cast a glowering, rankling look around the market square. Legendre had thrown down the whip and was handing the lad his shirt and coat. André snatched them out of his hand, and Legendre—a worthy man, not unkind—smiled indulgently. The two gendarmes stood at attention, waiting for orders, their faces wooden and impassive. Part of the crowd had already dispersed: the men silent and sullen, the women sniffing audibly. The younger ones—girls and boys—muttered words of pity or of wrath. Monseigneur was standing beside the door of his coach, helping the ladies to step back into the carriage. One of them—the one with the largnette—cast a final backward glance at André; then piped in a highpitched, flutelike voice:

"See, my dear Charles, so would a fallen angel have looked had the Almighty punished the rebels with thongs."

A man in the forefront of the crowd, close to Monseigneur's coach, laughed obsequiously at the sally. André saw him. It was Talon. Lucile stood beside her husband. When she met André's glance, she, too, gave a laugh, but quickly turned her head away. Then only did a groan rise from the boy's breast. It was a groan of an overwhelming, impotent rage. His breath came whistling through his teeth. He made a movement like a wild beast about to spring, but instinctively the gendarmes had already placed each a hand upon his shoulder and held him down. André was weak after the punishment, though he would not have admitted it even to himself; but his knees shook under him, and he nearly collapsed under the heavy hands of the gendarmes. M. le Curé murmured gentle words. "My son, remember that our Lord—"

André turned on him with a cry that was like a snarl. "Go away! Go away!" he muttered hoarsely. "I hate you."

But the Curé did not go away. He stayed to help the lad on with his shirt and coat; then, when André, avoiding the crowd, went staggering round a back street and then down the lane towards his mother's cottage, the kindly old priest followed him at a short distance, ready to render assistance should the boy be seized with giddiness and collapse on the way. Only when he saw Marianne standing at the narrow garden gate waiting for her son did he went his way back to his presbytery. Contrary to his usual habit, he did not take his breviary out of his pocket or murmur orisons while he walked. With his soutane hitched up around his waist, he strode along, obviously buried in thought, for now and again he would shake his head and then nod, as if in secret communion with himself.

The results of M. le Curé's agitation were, firstly, a lengthy interview with Monseigneur, and secondly a summons to Marianne Vallon to bring her son André up to the château. Monseigneur desired to see him.

André, of course, refused to go. "I hate him!" he declared when M. le Curé came to announce what he thought was great news for Marianne and the boy.

"Monseigneur," the priest had explained, "was interested. He is always so kind and so gracious, but when I spoke to him of André he was pleased to be genial, facetious; he toyed, as one might say, with the idea of doing something for the boy. Then there were the ladies. Madame la Marquise d'Epinay put in a word here and there, so charming she was, so sprightly. She spoke of André as the bronze Hermes, and though the latter we know is nothing but a heathen god, and I would not care to think that our André had any likeness to such idolatrous things, I could not have it in my heart to reprove the witty lady, especially as Monseigneur appeared more and more diverted. Then Mademoiselle Aurore came in—such a pretty child—her governess was with her, and I gathered at once she knew something about our André—domestics will talk, you know, my good Marianne—and Mademoiselle was even more interested than Monseigneur. She put her little hands together and begged and begged of her father that André might come up to the château, as she desired to see him. And Monseigneur, who since the death of Madame la Duchesse gives in to all the child's whims, gave me permission to bring our André to him."

The good Curé spoke thus lengthily and uninterruptedly, for Marianne, absorbed in her knitting, said never a word: she was never much of a talker, and André only glowered and muttered unintelligible words between his teeth. There was perhaps something a little unctuous, a little complacent in M. le Curé's verbiage. He was not forgetting that besides being the incumbent of this poor little village, he was also by birth a Rosemonde de Nièvre, and that by tradition and upbringing he belonged to the same caste as Monseigneur le Duc de Marigny de Borne, whose gracious sympathy in favour of "our André" he had been fortunate enough to arouse.

"I hate him! I will not go!" was all that could be got out of André that day. "You can drag me to that accursed château," he went on sullenly, "as you did to the whipping post, but willingly I will not go."

"But, my dear child," the Curé protested, "Monseigneur said—"

"Whatever he said," the boy broke in with a snarl, like an animal that is being teased, "may his words choke him!—I hate him!"

"You are overwrought and agitated, my boy," the priest said placing his well manicured podgy white hand on André's shoulder, who promptly shook it off. "When the good God and your dear patron saint have prevailed over your rebellious spirit, you will realize how much Monseigneur's kindness and Mademoiselle Aurore's intercession—"

"Don't speak to me of those women up at the château," André cried hoarsely, "or I shall see red!"

Marianne Vallon at this point put down her knitting. She knew well enough that to carry on the discussion any further today would only drive the boy to exasperation. All that he had gone through in the past few days had, in a way, made a man of him, but a man with all a child's unreasoning resentment at what he deemed an injustice.

M. le Curé took the hint. With characteristic tact he changed the subject of conversation, spoke to Marianne on village matters—the washing of surplices which she had undertaken to do for a small stipend, and finally took his leave, deliberately ignoring André's ill manners and glowering looks. At the door, however, he turned once more to where the boy sat, chin cupped in his hand, staring dully into the gathering shadows.

"Remember, my dear child," he said with gentle earnestness; all his small, worldly ways drowned in a flood of genuine sympathy, "that your future does not belong entirely to yourself: your sainted mother works her fingers to the bone so that you should be clothed and fed. She performs menial tasks, to which neither by birth nor upbringing was she ever ordained. Think of her, my lad, before you spurn the hand that can help you up the ladder that may lead you to an honourable career and give you the chance of repaying part of your debt to her."

Mother and son spoke little to each other during the rest of the day. Marianne appeared more than usually busy with knitting and sewing and spoke even less than was her wont. After sundown André went out from a tramp in woods and fields. Ever since the fatal day he had made a point of wandering over the countryside only after dark. He dreaded to meet familiar faces in the country lanes, dreaded to see either compassion or ridicule in the glances that would meet his.

Tonight his young soul was brimful with bitterness. Never before had he felt such an all-embracing hatred for everything, and every human being who had made possible the humiliation that had been put upon him. Childlike, he wandered down the lane past the house where lived talon and his wife, the prime authors of the whole tragedy. He stood for a long time looking at the house. There were lights in one or two of the window. The Talons were rich; they could afford candles. They were people of consideration. They got the ear of the Substitut and engineered his, André's, lasting disgrace. He hated them—hated their house, their garden, their flowers; he wished with all his might that some awful calamity would overtake them.

The fields around were bathed in moonlight; the air was fragrant and warm; a gentle breeze fluttered the branches of the forest trees, causing a gentle murmur to fill the night with its subtle sound. The scent of hay and clover rose from the adjoining meadows, and from the depths of the wood there came from to time the melancholy call of a night bird or the crackling of trigs under tiny, furtive feet.

Only a very few days ago André would have revelled in all that: the little cottontails scurrying past, the bard-door owl flying by with great flapping of wings; fantastically shaped clouds veiling from time to time the face of the moon. All would have delighted him, those few short days ago. Now he had eyes only for that house of evil. He watched its windows till the lights were extinguished one by one, and then wished once more with all his might that hideous nightmares should disturb the sleep of those whom he hated so bitterly.

# Chapter V

When André finally turned to go home again, it was close on midnight. Coming in sight of the cottage, he was surprised to see that, contrary to his mother's rigid rules of economy, there was still a light in the parlour. He pushed open the door and peeped in. Mother was sitting sewing by the light of a tallow candle. She looked up as he came in and gave him a welcoming smile. He thought she looked quite old, and her eyes were circled with red, as if she had been crying. But he pretended not to notice. Still, it was funny, her burning a candle so late at night when candles were so dear. And why did she look so tired and so old?

He asked no questions, however. Somehow he didn't feel as if he could say anything just then. He knew that presently his mother would come into his room to hear him say his prayers, to tuck him up in the old wool shawl and give him a last goodnight kiss. Of late he had refused to say his prayers. Le bon Dieu, he thought, only bothered Himself about rich and powerful people—nobles, bishops, and such like—s what was the good of murmuring prayers that were never listened to and asking for things that were never granted? When Mother said her prayers as usual beside his bed in spite of his obstinacy, he turned his head sullenly away. He had even caught himself wishing that she would leave him alone, once he was in bed: alone, nursing his thoughts of future retribution on all those whom he hated so.

Strange that he never had the desire to talk to his mother about all that went on in his mind these days. Strange, seeing that hitherto he had always blurted out everything that troubled him, poured into her patient ear the full stories of his peccadilloes, his adventures, anything and everything that passed through his mind. But now André had succeeded in persuading himself that his mother would not understand his feelings. She was, he thought, so patient and so devout that she would not sympathize with a man—a man!—who had been so deeply injured as himself. He felt that he had suddenly become a man—a man suffering an infinite wrong; and that Mother was only a woman, weak under the influence of priests and of their everlasting teachings of gentleness and humility. Men couldn't be gentle these days. They had suffered too long and too bitterly: crying wrongs, injustice that called to heaven for vengeance—only that heaven wouldn't hear. Well, if le bon Dieu wouldn't help the poor and the downtrodden to defend them selves against injustice, then they would fight on their own without help from anywhere.

Monseigneur and his sycophants! And those women with their perfumes and their silk dresses and their lorgnettes and their high-pitched voices! André hoped to God that he would live long enough to see them all eat the bread of humiliation as he himself had been forced to do.

At this point in his meditations Mother did come in. André did not hear her at first, for she had taken off her sabots and was in her stockinged feet. It was only when she stood close beside his bed that he turned his head and saw her.

Of course, he felt sorry for her. Women were women, and therefore weaker vessels, unable to take in the vast thoughts and projects of men. But they were dear gentle creatures whose ministrations were essential to the wellbeing of the stronger, more intellectual sex. Therefore André felt very kindly disposed towards his mother just now: he would not have admitted for the world, even to himself, that at sight of her dear old face, with its furrowed cheeks and eyes to often stern, and yet always full of love, a great yearning seized him to bury his head in her ample bosom, to forget his manhood and be a child again. However, all he said for the moment was: "Not yet in bed, Mother? Isn't it very late?"

To which she replied cheerily, "It is, my cabbage, and fully time you were asleep."

She then knelt down beside his bed. André ought then to have jumped out of bed and knelt beside her to say his prayers. This had always been the rule every since he was old enough to babble his "Gentle Jesus, meek and mild..." and clasp his baby hands; even when he began to feel himself a man, he had readily complied with the rule. But for days now, when Mother knelt beside his bed and murmured, "Our Father which art in Heaven," he had turned his head stubbornly away, nor had he looked at her till she had finished her prayers. Tonight, however, though he still felt wrathful and was too big a man to get out of bed, he kept his head turned towards her so that he could see her face. There was such a bright moon outside that he could see her quite plainly: her found flat face, her thin hair already streaked with gray, parted in the middle and fastened in a small tight bun on the top of her head. Her eyes were closed while she prayed with hands tightly clasped, her lips murmuring softly, "Forgive us our trespasses"; then all at once she raised her voice and said quite loudly, "As we forgive them that trespass against us."

"I won't! I won't!" André broke in involuntarily. "I'll never forgive them, never!"

But Marianne did not seem to hear. She finished her prayers and then remained for a time on her knees, gazing on the beautiful young face that meant all the world to her. Almost distorted now with wrath and obstinacy, it was none the less beautiful; with those large dark eyes that seemed forever to be inquiring, to be groping after something unattainable. Marianne's large, capable hand wandered lovingly over the hot, moist forehead and brushed back the unruly curls which fell, rebellious, over the brow. Without another word she pressed a kiss on the eyes, closed as she thought in sleep, and on the mouth through which the young passionate breath came in slow, measured cadence. Then she tiptoed out of the room.

André was not asleep. He had felt the kiss and tasted the salt moisture of his mother's tears on his lips. For a long, long while he remained lying on his back, with widely dilated eyes staring into the darkness above him. Through the chinks in the ill-fitting door he could perceive the feeble light of the tallow candle which still burned in the adjoining room. He heard the old church clock strike one, then the half hour then two. The moon had gone, the tiny room wherein stood the boy's small plank bed was in complete darkness, save for that dim streak of light underneath the door.

As noiselessly as he could André rose and tiptoed across the room. For a few seconds he listened, his ear glued to the keyhole, but all that he could hear was an occasional sigh, and once a sound like a broken sob. The door hung loosely on its hinges, he pulled it open. His mother was still sitting sewing by the feeble candlelight. André, leaning against the door jamb, stood mutely watching her.

She seemed very busy and never looked up once in his direction. She had a pair of breeches in her hands, had evidently been at work on them. Now she fastened off the cotton, broke it off, put down her needle. André watched her. She did look old, and there was a tear which had settled on the tip of her nose. She wiped it off with her apron and then held the breeches up with both hands to see if more darning was needed. Satisfied that they were quite in order, she laid them down on the table, smoothed them out with both hands, then folded them carefully and put them to one side.

André thoughts: "Those are my breeches. She has tired herself out mending them." And the words, which M. le Curé had spoken earlier in the day, came hammering into his brain: "Remember, my child, that your future does not belong entirely to yourself. Your sainted mother works her fingers to the bone that you should be clothed and fed."

That was true, for there she was, working for into the night, mending his breeches, while he...

"Mother!" he said abruptly. "Do you wish me to go up to the château and see those people?"

She didn't give a start; obviously she knew that he was there. She was standing now with one hand resting on the table and peering over into the darkness to try and see him with her blinking, tired eyes.

"André! Why aren't you in bed?" she asked. "Go back at once."

"Mother!" he insisted.

"Yes, André?"

"Do you wish me to go to the château and see those people?"

"It might lead to something good for your future, my child. M. le Curé said that Monseigneur was kindly disposed."

"I have no decent clothes in which to go," the boy muttered, his sullen mood not yet quite gone.

"There are your new stockings which I have quite finished," Marianne rejoined quietly, "and I have done mending your best breeches. You can wear you father's Sunday coat and his buckled shoes—fortunately he was a small man, and you are hear as tall already."

"Mother!" André exclaimed.

"Yes, André?"

"You have been working your fingers to the bone so that I should be clothed. M. le Curé said so."

"No, my child," Marianna said, smiling through an involuntary little sigh, "not to the bone."

"And did you sit up tonight because you—you—"

"I knew that you would want your best breeches—soon."

"You knew I would change my mind and go to the château?"

"Yes, André, I knew."

"How could you know, Mother?"

"I suppose your guardian angel must have told me. He knew."

"Mother!"

This time the cry came straight from the boy's heart. With one bound he was beside his mother and with his arms was encircling her knees. His tousled head was buried in her voluminous skirt. She fell back into her chair and drew the hot, aching young head against her breast. There, resting against that warm, downy pillow, all pretence at manhood was swamped in the grief of a child. André burst into a flood of tears, the first that had welled out of the bitterness of his heart since that awful day of disgrace. Marianne, with her kind fat arms wrapped round her most precious treasure, thanked God for those tears.

The tallow candle flickered and died out. The room was in darkness, only a pale light, the first precursor of dawn, came shyly peeping presently through the small, uncurtained window. The distant church clock struck four. It was more than an hour since Marianne had moved. The child had cried himself to sleep, squatting on the floor, with his head on her lap, her hand resting on his curls. From time to time a sob shook the young frame; then even the sobs were stilled, and Marianne, stiff with sitting motionless, would not move for fear of waking him.

# Chapter VI

If you should ever visit the Bourbonnais do not fail to go as far as Le Borne, on the outskirts of which stands the princely Château de Marigny. It is one of the most sumptuous survivals of medieval splendour, with its unique position on a spur of the Roches du Borne, commanding a gorgeous view over the valley of the Allier with its rippling winding stream, its spreading forests of beech and walnut and sycamore, its vine-clad slopes and picturesque villages—Val-le-Roi, Le Borne, Vanzy, and so on—peeping shyly through the trees.

Originally built in the twelfth century by Jean Duke of Burgundy, it was enlarged and enriched by each of his successors, until the great Duke Charles—known to history as the Connétable de Bourbon—as great in treachery as in doughty deeds, completed the work of making the Château de Marigny second to none in grandeur and magnificence. It was to him that King Henry VIII of England referred when he remarked to François I of France on the occasion of the meeting on the Field of the Cloth of Gold: "If I had so opulent a subject, I would soon have his head off."

François I had no occasion to follow his English friend's advice, for it was soon after that that the illustrious Connétable de Bourbon became a traitor to his country and sold his sword to the enemy of France, which was quite sufficient excuse for the King to declare the Duke's estates forfeit to the Crown. Some of these were subsequently sold and passed from hand to hand. The château, then known as Château de Borne, came into the possession of the Duc de Marigny, first cousin of King Henry of Navarre and a direct descendant of the Connétable who renamed it Marigny and added to his many titles that of De Borne.

Though the magnificence for which the old château was famous in the past—when 'twas said that Duke Charles kept five hundred men-at-arms within its precincts—was somewhat shorn of its dazzling rays, the present Duc de Marigny did, nevertheless, live there like a prince and entertain with lavish hospitality. These were the days, closely following on those of the Grand Monarque, when the king set the pace in splendour and prodigality and the great nobles thought it incumbent on them to emulate royal ostentation. It was the era of beautiful furniture and of exquisite silks and laces, of stately ceremonials both at court and at home, of gorgeous banquets, expensive food and wins, as well as of the aesthetic enjoyment of pictures, music, and the play. Money flowed freely into the coffers of those who had landed estates: the State favoured them, for not only were they free of taxation, but one privilege after another was conferred on them, and, quite naturally, they grasped these with both hands and then asked for more.

Cradled in the lap of luxury, wrapped up in cotton wool by sycophants and menials, they shut their eyes to the gather clouds of the inevitable Revolution. The cataclysm found them unprepared, scared, and astonished, like children wakened out of a dream. Most of them had not done blinking their eyes under the shadow of the guillotine. When they died, they died like heroes. They would have lived like heroes had they been given the lead, had they understood that the distant thunder of growing discontent among the people, the flashed of lightning of menace and revenge, were the precursors of a raging storm that threatened them, their traditions and their caste.

In this year of grace 1782 Monseigneur le Duc de Marigny, one of the richest and most distinguished members of the old French aristocracy, connected with the royal houses of Bourbon and Orléans, was certainly one of those who thought that most things were for the best in this best possible world. The only thing that ever troubled him was the occasional tightness of money. This was an unheard-of thing. The Duc de Marigny, cousin of kinds, short of money! In his father's day, my gad, sir! if there were no Jews to skin there were always those lazy, good-for-nothing peasants whose whole excuse for being alive at all was that they should provide their seigneur with everything he was pleased to want.

Those were the good old days. Now there was nothing but grumbling in the villages. Bad weather, poor harvest, bad luck. Eh, morbleu! Monseigneur knew well enough that the harvests were poor. If they weren't, he wouldn't be so terribly short of money; just when Aurore's birthday was coming on, too, and the château was going to be full of the most distinguished visitors that he had ever assembled under one roof. He was an amiable old gentleman, this descendant of the great

Connétable: he did not aspire to have five hundred men-at-arms under his orders, but he did expect his house to be second to none in the matter of hospitality and of splendour. And Aurore meant half the world to him. He had been married three times: the first two duchesses had failed in their duty of presenting him with an heir, the third one turned her face to the wall and died when a tiny baby girl was first put against her breast. Monseigneur quickly consoled himself and would no doubt have brought a fourth duchess home to grace the head of the table only that his reputation of Bluebeard had made the eligible young ladies of his own rank chary of accepting so dangerous a position. Moreover, little tiny Aurore had already entwined himself around his fickle old heart. He forswore the delights of matrimony for the more durable ones of fatherhood, and devoted all the time that he could spare from the study of his own comforts to the furtherance of Aurore's enjoyment of life.

It is, perhaps, a little difficult to imagine a girl in her teens taking pleasure in games and pursuits which in these modern days would rouse the scorn of a child of seven—difficult to visualize that bright sunny day in July, 1782, when Aurore's birthday party, consisting of twenty or thirty of her friends in ages ranging from thirteen to twenty-three, spent their afternoon in playing blindman's bluff or hide-and-seek in the terraced gardens of Marigny. In and out the bosquest and parterres they darted like so many gaily plumaged birds, filling the air with their laughter and childish screams of delight, the while Monseigneur le Duc in his boudoir was giving M. Talon, his bailiff, a bad quarter of an hour.

"Mort de Dieu! You old muckworm!" was one of the many pleasant ways in which Monseigneur addressed the unfortunate Talon. "Have I not told you that I must have five thousand louis before the end of the month?"

"Yes, Monseigneur," Talon replied obsequiously, "but—"

"There is no 'but' about it, my man, when I said 'must'—" Monseigneur broke in drily.

"The tallage has all been paid—the salt tax, the window tax—"

"Call it the harvest tax or any cursed name you choose, but find me the money, or else—"

"Monseigneur!" protested Talon, who was quaking in his buckled shoes, knowing well enough what menace was being held over his head.

"Or else," Monseigneur went on slowly, emphasizing his words, "you and your precious family quit my service; I have no use for incompetent menials."

"Monseigneur!" Talon protested again, and with hands upraised called Heaven to witness his loyalty and his competence.

"Ed, what? There is no 'Monseigneur' about it; and your sanctimonious airs, mon ami, are no use to me. I have thirty guests in the house; it is Mademoiselle's birthday. I have told you that before, have I not?"

"As if I could forget—"

"Very well, then. Even with your limited intelligence you must be aware that in order to entertain such distinguished persons I must have my larder and my cellars full. Well! I'm short of wine. You know that. You know that we sent to that thief in Nevers for some, and that the mudlark refuses to send the wine unless he is paid beforehand."

"I know that, Monseigneur."

"You also know that I am giving Mademoiselle a ruby necklace for her birthday. You wrote the order out yourself."

"Yes, Monseigneur."

"Well, then! That also has to be paid for," Monseigneur concluded with what he felt was unanswerable logic. "So do not dare to appear before me again without at least—mind! I say at least—five thousand louis in your filthy hand. Now you can go."

Talon's narrow hatchet face, usually sallow and bilious, took on an ashen hue. Through narrow deepset eyes he cast a furtive glance at his irascible master. But Monseigneur, having delivered his ultimatum, no longer troubled his august head about his unfortunate bailiff. No doubt experience had taught him that under threat of dismissal Talon had always contrived somehow to produce the necessary money. Monseigneur never troubled his head much whence that money came. He had never been taught to trouble his head about anything so mean and sordid as money. He paid Talon a liberal salary, gave him a good house, productive land, and every facility to rob and cheat him, in order that this man should take all such burdens to enjoy life without care or worry. Many a time had Talon heard this philosophy propounded to him by his master: he knew that argument and protests were worse than useless, and it is to be supposed that in an emergency like the present one it was safer to incur further hatred from Monseigneur's tenants than the displeasure of Monseigneur himself.

M. le Duc for the moment appeared to have forgotten Hector Talon's very existence; he had caught sight through the wide-open window of his darling little Aurore at play with her friends. There was a grand game of blindman's bluff going on, and the sight would have gladdened any old man's heart, let alone that of a doting father. Monseigneur's eyes gleamed with pleasure; the misfortune of "blindman" who measured his length on the sanded path drew a delighted roar of laughter from him. Talon thought and hoped that he was momentarily forgotten and that he could achieve his exit without hearing further abuse or further threats. As noiselessly as he could he turned on his heel and made for the door. Just as he was about to slip through it Monseigneur's pleasant voice once more reached his ear:

"That reminds me, Talon," he said lightly, "that my cousin M. le Marquis d'Epinay had a splendid idea last year when he was short of money. There was all that stony land on Mont Oderic and Mont Socride, you remember? It was no use to him, he couldn't make anything out of it. So he made the neighbouring communes buy it of him at his own price. I believe the rascals have done very well with it since. Well! There's that bit of land the other side of Rocher Vert. I don't want it. Let the communes of Val-le-Roi and Le Borne buy it of me. They can have it for three thousand louis and you can make up the other two out of the hoard which you have amassed through robbing me, you black-guard."

"The communes couldn't pay, Monseigneur," Talon protested, and then added very injudiciously: "As for me, how can Monseigneur think—"

"That you are a thief and a liar?" Monseigneur broke in, with a careless laugh. "Why, you villain, if you were a decent man you would have left my service long ago. You know that I only employ you to do my dirty work, which I couldn't ask others who are clean and honest to do for me. As for the communes, what I propose is a sound bargain for them: those peasants can make a good thing out of land, which you are too big a fool to turn to account. Anyway, that's my last word: and now, get out of my sight. I am sick of you."

Talon was as thankful to go as Monseigneur was to be rid of him. He slipped like a stealthy cat through the door, while Monseigneur, throwing cares and money worries off his broad shoulders, returned to the more agreeable occupation of watching his daughter playing at blindman's bluff.

Perhaps, if he had been gifted with second sight, M. le Duc de Marigny would not have felt quite so carefree: for then he would have seen his bailiff, Hector Talon, the other side of the door, pausing for a moment with claw like fingers resting on the handle. On his sallow face there was neither humility nor servility, only a cunning, mocking glance in the narrow, deepset eyes and a sneer upon the pale thin lips. What went on in the man's mind it is impossible to say. Did he long to turn on the hand that fed him? Did he foresee that, on a day not very far distant, he would be the one to command and Monseigneur the dependent on his good will? All unconsciously now, even good-humouredly, Monseigneur chose to snub and humiliate him. There was no conscious feeling of arrogance in so great a gentleman's treatment of his subordinates; just the belief amounting to a certainty that he and his kind were made of a different clay from the rest of humanity, and that God had preordained them to rule and the others to obey. All these thoughts and hopes did, no doubt, course through Hector Talon's mind as he stood on the other side of the door with his fingers on the handle. But Monseigneur knew nothing of that. He was not gifted with second sight and did not see the change of expression in his bailiff's face—just as he had only given one casual and careless glance at the boy at the whipping post whom the ladies had so aptly named "the rebel angel."

# Chapter VII

On this same afternoon when André Vallon, still rebellious in spirit, followed M. le Curé de Val-le-Roi up the wooded slopes that led to the château, the picture that was revealed to his gaze when he came in sight of the gorgeous old building, with its sumptuous gardens, its marble terraces, its towers and battlements, its stately trees and wealth of flowers, was one he never forgot. Vaguely he had heard the château spoken of by those who knew, as "magnificent"; vaguely he was aware that Monseigneur lived there in a state of splendour of which he, a village lad, had no conception, even in his dreams; and from the valley below, where on the outskirts of Val-le-Roi his mother's cottage lay perdu, he had often gazed upwards to the heights, where at sunset the pointed roofs glistened like silver and the rows of windows sparkled like a chain of rubies; but he had never been allowed to wander up the slope and see all that magnificence at close quarters.

Heavy gilded iron gates shut off the precincts of the château from prying eyes and vagabond footsteps; stern janitors warned trespassers against daring to set foot inside the park; and thus the place where dwelt those unapproachable personages, Monseigneur and his friends, had hitherto appeared to André like fairyland, or rather, like the ogre's castle of which he had read in the storybooks of M. Perrault—the ogre who devoured all the good things of this earth and always wanted more.

André was dazzled. The same enthusiasm that made him love the moonlight, the cottontails, or the hedgerows caused him to utter a cry of pleasure when he first caught sight of the château. He came to a halt and allowed his eyes to feast themselves on the picture. M. le Curé was delighted; he thought that the boy was showing a nice spirit of reverence and of awe.

"It is beautiful, is it not, André?" he remarked complacently.

But André's mood was not quite as serene as the worthy priest had fondly hoped. He turned sharply on his heel and retorted with a scowl:

"Of course it is beautiful, but why should it be his?"

"What in the world do you mean?"

"You call that man up there 'Monseigneur.' Why? This all belongs to him. Why?"

"Because..."

The good Curé droned on. André certainly did not listen; he stalked on once more, irritable and silent. He had asked a question for which, in his own mind, there could not possibly be an answer. True that something of the bitterness of intense hatred had, as it were, flowed out of him with the tears which he had shed on his mother's breast, but the spirit of inquiry, of blind groping after mysteries which were incapable of solution had, for good or ill, replaced the childish acceptance of things as they were. To him henceforth his mother's penury and Monseigneur's wealth were not preordained by God; they did not form a part of the scheme of creation as God had originally decreed. They were the result of man's incapacity to grapple with injustice; the result, in fact, of the weakness of one section of humanity and of the arrogant strength of the other.

Very wisely, M. le Curé had not pursued the contentious subject. Together the two of them found their way across the wide, paved forecourt and up the perron. Lackeys in gorgeous liveries opened wide the gates of the château, and André, feeling now as if he were in a dream, silent, subdued, all the starch taken out of him, all the rebellion of his spirit overawed by so much splendour, kept close to the Curé's heels.

They went through the endless rooms, across floors that were so slippery that André, in his thick shoes, nearly measured his length on them more than once. He caught sight of himself in tall mirrors, full face, sideways, walking, sliding, pausing, wide-eyed and scared, thinking that the figure he was coming towards him was some strange boy whom he had never seen before. At length the Curé came to a halt in what seemed to André like a fairy's dwelling place, all azure and gold and crystal, where more tall mirrors reflected a somewhat corpulent old man in a long black soutane, and a tall, clumsy-looking boy in an ill-fitting coat, with tousled hair and large hands and feet encased in huge, thick buckled shoes.

On one side of the room there were three tall windows through which André saw such pictures as he had never seen before. At first he didn't think that they were real. There were marble balustrades and pillars, parterrers of flowers and groups of trees, and a fountain from whose sparkling waters the warm sunshine drew innumerable diamonds. This fairy garden appeared peopled with a whole bevy of brightly plumaged birds that darted in and out among the bosquets and the parterres with flutelike calls and rippling music. At least, so it seemed to André at first. M. le Curé, tired out, hot and panting, had sunk down in one of the gilded chairs and was mopping his streaming face; André, attracted and intrigued by the picture of that garden and those birds, ventured to go nearer to one of the tall windows in order to have a closer look. The window was wide open. André, leaning against the frame, stood quite still and watched.

A merry throng peopled the garden; ladies in light summer dresses, some with large straw hats over their powdered hair, others with fair or dark curls fluttering about their heads, men in silk embroidered coats, with dainty buckled shoes and filmy lace at throat and wrist, were chasing one another in and out of the leafy bosquets, just like a lot of children, playing some puerile game of blindman's bluff, which elicited many a little cry of mock alarm and silvery peals of merry laughter. How gay they seemed! How happy! André watched them, fascinated. He followed the various incidents of the game with eyes that soon lost their abstraction and sparkled with responsive delight. He nearly laughed aloud when an elegant gentleman in plum-coloured satin cloth, his eyes bandaged, tripped over a chair mischievously placed in his way by one of the ladies—a girl whose pink silk panniers over a short skirt of delicate green brocade made her look like a rosebud: so, at least, thought André.

He quite forgot himself while he stood and watched. Like a child at a show, he laughed when they laughed, gasped when capture was imminent, rejoiced when a narrow escape was successful. M. le Curé, overcome by the heat, had gone fast asleep in his chair.

André, absorbed in watching, did not even notice that the crowd of merrymakers had invaded the terrace immediately in front of the window against which he stood. "Blindman" now was the young girl with the fair hair, free from powder, whose dress made her look like a rose-bud. With arms outstretched she groped, after the clumsy fashion peculiar to a genuine blindman, and her playmates darted around her, giving her a little push here, another there, all of them unheedful of the silent, motionless watcher by the open window. And suddenly "Blindman," still with arms outstretched, lost her bearings, tripped against the narrow window sill and wound have fallen headlong into the room had not André instinctively put out his arms. She fell, laughing, panting, and with a little cry of alarm, straight into him.

There was a sudden gasp of surprise on the part of the others, a second or two of silence, and then a loud and prolonged outburst of laughter. André held on with both arms. Never in his life had he felt anything as sweet, as fragrant, so close to him. The most delicious odour of roses and violets came to his nostrils, while the downiest, softest little curls tickled his nose and lips. As to moving, he could not have stirred a muscle had his life depended on it.

But at the prolonged laughter of her friends the girl at once began to struggle; also, she felt the rough cloth beneath her touch, while to her delicate nostrils there came, instead of the sweet perfumes that always pervaded the clothes of her friends, a scent of earth and hay and of damp cloth. She wanted to snatch away the bandage from her eyes, but strong, muscular arms were round her shoulders, and she could not move.

"Let me go!" she called out. "Let me go! Who is it? Madeleine—Edith, who is it?"

The next moment a firm step resounded on the marble floor of the terrace, a peremptory voice called out: "You young muck-worm, how dare you?" and the hold round her shoulders relaxed. André received a resounding smack on the side the face, while the girl, suddenly freed, staggered slightly backward even while she snatched the handkerchief from her eyes.

The first thing she saw was a dark young face with a heavy chestnut curl falling over a frowning brow, a pair of eyes dark as aloes flashing with hatred and rage. She heard the voice of her cousin, the Comte de Mauléon, saying hoarsely:

"Get out! Get out, I say!" And then calling louder still: "Here! Léon! Henri! Some of you kick this garbage out."

It was all terrible. The ladies crowded round her and helped to put her pretty dress straight again, but the girl was too frightened to think of them or her clothes. Why she should have been frightened she didn't know, for Aurore de Marigny had never been frightened in her life before: she was a fearless little rider and a regular tomboy at climbing or getting into dangerous scrapes; but there was something in that motionless figure in the rough clothes, in those flashing eyes and hard, set mouth which puzzled the child and terrified her. Here was something that she had never met before, something that seemed to emit evil, cruelty, hatred, none of his had ever come within sight of her sheltered, happy life.

Pierre de Mauléon was obviously in a fury and kept calling for the lackeys, who, fortunately, were not within hearing, for heaven alone knew what would happen if anyone dared lay hands on that incarnation of fury. The boy—Aurore saw that he was only a boy, not much older than herself—looked now like a fierce animal making ready for a spring; he had thrust one hand into his breeches' pocket and brought out a knife—a miserable, futile kind of pocket knife, but still a knife; and his teeth—sharp and white as those of a young wolf—were drawing blood out of his full red lips.

Some of the ladies screamed; others giggled nervously. The men laughed, but no one thought of interfering. Inside the room, M. le Curé, roused from his slumbers, had obviously not yet made up his mind whether he was awake or dreaming.

Just then the two lackeys, Léon and Henri, came hurrying along the terrace. A catastrophe appeared imminent, for the boy had seen them; knew, probably, what it would mean to him and all these bedizened puppets if those men dared to touch him. He was seeing red; for the first time in his life he felt the desire to see a human creature's blood. With jerky movements he grasped the flimsy, gimcrack pocket knife with which he meant to defend himself to the death. He met the girl's eyes with their frightened, half-shy glance and exulted in the thought that in a few seconds, perhaps, she would see one of her lackeys lying dead at her feet.

Not even on that fatal day when he had tasted the very dregs of humiliation had his young soul been such a complete prey to rebellion and hatred. Why, oh, why had he allowed his heart to melt at sight of his mother's wretchedness? Why had he ever set foot across this cursed threshold? Pay! Pay! Pay! Those were once his mother's words. Pay, while these marionettes laughed and played; pay, so that their bellies might be full, their pillows downy, their hair powdered and perfumed. He hated them all. Oh, how he hated them!

These riotous thoughts were tumbling about in André's brain, chasing one another with lightning speed while he was contemplating murder and hurling defiant glances at the pretty child, the cause of this new—this terrible catastrophe.

Ever afterwards he was ready to swear that not by a quiver of an eyelid had he betrayed fear or asked for protection. Asked? Heavens above! He would sooner have fallen dead across this window sill than have asked help from any of these gaudy nincompoops.

Be that as it may, there is no doubt that it was the girl's piping, childish voice which broke the uncomfortable spell that had fallen over the entire lively throng.

"Ohé!" she cried, with a ripple of laughter. "How solemn you all look! Pierre, it is your turn. Come, Véronique, you hold him while I do the blindfolding; don't let him go—it is his turn."

Her friend to whom she called was close by and ready enough to resume the game. Before Pierre de Mauléon had the chance to resist she had him by the hand, while Aurore tied the handkerchief over his eyes. A scream of delight went up all round. All seriousness, puzzlement, was forgotten. Pierre tried to snatch the handkerchief away, but two of them held onto his hands; the others pushed and pinched and teased. They dragged him along the terrace; they vaulted over the marble balusters; they were children, in fact, once more, tomboys, madcaps, running about among the bosquets and the flowers, irresponsible and irrepressed, while André, without another word, another look, turned on his heel and fled out of this cursed château, leaving M. le Curé to call and to gasp and to explain to Monseigneur, as best he could, what, in point of fact, had actually happened.

# Book II

## Chapter VIII

There are several biographies extant of André Vallon, some written by friends, others by enemies. No man who has played a role on the world stage has ever been without his detractors, and only a few have been without their apologists. To have really complete conception of Vallon's temperament, character, and subsequent conduct, it would be necessary to know something of his life during the ten years that followed.

He was little more than fifteen when he left his village of Val-le-Roi and went up to Paris under the aegis of M. l'Abbé de Rosemonde, who had obtained for him, after much tribulation, countless petitions, and untiring zeal, a scholarship in the College of the Oratorians in Paris, where a few years before this a young scholar named Georges Danton had pegged away at the classics, and where many young minds began nursing those thoughts of rebellion and agitation which were to render them famous or infamous in the annals of the greatest revolution of all time.

Some of these men, at the time that André Vallon went to the Oratorians, were already prominent in the public eye. Danton at this date was Conseiller du Roi, was calling himself Maître d'Anton and had a fine practice and a pretty young wife. Maximilien de Robespierre had finished his studies at the Collège Louis-le-Grand and was now a leading light of advocacy; and Camille Desmoulins was a notorious journalist. André, who had developed a hitherto latent ambition, and with such examples before him of success won by hard work, became as model a scholar as he had been a turbulent village lad. That it took all M. le Curé's eloquence and floods of his mother's tears to persuade him to go to college at all goes without saying, but he did go in the end.

How much it cost his mother to keep him in decent clothes while he was at college remained forever a secret within her ample bosom. As André grew to be a man he made a pretty shrewd guess at the hardships, which she must have endured in order to put by a few louis every year so that he should not cut too sorry a figure among his schoolfellows. Luckily for him, he never felt any sense of humiliation at his own shabby clothes or want of money to spend. He was so firmly persuaded that his mother's poverty and his own empty pockets were only transitory states, which would be remedied by himself when he was a man. And then, again, some of those whose names at this hour were on everybody's lips had been as poor as himself. Camille Desmoulins never had a sous from his avaricious father to spend on leisure or finery, and Robespierre's clothes were invariably threadbare.

Moreover, as the years went on, poverty became so much a matter of course, except in the case of a privileged or a dishonest few, that it ceased to have any significance. It was a matter of caste, that was all, and became such an accepted fact that for a family man not to be hungry, to have fuel on his hearth or shoes on his feet was to be something of an alien among his own class. Nor was it shame that stirred André's young blood to boiling when he saw his mother in her old age, still scrubbing floors or toiling up to the château to do the family washing; it was only passionate rage at his own impotence to drag her out of her penury, and ever growing better resentment at a social system which permitted the few to have all the good things of this world and allowed the many to go under for want of sufficient nourishment. That this resentment should lead a young mind to wholesale condemnation of the present régime was only natural, seeing that the King was an autocratic monarch, and that his word, and his word alone, made and unmade the laws.

In 1788 André Vallon was called to the bar and delivered, as was customary, his diploma speech in Latin. The subject set for the year was the social and political condition of the country and its relation to the administration of justice. A ponderous subject for a village lad to tackle, but even Vallon's detractors—and he already had a few—were ready to admit that he acquitted himself adequately, and that his Latin was faultless. The grave and reverend seigneurs of the law, on the other hand, sat up in amazement and rubbed their lacklustre eyes when they heard this young advocate from the back of the provincial beyond spout grandiloquent phrases, such as Salus populi suprema lex esto, and with wide gestures of delicately modelled hands strike a note of warning to those in high places—to all who had inherited power, influence, or riches.

"Qui habet aures auriendi," he thundered. "Audiat."

There could be no two opinions about it: it was an incendiary speech, even though there were no actual words in it that could be construed into excitation to reprisals or insurrection. On the contrary, it even concluded with a passionate appeal to those who had the ear of the malcontents to pause before they led the people blindly along the paths that led to revolution.

"Woe to him," he fulminated in conclusion, "who for his own advancement plays on the passions and the prejudices of the people. Woe to the instigator and the maker of revolutions!"

Thus ended his impassioned harangue, delivered in the language of Ovid and Virgil, leaving his learned audience marvelling at this young Cicero sprung out of a remote village, and gravely shaking their heads at the unorthodox sentiments to which they had been compelled to listen.

A week later André was at home, telling his mother all about it, courting her approval more ardently than he had done that of the leading lights at the Paris bar. There was something in Marianne Vallon's calm philosophy, in her acceptance of the inevitable, which by its very contrast appealed to André's rebellious spirit.

"You help me to keep my balance, Mother," he would say with all youth's impatience, when she talked as she often used to do in the past, of resignation and humility. "And God knows we shall all of us want it presently," he added, with a careless shrug and a laugh.

He went through all the fatigue of translating his Latin speech into French for her, so that she might understand and criticize. But he was quite proud of his achievement; he knew that he had left his mark on the somewhat somnolent brains of his fellow advocates.

"Maître d'Anton was present, Mother," he related, bridling up at the recollection of that proud moment when he saw the popular orator make his way into the hall. "I think he liked my speech, for I saw him nod with approval once or twice, and at the end he clapped his hands together, and I heard his stentorian voice shouting, 'Good! Very good indeed!'"

"A selfish and a cruel man," Marianne muttered under her breath.

"How can you say that, Mother chérie?" André protested. "He is a model husband and a devoted father."

"He was born lucky. Wait till misfortune overtakes him—"

"I hope it won't," André broke in gaily, "for he has offered me a clerkship in his office."

"Don't take it, André!" Marianne cried involuntarily.

"Why in the world no, Mother? It will be the making of me. Clerk to Maître d'Anton, Conseiller du Roi! Think of it!"

Marianne shrugged: "Conseiller du Roi?" she said with what would have been a sneer round a mouth less kindly. "That man, Danton, Conseiller du Roi? When he dreams of nothing but deposing his King—if not worse."

"He dreams of changing the whole aspect of the world," André protested with unwonted earnestness, "and God knows this old world wants a change."

Old Marianne shook her head. She was too old to imbibe all those principles which men with fine oratorical powers like Georges Danton poured daily into the ears of the young; too old also to hope for a change in the system which had brought her to her present state of indigence. In Danton's ways she foresaw disaster. "Once you set an avalanche sliding down the mountain side," she would say, "you cannot possibly stop its mad career. You are bound to be crushed beneath it in the end."

But André would retort proudly: "A man like Danton does not count the cost. He says and does what he believes to be right, and if he cannot carry his principles though, he will die like a martyr."

"And drag all those whom he has fooled to perdition with him."

"What grander death than that of a martyr?" André demanded, flushed with enthusiasm.

But Marianne, wise old peasant that she was, muttered: "Martyr? And for what cause, mon Dieu? For what?"

"The happiness of mankind!"

And so the boy would argue. He was only a boy still, after all, in spite of his Latin, and hero worship was in his blood. He became a clerk to Maître d'Anton, Conseiller du Roi, one of the greatest lights at the moment of Paris advocacy: a man, too, wholly unspoilt by success and prosperity. He had a way of persuading all those who knew in him intimately that his was a large, all-embracing nature, which only pined to see everyone around him smiling and happy.

He had a fine property in the country, a well-furnished house in town, a pretty wife and a boy whom he worshipped. Danton was at this time the most popular man in France, and André one of the happiest, for he felt that he had his chance, a chance coveted by every budding advocate who had delivered his Latin thesis that year. He walked hand in hand with the man who was called the Lion Tamer of France, for he held the savage pack of snarling felines on the leash. Marat, Desmoulins, and the others bowed to his moderate, sensible views.

"Wait," Marianne had said, "till misfortune overtakes him."

It did. Soon after André entered his office his only child died, the boy whom he adored. His wife was broken hearted; sought consolation in religion. Georges Danton, who worshipped her, would escort her daily to church, then rush round to the club and, in a hoarse voice, broken with sobs, would prophesy now the coming cataclysm. Shrewd, fat Marianne had proved indeed to be right.

In the wake of misfortune, Danton's moderation went to the wind, and during the most impressionable years of his life André's ears were constantly filled with his chief's ever more violent diatribes against the social regime, the ignorance and ineptitude of the King, and the venality of his ministers.

"They have eyes and see not; ears they have and hear not," Danton would thunder forth whenever news of riots in the provincial towns, already of frequent occurrence, looting of shops, firing of châteaux, were brought to his office. "Fools they are! all of them fools! Can't they see that their whole world is falling to dust about their feet, and that soon the rivers of France will be running with blood?"

André, whose young soul had always been inclined towards rebellion, would listen wide-eyed, trying with all his might to disentangle the right from the wrong in those tempestuous tirades. Danton was a man of immense influence. In the clubs his power was supreme, and it was the clubs that governed France these days; for it was in the clubs that ministers were made and unmade. Men of all ages, men of wide experience, bowed to Danton as to their greatest leader. And André Vallon was little more than a boy, with a boy's enthusiasm and generous impulses, and young blood ready to boil at sight of injustice and cruelty.

"Get me out an article for l'Ami du Peuple, André," Danton would often say to him when he came home, hoarse and tired from a noisy séance at the Cordeliers. "Revolution is in the air; it gathers strength. At Versailles the King fashions padlocks and the Queen plays at hide-and-seek. The people starve. Make no mistake: at this moment thousands of men are seeing their wives and children dying of hunger. Write it, André. Write it. Dip your pen in gall. Marat will print anything you write. For God's sake, don't mince matters! Up at Versailles they must be made to see, or the most awful cataclysm the world has ever known will drench this country with blood."

After which outburst he would go home to his young wife and with his ardent lovemaking help her and himself to forget their own grief and the misfortune of their country. But André would go back to his own dingy lodgings and try to put into words the turbulent thoughts of his chief. And whenever his mother shook her wise old head over these youthful lucubrations, he would excuse the more passionate passages by saying:

"It is impossible to stem the fury of the people now, Mother dear. All we can do is to lead it into as reasonable channels as we can."

"Your Danton tries to cure evil with worse evils, my child," Marianne retorted. "How can good come from evil? Take care, André! Men like

Danton have set their world rocking; when it falls together with a crash it will drag them along, too, into the abyss."

"They must take their chance, Mother," André rejoined with an impatient sigh. "We must all take our chances, for we cannot foresee what the end of it all will be."

But it was not often that he was in such a serious mood. Whenever he could obtain leave he would take the diligence to Nevers, and thence the country chaise to Val-le-Roi. He would burst in on his mother with the gentleness of an exploding bombshell, and thereafter for a few days, not only the cottage, but the country inns around, the lanes, the woods, the village streets would echo with his laughter and his big, sonorous voice.

# Chapter IX

The worst of the great political storm had not yet touched the outlying villages. The people, of course, were desperately poor, for the year had been one of the hardest the unfortunate country had ever known; a prolonged drought had been followed by terrible hailstorms on the very eve of harvesting; the price of corn was prohibitive, and the winter that ensued was so severe that even forest trees suffered from the frost. Poor? Of course they were poor! There was no such thing as a plump girl to be seen in any village: children were emaciated, their growth stunted, their future health hopelessly impaired. But life had to go on just the same. There was marriage and giving away in marriage; babies were born and old people died; and those that were not old clung to life in spite of the fact that it promised nothing but misery.

André Vallon's visits to Val-le-Roi were always something of holiday for all. He was so gay, so lighthearted. The news, which he brought from Paris, always seemed reassuring.

He would meet his friends around the bare tables of the village inn where, over sips of thin, sour wine, he would try to put heart into the men.

"It can't last, can it, André?" they would ask.

"Of course it can't. The darkest hour always comes before the dawn. There are some good times head for all of us. You'll see."

Then he would call to Suzette, mine host's pretty daughter, and sit her on his knee.

"Come, Suzette," he would say gaily, "help us to talk of something cheerful: of your pretty self, for instance, and of Jerome, whom you met last night in the lane. You did... don't tell me you did not... Give us a kiss, no, this instant, or I'll tell your worthy papa just what I saw in the lane last night."

And in the sunshine of his irrepressible gaiety some of them would momentarily forget their troubles.

"There goes that madcap, André Vallon," the older people would say when he went down the village street, singing at the top of his voice; "he was always a good lad, but his skin is too tight to hold him."

And they would tell each other tales of André's misdeeds when he was a boy, and of the worry which he had been to his mother: not a lad in the village whom he had not licked at some time or another, not a girl from whom he had not snatched a kiss. Twice he had been within an ace of being drowned; three times he had nearly smashed himself to pieces by falling from a tree or a rocky height; once he had tackled farmer Lombard's bull which was after him, and with just his two hands he had squeezed the life out of Bailiff Talon's savage dog.

"Such a beautiful boy, he was," the women said.

And the girls giggled as he went by, for those great dark eyes of his would look them up and down with disturbing, provoking glances. And some of them would pause and return the glance with a look, which was more than a hint, but André would only smile, showing a gleam of white teeth. But ne'er a look of tenderness did he cast in response, nor did the faintest whisper of love ever cross his lips.

Lovemaking? Yes! Any amount of it. André's young arms were forever reaching out for white shoulders or a slim waist; his full laughter-loving mouth was always ready for a kiss, but it remained at that: there was no girl for leagues around who could boast that she had meant more to André Vallon than the old mother whom he worshipped.

But the old mother knew—or rather guessed—that there was always something behind her son's flippancy in the manner of women and of love. She didn't know what it was, but there was no deceiving her—there was something. And there came a time when she made a pretty shrewd guess. She asked no questions, of course, but whenever the subject of the Château de Marigny and its inmates cropped up, a strange reserve seemed to tie the boy's tongue. He would become moody and silent, and if Marianne then pursued the subject, spoke of the hardships so bravely borne by Monseigneur, or said something of Mademoiselle Aurore and her angelic patience in all her misfortunes, André would suddenly jump to his feet and cry out with extraordinary vehemence:

"Don't talk to me about those people, Mother. I hate them!"

# Chapter X

But the time soon came, even in these remote villages, when agitator and demagogues would rub their hands with glee. They would stretch out their legs in front of their own hearths and declare complacently that the revolution, which they had foretold, had not only come, but come to stay. Distress had become general; with it stalked resentment and a fury of reprisals.

In the provincial towns bread riots were of constant occurrence; the starving people had taken to looting granaries and stores; in several cases shops, house, châteaux had been fired. Tub-thumpers were shouting daily to willing ears the deadly slogan: "Liberty and Equality."

Paris was full of men and women who had wandered to the capital from the neighbouring towns and villages, armed with scythes and other agricultural implements which had become useless, since there were no crops to harvest; starving, wrathful, and determined, they paraded the streets shouting for redress. At street corners, in the clubs, in public bars, malcontents waved their arms and spouted magnificent phrases about Liberty and the sovereignty of the people. Danton thundered forth his call to arms, to bloodshed and revenge.

Misery had sown discontent and reaped revolution. Less than a year later butchery had begun.

In September, '92, a brutish crowd, armed with pikes, scythes, old blunderbusses, and rifles, rushed through the streets of Paris, stormed the houses of detention that were overcrowded with unfortunate prisoners, and in cold blood massacred hundreds of men, women, and children, while Danton, the darling of the crowd, the all-powerful party leader, did not raise a hand to stop the carnage.

A Child of the Revolution

André Vallon, long before then, had given up his profession in order to join the army. France was besieged on every side: the whole of Europe had taken up arms against her, outraged at the excesses of this revolution which aimed at regicide and achieved wholesale butchery. The onus of carrying on a world war now rested upon the shoulders of men with no experience of organization or government. The responsibilities which hitherto had devolved solely upon the King and his ministers were theirs now; and they were already finding out that to depose the King, to wrest from him the control of civil and military administration, was quite one thing, but to defend the country against the foreign invader, with troops whom they themselves had taught to mutiny, was quite another. To rouse the people to insurrection had not been difficult, famine and misery had helped in the task; but to feed a whole nation and, at the same time, to raise an army strong enough to fight both Austria and Prussia, was not quite so easy.

Already these new masters of France hated and despised one another. Five out of the six ministers who formed the Executive were timid and vacillating. Danton alone dominated them. He, too, was ignorant of the essentials that make up a stable government, but at any rate was a man—a lion amid a flock of sheep.

His impassioned oratory, his powerful voice, his immense patriotism, helped to raise an army of recruits, to send them to the frontiers, insufficiently armed, insufficiently clothed, empty bellied and undisciplined, but full of enthusiasm for la patrie in danger. There is nothing in the world that quite comes up to the love of a Frenchman for his country. France is a beautiful country; every corner of it is beautiful, and its sons love it with a love that in a way transcends the patriotism of every other nation. La patrie is a word that cannot be rendered in any other language—it is not a question of home, of family, of race! It is just France! And there are few pages in the world's history so pathetic and yet so magnificent as this epic of raw, untrained, famished recruits, dragging their shoeless feet along the muddy woods of Champagne, on whose sacred soil the King of Prussia was advancing with his well trained, highly equipped army, and, with the sheer enthusiasm of love for their country and determination to defend her against foreign invasion, keeping the whole of Europe at bay.

At home now there remained, in addition to the women and children, only the halt and the maimed, a few youngsters too débile to bear arms, the only sons of widowed mothers, who were exempt from military service, and the fathers of growing families. Quite a crowd, nevertheless, and one that, in the opinion of the Executive up in Paris, must be made to bear its part in furthering the glorious Revolution.

Inflammatory placards were posted up at every street corner and every crossroad, proclaiming the sovereignty of the people and headed by Danton's declaration: "We must govern by fear."

Terror had become the order of the day. Men and women—peaceable and respectable citizens—went in fear of their lives. Every crime had become permissible; every act of violence was considered patriotic; every outrage was not only condoned but commended; so long as they were directed against those who, through their selfish enjoyment of life, their riches, their contentment and luxury, had proved themselves traitors to their country and enemies of the people.

And men in three-cornered hats and cloth coast ornamented with brass buttons, pot bellied and bleary eyed, were sent round the provincial towns on a tour of active propaganda. Hoisted on tables outside the taverns they harangue the famished crowds, denouncing the traitors that caused all the sufferings of the people, and foretelling an era of plenty, which certainly would soon come if only France were swept clean of King and aristocrats.

At first the crowds listened in sullen silence, and in some places it took the rogues some time to work the people up to a state of effervescence. They were all so poor and so hungry that in most cases all they wanted to do was to sit still and brood over their wrongs. But the demagogues were no fools; they knew their business. It was not inertia they wanted, or acceptance of penury. They were out to make trouble and to stir up strife. Within half an hour they had hurled sufficient invectives against the owner of the nearest château—his hoard of wheat and fuel, his cellar full of good wines—to work up the lethargic blood of these ignorant folk into a state of frenzy. The poisonous suggestion of reprisals began to filter down into receptive brains, and men who saw their wives and children dying for want of food began lending a more attentive ear to these prophecies of a panacea for all their ills.

"Liberty!" and "The sovereign will of the people!" The great slogans, thundered at them day after day, began to make an appeal to their empty stomachs and frozen limbs. If liberty meant taking what you want, eating your fill, and drinking good wine; if it meant covering your wife's emaciated shoulders with a warm shawl and putting shoes on your children's feet, then liberty by all means!

In the villages the tavern orators were for the most part local malcontents or ambitious rascals who had nothing to lose and everything to gain by a complete upheaval of the social system. Subsides for carrying on the propaganda came from the clubs in Paris. It was a paying game, carried on in one village by a defaulting clerk, in another by a dishonest servant or perhaps it would be an absconding lawyer, or even an unfrocked priest.

At Val-le-Roi it was Hector Talon.

Talon was still nominally steward to Monseigneur le Duc de Marigny, but the place had become a sinecure. The estates had become so impoverished that they were no longer worth administering. Talon knew well enough that the days of Marigny in its present condition were numbered. Either the owner would emigrate—as so many of his kind had done, in which case the whole of the property would be confiscated—or he would be arrested on some pretext or other and sent to the guillotine. And it was quite a usual thing for faithful servants to share the fate of their masters.

Now, Talon was quite determined not to share any untoward fate with his employer or with anyone else. He wanted to be on the right side. Not only now, but in the future.

Indeed, Hector Talon was no fool. He knew as well as anybody that the present state of affairs could not possibly last; that presently—in three, four, or even ten years, perhaps—tempers would quieten down, and when all these assassins who were now in power had butchered one another, an era of moderation would then assert itself. And—who knows?—it was just possible that the reaction would be so great that the political pendulum would swing right over to the old regime.

Fortunately for him, Talon was an adept as dual rôles. Monseigneur— or cidevant Marigny, as he was contemptuously designated by his former sycophants—lived a solitary life up at the château, like an eagle in its eerie, with only his daughter for company and a couple of his old servants to wait on him. Talon was, as it were, the only link between him and the seething world down below. It was easy enough to throw dust in his eyes and to persuade him that the interests of respectable citizens, be they bailiffs, or ex-dukes were identical. There certainly was the Curé of Val-le-Roi, the Abbé de Rosemonde, who had kept up friendship with De Marigny and who might have enlightened him as to the real worth of Hector Talon; but the old priest was one of those entirely childlike natures which never see anything that is not thrust under their very noses, who never seem to know anything of what goes on around them, and whom it is the easiest thing in the world to hoodwink.

Talon, therefore, had a clear field up at the château for his role of faithful administrator entirely devoted to his employer's interests. But in the village taverns, surrounded by all the malcontents of the countryside, adulated and puffed up with his own importance, he gave lip service to Danton and Marat, spouted insults at every man or women who had ever owned a hectare of land, and spat out the venom of malice and envy which was the accumulation of years.

Of a truth, he was on the safe side. During the past lean years his corpulence had melted away; he was thin now and more bandy-legged than ever, with wide, bony shoulders and hollow belly. His head rolled about on his long, lean neck, crowned with a stubble of short, tawny, ill brushed hair; his lips were thin and his mouth awry; his chin was pointed, and his hollow cheeks were darkened with the bristles of an unshaven beard. And under overhanging brows his eyes, which had a yellow tinge in them, were always veiled by heavy, blue-veined lids. Unlike the regular army of tub-thumpers, he affected the meanest and dirtiest of clothes, a ragged shirt which had not seen the washtub for months, breeches that hardly covered his lean thighs; his shanks were bare, and his feet were thrust in sabots stuffed with straw.

But he had a powerful voice and a good delivery and an easy choice of words. For the most part he drew his inspiration for his most inflammatory speeches from articles which he picked out of various Paris journals.

"Liberty! The time has come, citizens, not only to talk of liberty, but to fight in her sacred cause!" his was one of his favourite tirades. And then he would go on: "Let us take up arms like our brave soldiers on the frontier and engage in a hand-to-hand struggle against tyranny, against all those vampires who suck our blood and strive to break our will. France needs you, citizens, every one of you; she needs your help to gain that freedom for which she pines; she needs all your strength, all your courage. She needs the patriotism of self-sacrifice. To arms, citizens, to arms! Think no longer of yourselves or of your wives or children! Think only of liberty. And if in your heart you should reckon the cost of your lives, then remember that there are forty-thousand palaces, châteaux, and abodes of the rich, half the wealth of France, that will become yours in payment for your valour and for your loyalty."

And after he had delivered himself of this oratory he would go home, put on a cloth coat and breeches, woollen stockings and buckled shoes, and make his way up to the château, and fill Monseigneur's ears with protestations of his loyalty.

His wife sometimes gave him a word of warning.

"If the old crow should hear of your oratory..." she would say.

"He wouldn't believe anything against me," Talon retorted with a complacent snigger.

"Rumours do travel," Lucile insisted. "I heard in the village, for instances, that it was you who egged that crowd on last night to set fire to the mill and the granaries."

Talon nodded. "Quite true," he said drily. "I did."

"What was the good? The granaries were empty, and they'll want to burn the château down next."

"I hope they do."

"What? Set fire to the château?"

"No. Only threaten to."

Lucile Talon was silent for a moment or two. By the feeble light of a flickering tallow candle she could only partly see the expression on her husband's face. It was not pretty at this moment, and Lucile gave a slight shudder as she turned away and busied herself for a time with her household affairs. But presently she came back into the parlour and sat down at the table opposite her husband.

"You have a plan in your head, Hector," she said decisively. "What is it?"

Then, as he made no reply, only stared and stared into the flickering flame, she added: "You won't tell me?"

"It is too vague at present," he replied at last, "for you to understand."

And Lucile saw the yellow gleam in his eyes, shining like the light in the eyes of a cat.

# Chapter XI

It was eleven years almost to a day since M. l'Abbé de Rosemonde, Curé de Val-le-Roi, had toiled up the slope to the Château de Marigny with his young protégé, André Vallon. Then, as now, a hot July sun flooded the pointed roofs with silvery lights. Only a few white fleecy clouds flitted across the cobalt sky. The birds sang in the forest trees; the branches of walnut and sycamore quivered under the breath of a gentle summer breeze. In the valley below, the Allier gurgled softly among the reeds, and the weeping willows along its banks set forth their sweet, sad sighing through the noonday air.

Nature, lovely and impersonal, seemed by her serene beauty to mock at all the turmoil, the hideousness created by men. "Look at me," she seemed to say. "My laws are immutable. I destroy nothing without cause. Death in my infinite wisdom is only the maker of life."

M. le Curé looked about him and sighed. He could almost have wished that God's world would cease to be beautiful since men no longer had eyes to see the glory of His creations. He was an old man now. These last few years had put a heavy burden upon him. Torn between his hatred of the present godless regime and his desire to do what little good he could among these poor misguided folk to whom he had ministered for more than thirty years, he had at last decided to take the oath of allegiance to this impious government which he abhorred, simply because he did not wish to leave Val-le-Roi to its fate. In spite of threats, in spite of persecution, he had managed so far to keep his church open, to hold occasional services, to visit the sick, and to administer the sacraments.

On this beautiful morning in mid-July when he came in sight of the château, he experienced the same heartache, which assailed him every time he noted the slow but sure ravages of neglect upon the magnificent pile. It was many years now since flowers had graced the parterres of the garden and thrown their gay note of brilliance against the subdued colouring of the age-old stonework. The bosquest now were withered; the fountains still; marble balustrades and terraces were covered with the soil and litter of years.

The Abbé sighed again and wearily made his way up the perron. The monumental gates opened at a touch; the cracked bell which he pulled echoed weirdly through the silent halls. There were no servants in gorgeous liveries now to wait on visitors; no sound of gaiety or laughter came reverberating through this silence, which seemed as solemn as that of a tomb. The old priest crossed the vast hall and made his way up the great marble staircase and through the length of the gorgeous apartments, which stretched en enfilade to the farthest angle of the château. Here he came to a halt and knocked at the door that faced him. A woman's voice called, "Entrez!" and he stepped into the room.

At sight of him a young girl jumped up from the low stool whereon she had been sitting, threw down a book, and came to greet him with hands outstretched.

"M. l'Abbé!" she cried. "How kind of you to come, and in this heat, too! Do sit down. You must be tired. Papa and I were just saying that perhaps you would not come till later in the day."

The good Curé took the two soft white hands that were so eagerly tendered him and then turned to pay his respects to Monseigneur. Like the Curé himself, Monseigneur le Duc de Marigny had in the past few years become a very old man. Misfortune and anxiety had put a quarter of a century onto his years. Like so many men of his generation and caste, he had made a splendid effort to bear with outward fortitude the terrible calamities that well-nigh overwhelmed him, but obviously the fortitude had only been on the surface. Every line on his face showed that he had suffered and was suffering terribly. He had the appearance of a martyr, conscious of his martyrdom. He had see his friends, his relatives, one by one, either driven to exile or to death, and calmly awaited the hour when he would be called to share their fate. Were it not for his daughter he would have welcomed that hour, nay! Even have gone forward boldly to meet it. But there was Aurore, his child, the darling of his shrivelled heart. Because of her he was willing to shelter beneath the protection, which his near relationship with that infamous Duc d'Orléans, who had cast his vote in favour of the death sentence on his cousin and King, had so far given him. Because of his cousinship with that man he had escaped persecution at the hands of the Committee of Public Safety: his name had not as yet appeared on the list of the "suspect." He accepted this slur upon it for Aurore's sake, but had suffered agonies of humiliation for this immunity. In his eyes today, dimmed not so much with age as with unshed tears, there smouldered the fire of bitter resentment. Not even to his daughter, not even to the kindly priest, his one remaining friend, did he open out his innermost thoughts, his desperate longing for revenge.

On this occasion, as indeed always, he greeted the Curé with the greatest friendliness. Cut off from all his friends and all his kindred, the Abbé de Rosemonde seemed like a last link with the happy past. They had become like two old cronies, these two, not talking much to each other, because there were so few pleasant things to talk about, but they often had friendly bouts at chess or piquet, and instinctively the old Duke felt the soothing influence of his friend's Christian philosophy.

Aurore had put a chair in a convenient position, and the Abbé fell into it, panting and blowing, for the day was hot and the climb up the hill steep.

"I wish I could offer you a glass of wine," Monseigneur said with a fretful little sigh, "but I have not a bottle left in the cellar."

Aurore poured out a glass of water for the old priest, who drank it eagerly, and then set to with great energy to mop his streaming face and neck.

"The best wine in the world, Monseigneur," he said cheerfully, "is this fresh water from the well. I am not tired, I assure you, my dear little Aurore, and even if I were, your smile would comfort me more thoroughly than the finest bottle of Burgundy."

Monseigneur gave a significant grunt and turned his head away.

"Well!" the priest went on after a moment or two. "What news?"

"The very best," Aurore de Marigny said eagerly. "I found the box I told you about, and, oh! M. l'Abbé, it is full, full of lovely things—stockings and shirts and petticoats. They will be so useful for many of the poor mothers this winter."

She chattered away in great excitement, her eyes sparkling and her cheeks flushed.

"And they won't as much as say 'Thank you!' for them," Monseigneur put in drily.

"Oh, yes, they will!" the girl asserted. "And even if they don't..."

She gave a little shrug. What cared she if she got thanks or no, so long as she could find something to do, something in which to interest herself, to make time slip by a little more swiftly? The days were so long and so dreary! Nothing to do, nothing to think of or to hope for, save to bring now and again the ghost of a smile on Papa's face. To help M. l'Abbé in his charitable work was a perfect godsend, now that she saw her youth slipping by before she had begun to understand the true and inner meaning of such things as happiness and love. She was barely nineteen when her world began to crash about her feet, when she first came face to face with ill will, malevolence, even hatred. Until that hour the world had been one great thing of beauty. Loveliness was the very essence of her young life. She inhaled love and adulation with every breath she drew. When she took her walks abroad people got out of her way to allow her to pass. Glances of admiration accompanied her all the way she went. Gentle expressions of respect, often a murmured blessing, were the words that most often rang in her ears.

Then suddenly came the crash: an awful cataclysm seemed to sweep the whole of her past into an immeasurable abyss. Glowering looks, sullen glances, objurgations, even insults were cast at her, until she no longer dared to set foot beyond the precincts of the castle. One by one the servants, who she thought loved her, who had seen her grow up from babyhood, fled from the château as from a plague-ridden spot. And slowly her childlike mind began to unfold: it had been closed hitherto to outward things, as is a flower bud sheltered beneath a canopy of leaves. But soon her quick intelligence grasped the true significance of what was going on around her, and the Abbé de Rosemonde, with the utmost gentleness and care, helped in the development of her understanding.

Aurore de Marigny never took a gloomy view of life. She accepted a great deal, which was rousing her father's bitter resentment, as inevitable; as she was very young, she never gave up hope. These years of indigence and anxiety were only transitory: of this she was sure. But while she did her best to infuse some of that hope into her father's soul, she would in the loneliness of her little bedroom shed many a bitter tear over her lost youth. Better times might come presently—they certainly would come, she knew they would—but she would be old by then; her beauty would be gone along with her youth; she would no longer be desirable; she would never learn the great lesson of life, the lesson of Love.

# Chapter XII

Aurore had dragged the good old Curé along interminable corridors, and up interminable stairs to a distant attic, where, beneath the old oak beams, covered with dust and cobwebs, and ancient black leather trunk stood open, with most of its contents already scattered about the floor.

Aurore went through them methodically, and M. le Curé nodded approval, or the reverse, as she held up the garments one by one to the dim light.

"These stockings are strong," she said. "They'll do for Legendre's children. This shawl we'll give to Marianne Vallon; she has nothing of the sort, poor thing. These silks are not much use, but what do you think of these cloth breeches? They are just the right size for Chabot's boy. Oh! And do look, M. l'Abbé, here is a beautiful travelling coat, warm and thick. You'll have to think of someone for whom it would be really useful."

She was squatting back on her heels, turning a great heavy cloth coat over and over.

"It is rather moth-eaten in places," she said ruefully, "but that wouldn't matter much. I believe it was Papa's travelling coat when he and Maman used to post in Paris..."

She paused with the coat in her delicate hands and looked up at the priest with a troubled expression in her eyes.

"M. l'Abbé," she said abruptly, "do you think it would be possible to warn Papa against that awful Talon?"

The Curé looked astonished, not to say shocked.

"My dear child!" he exclaimed. "An old and faithful servant!"

"He is not," Aurore said decisively. "I am sure he is not. He is a hypocrite Val-le-Roi he talks softly to Papa Val-le-Roi "

"My little Aurore, you must not say those things. Where is your Christian charity? What has poor Hector Talon done?"

"He incites the people down in the village against us."

"But what makes you say such a thing? You really haven't the right
Val-le-Roi "

"M. l'Abbé, listen to me," Aurore rejoined firmly. "You know
Marianne Vallon down in the village?"

"I do. A good woman and—"

"She is a good woman, I daresay, though she seems to hate us."

"No, no, my dear child. You must not jump to conclusions like that.
Marianne is a very unhappy woman. Her only son, whom she adored,
went to the war a year ago and has not been heard of since. She feels
rather bitter about everything. But hatred? No! No!"

"Well, that is as it may be," Aurore rejoined with some impatience;
"but she said something yesterday which has confirmed my opinion
about Talon. I suspected him long ago, but since yesterday..."

"Well? And what did Marianne say?"

"That it was Talon who egged on those people to fire the mill and the
granaries."

The Curé raised his hands in protest.

"Oh!" he exclaimed. "I cannot believe that."

"Then you think that Marianne Vallon deliberately told me a lie?"

The old priest felt cornered. His brain, which was not over brilliant,
though intensely kindly, had to make a choice between calling a man a
traitor or a woman a liar. He shrank from either conclusion; he

hummed and hawed and did his best to avoid Aurore's searching eyes. In the end he compromised.

"Talon," he said, "may have said something that those poor people misunderstood. And there is no doubt, alas! That, with their minds turned away from God, the devil has a great hold over their souls. But I am sure," he added hopefully, "that they have already regretted their action of the other night."

"Only because they found the granaries empty," Aurore concluded with a shrug.

What was the use of arguing? This incorrigible optimist was as surely courting disaster as was her father with his bitter resentment. She gave an impatient little sigh and returned to the more pleasing subject of stockings and petticoats.

# Chapter XIII

Indeed, Aurore de Marigny's anxiety would have turned to real alarm could she have guessed Talon's purpose in coming up to the château today.

He made his way quite unceremoniously to the small boudoir where Monseigneur usually sat, entered without knocking and with all the assurance of a privileged guest, rather than of a servant. Charles de Marigny always writhed at this show of independence on the part of his once obsequious bailiff. In spite of his outward stoicism, he had not yet become accustomed to those principles of equality, which placed the caitiff on a level with the seigneur. Every time that Talon came into his presence with the swaggering air of an equal, and the suggestion of sympathy and protection more galling than enmity, Monseigneur would grind his teeth and clench his hands in an effort not to strike the insolent varlet. But he had enough sense to realize that, as far as the future was concerned, his safety, and perhaps his life and that of Aurore were dependent on this man's goodwill: so he swallowed his wrath and returned Talon's casual greeting with as much heartiness as he could.

With scant ceremony the bailiff took the chair lately occupied by the Abbé, poured himself out a glass of water, drank it down, and remarked with an attempt at jocularity:

"No more Burgundy in the cellar, eh? Well! Never mind, better times will be coming soon."

Then he talked about the weather, commented on the latest news from Paris, seeming not to notice Monseigneur's absorption. At last Charles de Marigny broke in impatiently:

"Well, what about the granaries?"

Talon sighed and dolefully shook his head.

"Burnt to the ground. Nothing saved."

"And the mill?"

"Alas!"

Monseigneur had made a vigorous effort to control his temper, but with each curt answer from his bailiff the veins on his temples stood out more and more like cords, and he pressed his lips tightly together because he felt that his breath was coming and going with a hissing sound. All of which Talon did not fail to notice, even while he appeared absorbed in picking at the nails of one hand with those of the other.

"And," Monseigneur asked, after a moment or two when he thought that his voice would sound steady, "what have you done about it?"

"I, my dear sir!" Talon exclaimed, "What do you suppose I can do?"

This easy familiarity, this jaunty "my dear sir" required yet another effort on De Marigny's part to keep his temper. He did it, nevertheless, forced himself to appear at ease with this man the very sight of whom he detested, and after a moment he said with quiet deliberation:

"I ordered you, some time ago, when that raffish mob fired my bakery, to let the miscreants know that for every building of mine which they destroyed I would raze one of their cottages to the very ground."

"But, my dear friend—" began Talon in protest.

"I am not your dear friend," Charles de Marigny broke in, on the fringe of exasperation, "but your employer! I gave you certain orders. Did you execute them?"

"I did my best. I threw out hints. I warned them, but I dare not do more."

"Your warnings were no use, apparently. Two valuable granaries have been wantonly destroyed: also the mill, which cost thousands to build only half a dozen years ago: find me a handful of honest men—men who will do what they are paid to do. Choose any two cottages in the village you like, evict the tenants, and let not one stone remain upstanding."

"Monseigneur!" Talon exclaimed with a gasp.

"Ah!" De Marigny rejoined with a sneer. "It has brought you to your senses, too, has it? You realize that I am not your dear friend but a man who has not forgotten either his position or his rights? Those devils up in Paris talk of a government by terror. Terror, they say, is the order of the day, and they remain in power because they govern by fear. Terror is going to be the order of the day on my estate. An eye for an eye, a tooth for a tooth. a cottage for my granary; a house for my mill. Find me the men, Talon: I'll show those dastardly ruffians down there that I am still their lord and master."

Charles de Marigny had worked himself up into a state bordering on frenzy. All his common sense, his stoicism had fled to the winds. He had nursed his resentment, his longing to hit back, for so long that all this wanton outrage against his property he lost all sense of proportion, and seized the opportunity to strike, and strike again, not counting the cost of the deadly danger. If he had been perfectly sane at the moment he not only would have realized the folly of such arrogance, but he would not have failed to notice that his bailiff, far from appearing horrified at the monstrous suggestion or frightened at its probably consequences, sat huddled up in his chair with his bony hand across his mouth.

Talon was doing his best to conceal the sneer that lurked around his lips and the gleam of triumph that shot through his eyes. For months now he had worked for this: to bring this arrogant fool to a state of exasperation had been the aim and object of all his scheming and his double game. Those whom the dogs wish to punish they first strike with madness. Talon knew no Latin, but he did know that he had at last succeeded in bringing to the point of frenzy the man on whom depended the success of all his well-laid plans.

"Monseigneur," he murmured again. "You don't seem to realize the temper of the people..."

He had shed his easy familiarity as he would a mantle; he was obsequious, servile, cringing now.

"It is time they realized mine," De Marigny retorted proudly. "I or that rabble. One of us must be the master here."

"Unfortunately they have the power... and the numbers. You are alone."

Monseigneur said nothing for the moment. He sat staring out of the window through which he could perceive over the treetops the ruins of his mill and his granaries. It seemed as if his outburst had tired him out. He looked, all of a sudden, like a sick and weary old man; the blood was ebbing out of his temples; he closed his eyes for a moment or two, and a long sigh broke through his trembling lips.

Talon drew his chair a little closer to him, and, sinking his harsh voice to an insinuating whisper, he said:

"Why not turn your back on the rabble? Get away to England or Belgium... emigrate. So many of your friends have done it..."

Monseigneur made no reply; but Talon, whose keen eyes were watching every change on the proud, expressive face, saw a sudden softening of its lines, as if an invisible hand had passed over them and erased all that were hard and cruel. And in the eyes there crept a look, which was almost one of yearning.

"So many have done it," Talon reiterated. "It is the only road to safety."

But, as quickly as they had come, softness and yearning had already vanished from De Marigny's expression; once more the eyes became hard, the mouth obstinate.

"I'll not go, Talon," he said forcefully, and brought his clenched fist down on the arm of his chair. "I will see this devilry through to the end. I will hold the fort against this rabble, though, as you say, I must do it alone, but nobody shall lord it over Marigny while I live."

"It wouldn't be a case of any one 'lording' it," Talon murmured, "only of a temporary arrangement. Scores of gentlemen have done it... and it is the safest plan."

He waited a moment or two, then he added:

"The safest plan for you and Mademoiselle Aurore."

This time the blow had gone him. Charles de Marigny could not suppress a cry of anguish.

"Aurore!"

"But," he went on slowly, speaking as if to himself, "if we go—if we—if we emigrate—those devils will confiscate the whole of my property, and—"

Talon had to make a great effort to conceal the gleam of satisfaction that shot through his yellow eyes: Monseigneur had started to argue the point—and that was the first sign of defeat.

"Only nominally," he said. "The whole plan is of the simplest—as I said just now—a temporary arrangement...."

"What temporary arrangement?" De Marigny asked with a frown.

"A paper making the property over to—to—a faithful servant—just a temporary arrangement, as I say—the other party under-taking to restore the property to its original owner on demand. It is done every day, my friend. Half the estates in France, at this moment, are nominally the property of men who have under-taken to administer them on the quiet, till times are better...."

"In this case you mean yourself?"

"Oh, I don't know that, my good sir. The risks are very great, you must remember."

"How do you mean—the risks? There are no risks, except for the unfortunate owners who put themselves at the mercy of knaves."

"Only for the time being—always supposing that those others are knaves. But when life is at stake—and not only one's own life, but that of others who are very dear—well, one must take certain risks. And there is little risk in trusting a faithful servant who has looked after your interests for twenty years."

Talon had a persuasive tongue, and as soon as he noted that his suggestion had made a breach in Monseigneur's armour of pride and obstinacy, he pressed his point home. It was done every day. The sale of the estate was nominal. The price paid in worthless bits of government bonds. Talon had once more dropped his show of servility. He "dear sir"-ed and "my dear friend"-ed De Marigny because he had not rejected the proposal with scorn but was pondering over it. Half the battle, then, was already won, and Talon saw himself in possession of Marigny, at any rate for a number of years, long enough to build a good nest egg and then to flit out of the country if times changed back to the old regime and he was summarily dispossessed.

"You, as the owner, would run no risk," he went on more glibly. "The risks would all be mine, if I undertook the task, for I might be denounced as a traitor for my devotion to you. But you! Why, my dear friend, you could go away to England or Belgium with Mademoiselle Aurore, and when you came back to Marigny four or five years hence—the present state of things cannot last longer than that—you will find your estates impoverished, no doubt, but your house standing where it did."

He rose, preparing to take his leave. He knew well enough that he had sown the right seed in fairly receptive soil and that to say more just now might imperil the happy issue of his fight. Whether, when once more left to himself, Charles de Marigny would return to his state of arrogance and frenzy or ponder more deeply over his bailiff's suggestion was on the knees of the gods. It was no use thinking that the battle was already won. It was not. There was a chink in the armour of obstinacy, and that was all.

"I'll bring you the papers in a day or two," he said casually, as he took his leave. "It is quite a simple affair. You acknowledge having received a certain sum from me for the sale of all your properties wheresoever situated, and I sign an undertaking to restore them to you on demand and the repayment of the money."

"On demand?"

"Why, yes! You are not likely to return to this hell upon earth, are you? Unless times have much changed."

And Charles de Marigny, as if wear of struggle and argument, assented somewhat lamely.

"Yes, yes, Talon. Quite right! You are right, I am sure, and you mean well. Bring me the papers; I'll look at them."

"In the meanwhile I'll give it out more decidedly that if any more arson occurs on your property you will give as good as you get."

"Yes, yes!" Monseigneur assented, his exasperation getting, at last, completely the better of his good sense. "Do what you like, but, for God's sake, get out of my sight now! I am sick of you and your ugly face."

Talon grinned. Memory took him back to those days before the great upheaval, when Monseigneur le Duc de Marigny was in the habit of thus dismissing his obsequious bailiff. Times had changed, but not Monseigneur. Talon knew well enough that beneath a great deal of show of stoicism the old Adam could always be reckoned with. Because of that old Adam of arrogance and tyranny he would gain his point. Monseigneur would be forced to yield Marigny up to him or perish at the hands of an infuriated mob.

And Hector Talon made his way home, satisfied with the morning's work.

# Chapter XIV

By the time that Aurore and the Abbé Rosemonde had finished sorting out the treasures of the old leather trunk Talon had left the château. Aurore found her father looking thoughtful.

"That rascal Talon," he said presently, speaking as it were to himself, "is no fool. His advice is sound." He drew the girl to him and looked searchingly into her eager young face. "My little Aurore," he went on wistfully, "would you like to put all these horrors behind you and seek refuge somewhere where we could have peace?"

"You mean—emigrate, Father?"

"Why not?"

"And lose Marigny? They confiscate everything if one emigrates."

"If it could be done without losing Marigny?"

"Even so...?"

"You don't want to go?"

"I want to do whatever you think is right; but—I love Marigny." And Aurore's dreamy eyes, full of a vague yearning, swept over the beautiful vista around, the wooded slopes, the distant ribbon of the Allier whispering among the reeds, the steeples of the village churches peeping out between the clumps of sycamore and walnut. All this meant home to her. She had never known another. Even the palace in Paris had been but a pied-à-terre for her: Marigny alone was home. "I love it," she reiterated with a sigh. "I know every tree in the forest, every shrub in the coppice, the call of every bird. To go away into the unknown frightens me, somehow."

"Now, that is sheer childishness, Aurore," her father said sternly. "My dear Abbé, help me to get those silly fancies out of her head."

The old priest had stood by in discreet silence, ostensibly engrossed in looking over again the old clothes he was going to distribute in the village. At Aurore's outburst he looked up, and now that Monseigneur appealed to him he came and placed a hand on the girl's shoulder.

"I should miss you terribly in the village, my child," he said, "but I agree with your father. If it can be done, it would be wiser to go away. It will only be for a time."

"Do they hate us here so much as all that?" she asked. Probably she would have broken down then and had a good cry. It seemed so cruel that, in spite of every effort towards forgiveness and charity, it was impossible to combat that hatred which a lot of irresponsible and cruel demagogues had instilled into the hearts of the people of France. But Aurore met her father's anxious, loving glance fixed upon her: young as she was, she knew that he depended on her for every tiny gleam of joy or happiness that she was able to give, and also that at sight of her grief his bitter resentment and suffering would increase a hundredfold. So she swallowed her tears, gave her father a good kiss, then turned once more to the old priest, smiling through her tears:

"Let us go straightway to the village now, M. le Curé," she said. "I do want the Legendre children to have those stockings soon. And," she added with a light laugh, "I have not yet done my marketing today."

It was late afternoon when Aurore de Marigny made her way back from the village toward the château. Jeannette was with her and carried her market basket. She was an elderly woman who had served the ducal family almost from childhood, when she began life as a scullery wench. She had lost mother, father, kindred, one after the other, and gradually her whole life became entirely dependent upon the château. When approaching middle age she had married Pierre, one of the men-servants, and after that had carried on just as before. She never had any children. Somehow she had never wanted any. And then when, one by one, the other servants of the château ran away, terrified lest they should be identified with unpopular aristos, Pierre and Jeannette had stayed on, chiefly because they had nowhere else to go. What few services were required of them—the little bit of cooking and cleaning—they did quite ungrudgingly but without enthusiasm. They seemed to have become a pair of automatons, with undeveloped brains and a vague protective instinct towards Aurore de Marigny and Monseigneur who gave them shelter and food.

Together Aurore and Jeannette walked rapidly along the road, which at this point follows the riverbank until it branches off to the wooded slopes which lead up to the château. They had gone past the last two or three outlying cottages, and the road stretched out before them like a white ribbon, sunbaked, dusty, and solitary. They had seen no one for some time when, suddenly, a man came into view around a bend, walking slowly towards them. He looked wearied, ragged, and dirty, but in this was no different from many other wayfarers on the high roads these days; but there was something in his limping gait, in his stooping shoulders, and in his head, which fell forward on his chest and rolled round and round as if insecurely held by his neck, which gave the idea of fatigue verging on complete collapse.

As the man drew nearer Aurore perceived that he wore a military coat and breeches, both in the last stages of decay, and that he had no shoes on his feet, which were bleeding and covered with grime. His head was bare, and a shocked of chestnut-brown tousled hair fell like a mop over his face. Aurore noted, also, that the right sleeve of his tattered coat was hanging empty.

Obviously, a miserable soldier, making his way home from the war. As he came close up to the two women he stumbled and would certainly have fallen had not Aurore put out her arms. Instinctively, with his one hand he seized hold of hers, and remained quite still for a moment or two, trying to steady himself and clinging blindly to this unexpected support. Then he raised his head and shook the mop of hair away from his face. Aurore encountered a pair of dark eyes, lacklustre and glassy, and with an unseeing vagueness in their dilated pupils. She did not dare move for fear of seeing the man fall at her feet, but she half turned her head to Jeannette and said quickly:

"That drop of wine in the small bottle... give it here...."

At sound of the voice the glassiness went out of the man's eyes. The pupils contracted, and a deep frown appeared between his brows. He seemed suddenly to realize that the prop, which supported him was a woman's arm, and with a great effort he steadied himself on his feet. A curious light flashed from his eyes, which seemed to sweep Aurore from head to foot.

Jeannette muttered something about wasting good stuff, which had cost so much to procure, but Aurore spoke impatiently:

"The bottle, Jeannette! Quick!"

Under the man's curious sweeping glance she felt her cheeks flushing, but still she did not move, holding out her arm quite stiffly until his hold on it relaxed. Then she frowned and turned her head away, for the man was staring at her still, and there was something in that stare, a certain contempt or even enmity, which almost caused her to take to her heels and run. But she held her round, and when, presently, Jeannette handed her the bottle, she took it and held it out to the man. With a sweep of his arm he brushed it away, then threw back his head and laughed. It was a strange laugh, hard and mirthless, which caused the suspicion of a shiver to run down Aurore's spine—a shiver not of fear (for what was there to fear in this miserable, maimed creature?), but of recoil, as if in the presence of something weird and not altogether earthly. But that was only a momentary weakness: the man looked so unutterably wretched that tears of pity, never absent from the depths of Aurore's sympathetic head, welled up to her eyes. Instinctively she felt, however, that pity in this case would be unwelcome; repulsed, perhaps, with that contempt which still lingered in the man's eyes; so she closed her own for a moment or two, lest the tears trickle down her cheeks.

When she opened them again the man had passed by.

"Come, Jeannette," Aurore said quickly, "let us get home."

Jeanette, stolid and silent, had rearranged the market basket and started to walk beside her mistress.

"Thank goodness," she said, "this good wine was not wasted. It would have been a sin to deprive Monseigneur of it for the sake of that down-at-heel vagabond."

After a while she added: "You know who that was, don't you, mademoiselle?"

"No," Aurore replied. "How should I?"

"It was André Vallon. I knew him at once, though he looks a miserable bag of bones now."

"André Vallon?"

"Marianne's son. Mademoiselle must recollect."

"But how should I?" Aurore reiterated frowning.

Mechanically, however, she had paused for a moment and turned round to look at the retreating figure. Strangely enough, the man, too, had paused and looked back; and once more their eyes met. There was a distance of some ten metres between them now: the man, whoever he was, shrugged and laughed as soon as he had caught her glance; then he turned and went his way; but Aurore was again conscious of that vague sense of terror, as if something fateful and irresistible had come across her path. It was nonsense, of course. Again and again she said to herself: "What is there to fear?" Unfortunately, these days, inimical glances were more familiar to her than kindly ones; she was accustomed to looks of derision, even of hatred, to threatening words and menace of violence. The wretched vagabond who had just gone by had not spoken; had threatened with neither word nor gesture; but never in all these fateful days had she encountered a glance so full of latent contempt and almost unearthly hatred.

"Tell me about this—this André Vallon—was that the name?" she said presently to Jeannette, while together the two of them walked up the slope.

Jeannette, whose powers of narration were limited, began a long and involved tale on the subject. She talked of André and his mother; of the boy's early turbulent life in the village, which ended abruptly and violently in a public whipping in the market square for disorderly conduct. Jeannette could not remember the details, but she had heard it said in the village that young Vallon had sworn deadly enmity against all those who had been present and seen his humiliation.

"He went up to Paris after that," Jeannette went on to relate, "and got under the thumb of that murdering blackguard Danton. So I shouldn't wonder if he has become just such another assassin himself. I shouldn't care to meet him alone on the road. But, as I used to say to his mother long ago, she would spoil him. She let him think he was somebody, though he was nothing better, even in those days, then a young ne'er-do-well. And the woman spoilt him, too, because he had flashing eyes and a way with him. Dirty young blackguard, I call him."

She went meandering on, not caring whether her mistress listened to her or not. She had the usual anecdotes to tell of André's turpitude, and the perpetual mischief he would get into, causing his mother endless worry.

Aurore only listened with half an ear. Vague memories floated through her mind of a glorious day such as this in mid-July. Her birthday. Her young friends. A game of blindman's bluff. And then the face of a boy with flashing black eyes, a shock of chestnut hair from which the hot sun drew glints of shining copper, and of a brown, slender hand holding a futile, useless pocket knife.

It all seemed like a dream now. Later on she had heard the story of the same boy being publicly whipped in the market square for having killed Hector Talon's savage dog, and she remembered feeling sorry for him, because already in those days she had instinctively disliked Talon. How it all came back now! Her pity for the boy, her dread at sight of his flashing dark eyes and of his beautiful face convulsed with rage because Pierre de Mauléon had slapped his cheek. And the heavy scent of earth which had offended her nostrils when, blindfolded, she fell against his breast.

# Chapter XV

Soon the news was all over the countryside that André Vallon had come home from the war, and the very next day Marianne's doorstep was besieged with people who not only wanted to see the boy, but wished to know just what was going on over in Champagne or Verdun; whether the King of Prussia was really marching on Paris, or whether he had been defeated by the brave national army and was now in full retreat.

Somehow, too, it had become known that André had both won his epaulettes and lost his left arm at Valmy, where the King of Prussia had suffered a severe defeat. Rumours of that victory—one of the rare ones—had penetrated as far as Val-le-Roi; Danton had made grandiloquent allusions to it in the National Assembly, had talked volubly about "our glorious troops, our valorous soldiers who were sweeping the whole of Europe clean of tyrants and militarism." He spoke of "their heroic deaths, fighting in the glorious cause of liberty," and "sacrificing their noble lives with the smile of martyrs going to glory, so that the world might, at least, be safe for democracy."

What he did not talk of were the unspeakable privations, the almost unbelievable hardships, which, indeed, had been endured by the troops with a stoicism and heroic obstinacy almost without parallel in the history of the world. André himself never spoke about that. That he had suffered, and suffered terribly, along with the troops which he had helped to lead to victory, could be seen by the unnatural glitter that came to his eyes whenever friends pressed him to tell them something of that well equipped and well fed army of Prussians and Austrians who were attacking France just because she had thrown off the shackles of tyranny and led the vanguard to an era of equality and of liberty. An almost cruel curve would then distort André's lips when he spoke of the Austrian officers in their smart uniforms, or the Prussian troops with their good boots and well filled bellies, all fighting in the cause of those aristos who had so complacently shaken the dust of starving

France from their high-heeled shoes and were disporting themselves in comfort and safety in Belgium or England. And he would glance up into the distance, where, outlined against the summer sky, the pinnacles and pointed roofs of the Château de Marigny towered above the treetops, and the look in his eyes became almost one of frenzied hatred, whilst words such as Danton himself would have emulated came hoarsely from his parched throat. He hated them. Heavens above, how he hated them all! It was a hatred akin to physical anguish, one that had been born in his heart when he was a mere child, on that day of bitter humiliation when he had stood naked at the whipping post, exposed to the mocking gaze of those aristos with their perfumed hair and bejewelled lorgnettes. That had been a boy's hatred, but now it was the hatred of a man filled to the soul with bitter resentment and the yearning for some measure of revenge.

But it was when the gleam of that resentment glittered most vividly in her son's eyes that Marianne's podgy, toil-hardened hand would descend with a soothing pressure upon his shoulder. Her calm philosophy would express itself in a few clumsy words, and André would pat that kindly hand and kiss it and make a big effort to subdue the paroxysm of his fury.

"All I long for, Maman chérie," he would say, as calmly as he could, "is that I may live long enough to see the destruction for this old world and the rebuilding of the new. Nothing else will do, my dear one, but complete annihilation of everything. There is corruption everywhere; uncleanness, crying evils too deeply rooted to be remedied. The world is overgrown with tares; nothing but a world conflagration can render it clean again."

At which Marianne would nod her head and reply gently: "The worst tare of all, André, is hatred. How can you reap anything but conflict if you sow that?"

"It is not hate, Mother, that will set the world aflame, but justice. Something has got to be done. Those who have mocked at misery and done nothing to alleviate it must be made to suffer. Those who have enjoyed life, who have always eaten and drunk their fill—they have got to learn what it feels like to be so cold—so cold that your chattering teeth seem ready to fall out of your jaws and to feel your belly so hollow that you would gnaw the flesh off your own limbs. They have got to know something of suffering, Mother. It is justice, and it has got to be."

But Marianne would still shake her wise old head. Justice? When had there ever been justice in this old world in which she had lived long and endured so much? There had been no justice in the days that were past, when up at the château—whither she trudged day after day, in order to do the family washing—she saw buckets full of meal and skim milk thrown to the pits, and fat, meaty bones given to the dogs, which would have kept her and her boy free from hunger. Was there justice now, when soldiers who were fighting for France were allowed to starve while the great orators up in Paris held banquets and feasts in the name of Liberty?

Justice? God alone held its scales, and no man knew how He would administer it in the life that was to come.

# Chapter XVI

It was while the excitement of André Vallon's homecoming was at its height, and the imagination of the countryside stirred by his account of the heroism and endurance of the national army, that Hector Talon took the opportunity of recruiting half a dozen ruffians to fulfil that act of madness ordered by Monseigneur by way of reprisals for the burning of his granaries and his mill.

With ferocious spite he had already selected the cottage of Marianne Vallon for the dastardly deed and chosen the day when André himself was absent from Val-le-Roi, having gone to Nevers on business of his own. He also selected another cottage close by, which was the property of the widow Louvet, who had four children and a small competence left to her by her husband, at one time a prosperous farmer who, some time before his death, had fallen on lean days and been forced, like so many others, to sell most of his land. Those two cottages, then, isolated from the rest of the village, had been marked by Talon for destruction. The six ruffians, whom he had recruited in absolute secrecy and for a small sum from one of the distant villages, arrived in the early morning armed with sabres and bayonets, clad in cloth coat and breeches, and wearing red caps on their heads. They proceeded first to one cottage and then to the other, and summoned the women to clear out of them at once. As they refused to move, the ruffians seized them and the Louvet children and forcibly ejected them from their homes, after which act of brutality, they set fire to the cottages. When these were well ablaze they incontinently took to their hells, and no one had set eyes on them since.

The news of the outrage spread like wildfire, and soon the entire population of three villages flocked to the scene of the disaster.

Strange how rumour does travel in these lonely districts! The firing of shops or stores, of granaries or timber sheds, were of frequent occurrence these days, and usually the crowds that gathered round the conflagrations were made up, in addition to the ruffianly incendiaries, of a few young rapscallions intent on mischief and some poor half-starved vagabonds—men and women—who hoped to pick up something out of the wreckage. There were also those who came to shout, "Vive la liberté!" at the instigation of the professional tub-thumpers, who took the opportunity of egging the crowd to worse mischief still.

But in this case it was different. People came from Le Borne and Vanzy, from Auberterre and Barbuise; for hours the road, the lanes, the towpaths, were dotted with dark figures hurrying to the scene. Men in ragged shirts and shoeless; women in tattered kirtles; children, half naked, clinging to their mother's hand; but there were also the farmers from Aubeterre or Vanzy, who came driving in their carts, and there was the lawyer from Le Creusot in his carriole, and the leech from Barbuise, who was on his rounds.

For an hour or more the cottages were ablaze. They were stone-built, with heavy wooden rafters and age-old beams, which were a ready prey for the flames. There was very little wind, and the sky was leaden. Great storm clouds, tinged now with crimson, came rolling in from the west. Huge columns of smoke rose, writhing and twisting, to the sky mingled with showers of spluttering, hissing sparks.

The men worked wonders, some of them risking their lives in a heroic endeavour to save the women's goods. There had been a prolonged drought since June and very little water in the wells, but many men defied the flames while they dragged poor bits of furniture, bedding, or clothing out of the blazing buildings. The women stood round, staring wide-eyed at this disaster, which they could not comprehend. It was so un-understandable, meaningless, wanton. The destruction of bourgeois or aristo property, yes! They understood that well enough, because those that were well-to-do were the enemies of the starving people of France—at least, so the great orators up in Paris were never tired of dinning into the ears of all and sundry. But cottages! The dwellings of the poor, the home of a widow and of a mother of children! That was beyond human comprehension.

The widow Louvet, with her children gathered about her knees, was squatting by the side of the road up against the hedge with a crowd of sympathizers all round her. She mostly had her apron over her face, feeling, she said, quite unable to bear the sight of that awful conflagration. She seemed quite incapable of lending a helping hand, even in the simple effort of dragging her goods out of the way of the crowd. When her apron was not over her face she just stared in front of her, or else at her children, and through quivering lips murmured agonizing, "Mon Dieu!"s and "Sainte Vierge!"s. "What will become of us now?"

But Marianne Vallon neither cried nor prayed. In her own quiet, stolid way she did her share in endeavouring to rescue her goods. She worked like a man: and when all her little bits of furniture were in safety, she went over the Louvets' cottage and helped in the work of salvage there.

"Voyons, Citoyenne Vallon," one of the men said to her when she attempted to go too near the blazing building. "Keep your distance. The place is dangerous."

She said nothing, only shook the men off who tried to restrain her. There were the children's paillasses to get out of the way, and their few bits of clothing. The men had gotten these out of the cottage, but they were too near the fire still, and flying sparks might set them alight.

"Take care, Citizeness Vallon!" the women shouted to her. "Let the men do what they can."

Marianne was stooping at the moment. She had hold of a bundle of bedding with both hands and was dragging it out of the way. Her bulky shoulders were bent to the task: the scanty gray hairs clung to her streaming face. The bedding was heavy and awkward to handle, but so precious; so very precious, with all those poor sickly children wanting to sleep comfortably o' nights.

"Take care, Citizeness Vallon!" the women screamed. "It isn't safe!"

"Let the things be!"

"Take care!"

And the men all at once gave a terrific shout, "Out of the way!"

One of them tried to get a hold of Marianne to drag her to safety, but she was large and heavy and bulky, and she was bending to her task, not seeing what was going on and heedless of the shouts of warning.

And suddenly a sheet of fire came bursting from the cottage: it was followed by a thunderous crash as the roof fell in, scattering bits of wood, stones, and tiles in all directions.

A cry of horror arose from every throat, drowning the roar of the flames, the hissing of sparks, the din of falling timber and crumbling stones. Beneath a huge smouldering beam Marianne Vallon lay, huddled up and lifeless, still clasping the bundle of bedding in her arms.

# Chapter XVII

Now only the blackened stone walls were left standing, with the empty holes where the tiny windows had been staring out on the scene of devastation like hollow, sightless eyes. An evil-smelling sooty smoke still found its way out of the smouldering ruins, and now and then a volley of sparks rose up hissing to the stormy sky. A suffocating smell of hot paint and burning refuse hung in the air, and the lamentations of women, the whimpering of children, and the dull murmur of men's voices seemed like eerie sounds that came from the Stygian creek.

No one knew exactly what to do or what to say. The catastrophe was so appalling that, beyond sullen murmurs, those who had witnessed it appeared tongue-tied. Paralyzed they were with the horror of it. The death of Marianne Vallon was the culminating point in the over-whelming disaster. And André himself was away. He had gone to Nevers the day before to see about a lawyer's business, which he wanted to take over now that he was no longer fit to rejoin the army. He had been full of hopes of a brighter future for the mother whom he adored. No longer would she have to wash and scrub for him. There was so much litigation these days that any lawyer with brains was certain of a good income. And André Vallon was well seen in his high places: he had been clerk at one time to no less a personage than Georges Danton, the idol of the people, who thought the world of him. Oh! There was no doubt about it, the world held compensations for a man like André Vallon. He had lost an arm but not an iota of his brains, and though the terrible hardships, which he had endured in the campaign against the Prussians, had to a certain extent impaired his health and embittered his temper, he had still two priceless posses-sions—youth and an iron constitution.

He was going to be so happy! And now this awful, this overwhelming cataclysm. Who was going to tell him? Who would be bold enough to face that son with news of his mother's death under such tragic cir-cumstances? The women discussed it but could offer no advice. All they could do was to stretch their arms up to heaven and ejaculate, "Jésus! Mon Dieu!" even though they knew well enough that appeals to the deity were now forbidden by law. The men were torn between the desire to run away, now that they could do nothing to help in an active way, and the longing to fasten the guilt of the whole thing on somebody. For somebody had done this awful deed. The ruffians who had ejected the women and children from their homes had taken to their heels. True enough! But the countryside could be scoured for them, and, by dint of menace and other more forcible arguments, they might be made to confess in whose pay they were. Strangely enough, no one suspected as yet that the monstrous order had emanated from the château.

In the meanwhile, those among the crowd who had business of their own to attend to were gradually trying to get away. Perhaps at the back of their minds there arose the fear that some sort of mischief would surely come out of this. Vallon would turn up presently, and the devil alone knew to what lengths his fury would go. He already held the people around in the hollow of his hand and could lead them whithersoever he chose. With his mother lying dead at his feet through an outrage as yet inexplicable, something of the rage of a tiger unleashed might carry him and his sympathizers to excesses, which presently might know no bounds. When the temper of the rabble was worked up no one knew how things would end, and it was best to be home and keep gates and doors well barred and bolted. And so the farmers in their carts, the leech in his carriole, the keepers of neighbouring village stores, drifted away one by one.

"If you meet Vallon, tell him!" was shouted after those who were going in the direction of Nevers.

And Farmer Lameth, from over Le Borne way, going homeward in his cart, did presently meet André Vallon, who had borrowed a carriole in Nevers and was leisurely driving home. Farmer Lameth pulled up.

"Terrible doings up at Val-le-Roi," he called out to André. "You should be there, Citizen Vallon."

"Why? What has happened?"

"Two cottages have been fired, and families turned out of their homes."

"Name of a dog...!"

Farmer Lameth hesitated a moment or two. Already he did not much like the look in André's face. What would it be presently—when he knew?

"One of them is your mother," the worthy farmer added tentatively.

"My mo—!"

This time it was the devil himself who kindled the flame in André's eyes. He whipped up the nag, and the carriole started off with a bump upon the stony road. Farmer Lameth turned in his seat and called out once more:

"Citizen Vallon!"

André did not slacken speed, but he too turned in his seat and shouted back:

"Yes! What is it?"

"There's more trouble there than you think—"

But André did not really listen. He whipped that poor old nag as he had never whipped a horse before. Never had the road seemed so long. Trouble indeed! He would see to it that there was trouble and to spare for whoever had lain hands on his mother's property and turned her out of her home. Trouble? There would be trouble in Val-le-Roi such as there had never been even in Paris, even in Versailles! Trouble? My God!

# Chapter XVIII

"Here comes Citizen Vallon."

"No."

"I tell you 'yes.'"

"And he's driving like the devil!"

Instinctively the crowd had closed up right across the road, barring the way to the smouldering cottage and standing in a dense mass round the recumbent figure over which someone had reverently laid an old tattered shawl. The men had succeeded in moving away the beam and the bundle of bedding, and Marianne Vallon now lay on one of the paillasses which she had rescued from the flames: her hands had been folded across her ample bosom, and the thin gray hair smoothed away from the marble-like, wide forehead.

There was no other feeling in the heart of anyone there at this moment but intense pity for the bereaved son and an awed wonder as to what would happen next. Even such men as Tarbot, the ex-butcher of Vanzy, and Molé, the wheelwright, two of the most desperate ruffians the Revolution had engendered in any village, were silent and uncertain, and determined to delay as long as possible the terrible revelation that would bring such overwhelming grief to a devoted son. So they all stood like a solid phalanx, shoulder to shoulder, around that still and inert mass, while a carriole came rattling down the road, and a miserable nag, all skin and bones, thick with dust and lather, charged straight into them. It is very difficult to stand up to a charging horse and vehicle, even though the horse is but skin and bones: the crowd gave way, and André jumped down from the carriole. The men tried to restrain him, but with his one arm he shook them off and forged his way to where his mother law, with eyes closed, her hands folded across her bosom, her body covered with a shawl.

He was in the midst of a crowd, and he would not let them see what he felt. Not a word came through his lips, and the cry that had risen to his throat was smothered and deadened with a mighty effort of will. He knelt down beside his mother and, with his hand on her ice-cold forehead, he looked down on her face and listened. No need for the others to tell him. Death was all too plainly writ on those beloved features, so stark and set, and the slightly parted lips through which so many words of quiet philosophy had often passed in order to comfort and to calm him. The eyes were closed, and André bent down and kissed each rigid lid; the hands were folded as they had so often been in prayer when she had knelt beside his bed. Her heart was still—that great, big heart of hers in which there had never been room for hatred and bitterness.

Oh, no! There was no need for others to tell him. He knew the moment that the crowd parted and he saw her lying there with the tattered shawl over her that she was dead. A slight noise among the crowd, a sigh, no doubt, or a smothered sob, recalled him to the fact that there were others there. Very gently he drew the old shawl right over his mother's face, and then he rose to his feet. There was not a drop of blood in his cheeks: his face looked as pale as that of the dead woman at his feet, but in his eyes now there were smouldering flames of fury that would not be quenched save in revenge.

"What has happened?" he asked curtly.

A dozen voices were raised at once. Floods of eloquence so long held in check poured into his ears in full.

"The two cottages were fired."

"Six ruffians laid hands on the women."

"The widow Louvet and her four children are homeless."

"Your mother was killed in an endeavour to save some of the children's belongings."

"The roof fell in. A heavy beam knocked her down."

"She must have died instantly."

"Hold on!" André shouted, drowning the tumult with his stentorian voice. "Who fired the cottages?"

"Six ruffians there were—"

"In cloth coats and breeches—"

"And with shoes on their feet."

"Who saw them?"

The widow Louvet—she with the four children—had given up crying and moaning and staring into vacancy. The far greater tragedy of Marianne Vallon's death had put her own misfortune in the shade. Thus directly appealed to, she was ready to come forward with her tale. She had seen the six ruffians, of course: had they not turned her out, her and the children, out of her home, and at the point of their bayonets? She couldn't resist. What could she do? They had turned her out, and she was afraid the children would be hurt. Then the ruffians had set fire to her cottage. They had piled up straw in the middle of the kitchen floor and set it alight. Some of them stood by to see that the straw had caught on properly; the others went on to the house of Citizeness Vallon.

"Was no one about, then, to stop them?"

Apparently not. They all shook their heads. It had all been done so quickly.

"After that the reprobates took to their heels."

"And no one after them?"

Again they all shook their heads.

"Your mother tried to save the children's bedding—" the widow Louvet began dolefully, and suddenly paused, for the look in André's face was so terrifying that it froze the words on her lips.

"And I am not here," he murmured, "to tear their entrails out of their filthy bodies..." And suddenly he threw back his head and his glowing eyes searched the faces in the crowd.

"Can any of you guess," he asked quite quietly, "who is at the bottom of this?"

Not only had they guessed, but they knew. Had not Hector Talon—that double-faced hypocrite—had he not thrown out hints that more than a week ago that Marigny, up at the château, had threatened—nay, commanded—reprisals for the firing of his granaries? Some of them murmured the name of Talon, but André gave a harsh, scornful laugh.

"Talon?" he said. "Yes! We'll deal with Talon presently, for of a certainty he is in this villainy up to the neck. But," he went on more slowly, so that every word told and struck the ears of the crowd like the knell of an inevitable doom, "it is that devil up there who must account for today's infamy."

He paused a moment and then added:

"I am going up there, anyway, in order to make sure. Who comes with me?"

The response was unanimous. Indeed, it seemed as if a great sigh of relief went through the assembled crowd. Not only the men, but also the women. The sense of awe engendered by the magnitude of the catastrophe and the death of Marianne Vallon was beginning to wear away. There were men here who had begun to think of reprisals and who read in André's white, set face, in the almost tigerish fury in his glowing eyes, that passionate desire for revenge for which they themselves had so often thirsted. Men like Tarbot, the ex-butcher, and Molé, the wheelwright, had also brooded over the wrongs of their caste until they hungered for an opportunity to bring aristos to shame, or, better still, to the guillotine. They had seen around them such scenes of misery, humiliation, starvation, and tyranny that their hatred of tyrants and oppressors had turned to savage lust for the sight of blood.

There was no question here of philosophy or moderation.

How are you going to preach forgiveness and moderation to a starving crowd? There is no tongue sufficiently eloquent to find words that will pour the soothing oil of forbearance on a raging sea of rebellion. One

Voice alone could do that, and did it nigh two thousand years ago, but today that Voice is still: It only speaks mutely from the Cross.

"Citizen Vallon," one of the men said decisively, "we will help you in your revenge."

André nodded in silence. He could not trust himself to say much. Not yet. There was always the fear of breaking down, of showing weakness, which he was far from feeling. He hardly dared look on that so still form beneath the ragged shawl: the folded hands showed all too plainly, and the swell of the ample bosom against which he had so often as a child cried himself to sleep. No, indeed, he dared not look, for sobs threatened to choke him, and he might cry out his agony of grief. But he still had a task to accomplish, a duty to fulfil.

"A few sticks to make a stretcher," he said curtly.

"Where'll you take her, André?" one of the women asked.

"Back home."

"It is burnt to the ground."

"I know that."

They asked no further questions, for already André was busy breaking down branches of trees. The men helped: some of them had tools, others went to fetch what they could. A stretcher was soon improvised, and they lifted the dead woman on it. André and Tarbot, the ex-butcher, carried her to her ruined cottage, most of the others following.

Tarbot, looking down on the dead woman, asked:

"Where shall we put her?"

"In there," André replied.

They put the stretcher down, and André went deliberately up to the cottage door and started clearing away the charred débris which encumbered it. The other men lent a hand, and when the entrance had been cleared André and Tarbot went back to get the stretcher. They had just stooped to lift it when the Abbé Rosemonde was seen hurrying down the road. He had heard the news and came panting along as fast as his shaking limbs would carry him. He had tucked his soutane up round his waist: he was hatless, and his gray hair clung to his streaming forehead.

"I don't want to see him," André said abruptly. "Keep him away."

But the Curé forged his way resolutely through the crowd.

"André, my child," he cried panting, "I only just heard the news. I came as fast as I could."

André paid no attention to him. In silence, with the aid of Tarbot, he carried his burden into the ruined cottage.

"We'll lay her down here," he said, "until such time as—"

"André!" the old priest called.

"Go home, Citizen Curé," Tarbot said roughly. "Can't you see that you are not wanted here?"

He and André had taken the dead woman to the centre of what had once been her parlour. The floor was littered with rubbish. They cleared a place on which to deposit the stretcher. Above, through a wide, yawning gap in the roof, there was a vista of a leaden sky of gray clouds which hung, low and heavy, presaging the coming storm.

André collected what there was left of charred wood and spread it around the stretcher.

"Straw would be better," he muttered.

"What are you going to do, Citizen Vallon?" Tarbot asked.

The others had come to a halt all about the doorway. Behind them the old priest was still striving to elbow his way through the crowd. André drew his flint and steel out of his pocket and used them vigorously, trying to draw a spark. The men understood.

"Straw would be better," one of them said. Another added: "I know where to get some," and turned toward the road. This made a gap through the crowd, and the old priest pushed his way in.

"André!" he cried once more. "Your mother...!"

André paid no attention to him. He was busy with his flint and steel, trying to get little bits of wood alight. But the fire had done its work, the charred wood fell into ashes and would not burn.

"Young Legendre has gone to get straw," said one of the men.

"This is sacrilege," the old priest protested loudly. "André, in your dead mother's name..."

At this André looked up. "My mother is dead," he said roughly; "she doesn't want you."

"You may not want me, my child," the old priest retorted firmly, "but she would."

Then, as André said nothing more, only went on stolidly striking flint against steel, the Curé said forcefully:

"Remember, my son, that from above she can still see you; how think you she would view this awful sacrilege? Voyons! Voyons, André," he went on more gently, "do not harden your heart in rebellion against the will of God. Let me come near the dear old soul, and we'll pray together that she may have eternal rest. She would have wished it, you know."

And though resentment and bitterness were tearing at André's heart, he knew that the priest was right. Old Marianne, could she have said the word, would have rebelled against this desecration of her body: she would have wished for Christian burial, to the accompaniment of prayer and the ministrations of the Church. To the end of her hard life she had remained a professing Christian, clinging to the simple beliefs of her youth, weeping over the godlessness of this new regime, over the spirit of rebellion which it had fostered in her André's heart, abhorring the tyranny of man which had brought so much misery on the poor people, yet bowing with quiet philosophy to the inscrutable will of God.

André knew all that. "She would have wished it, you know." The priest's words found an echo in his aching heart. For a few seconds still did he hesitate, did his pride war with his love for the dead. The others watched him in silence while the women wept. Here was something that was past their comprehension, something that awed and silenced them and for the time being made them forget their passions and their hatred. Then André, without another word, put his flint back into his pocket and rose to his feet. He stood aside, and when the priest knelt down beside the dead and began murmuring his prayers, he watched him silently for awhile and then walked quietly out of the cottage.

# Chapter XIX

But under the stormy canopy of the sky the spell was broken.

"We'll help you, citizen Vallon. Let's to the château!" was the universal slogan.

"But first of all for Talon!"

The cry came from André. It was harsh and cruel like that of a young tiger scenting its prey. The others did not quite understand.

"Talon? Why Talon?"

"Because," André said, "such an abominable deed could never have been carried out without the aid of Hector Talon."

Why indeed Talon? Because he was the man whom André hated only one degree less than the people up at the château. Why Talon? Because André had a longing to see him dragged here by the heels through the dust and to see his yellow eyes turn glassy with the agony of deathly terror. Talon the hypocrite! The mealy-mouthed sycophant!

"Who will go and fetch Talon?"

There were any number of them there willing enough to start the day's work by baiting Talon. They went off in a body to fetch him. They dragged him out of his house. Pushed along, heckled and jostled, they brought him to the scene of the disaster, face to face with André Vallon.

They had dragged him along, and he had come, and on the way he had mapped out his line of action. Not without due deliberation had he planned the monstrous outrage, nor without due regard to the consequences, unpleasant to himself, that might ensue. He had foreseen the rage of these people, their lust for revenge; he had reckoned on their passions as a lever for finally persuading Marigny to emigrate. He had even been prepared for a certain measure of danger to himself—danger, which he would know how to combat. But what he had not reckoned on was the death of Marianne Vallon.

Nevertheless, he faced the crowd boldly. Whatever terror he felt, he did not let them see; nor did he flinch when André, towering above him, laid such a heavy hand on his shoulder that his knees gave way under him.

"So there you are, Citizen Talon," André apostrophized him coolly. "I suppose you know who I am?"

Talon looked up at the young face, dark and distorted with fury, and blinked his yellow eyes.

"How should I not know you, Citizen Vallon?" he said smoothly. "I have known you ever since—"

"Ever since you had me whipped for killing your brute of a dog, eh?"

"That is past history, Citizen Vallon," Talon said jocosely; "you are a man now."

"While you have remained a worm," André retorted: "such a worm that I have a mind to tread on your face, just for the pleasure of seeing you wriggle."

The men laughed, but Talon did not flinch. He even contrived to shrug and to smile. He was clever enough to know that a bold face and an arrogant air would be his best safeguard against aggression. Some of these men here—the rougher ones—were his friends. They knew him to be a man of influence. They had listened to his oratory outside the village taverns and had heard men in high places speak of Citizen Talon as a good patriot. And Talon knew that they would not dare touch him, even though André Vallon, the savage young brute, did his level best to incite them to murder. He kept up his jaunty air, and, only pulling a wry face, he said indulgently:

"You were always good at jesting, Citizen Vallon."

"I am not jesting now," André rejoined. "I want to know who gave the order for this abominable outrage."

"You mean the firing of the cottages?"

"Who ordered it? Tell us! Speak, why don't you? Speak, or I'll tear the words out of your filthy throat."

Talon put up his hands and gazed at André with an air of innocence.

"Easy! Easy! My friend," he said, "how should I know?"

"You are Marigny's menial—you must know...."

"Then if you've made up your mind..."

"It was Marigny who gave the order?"

"I don't know," Talon protested. "I swear I don't know."

"You lie!"

Talon shrugged his lean shoulders.

"You lie, I say," André reiterated roughly. "Speak the truth, man," he went on more calmly, "it will be better for you. The aristo gave the order, is that it?"

But Talon would admit nothing. He knew nothing, he declared: vowed that he could not believe Marigny capable of such a thing. As for himself, he knew nothing. Nothing. He had been more shocked, more distressed than anyone when he first heard of the disaster.

"Lies! Lies!" André retorted roughly. "Shall we to the château, citizens, and find out the truth for ourselves?"

A murmur of assent went the round. The truth? Why! They all knew the truth. André had known it all along, from the moment when he saw his mother lying dead and that awful red mist rose before his eyes. Marigny! It was Marigny who had done this loathsome deed. Murder, deliberate and most foul, lay at the door of that arrogant man up there, who, like his kindred and his king, had not yet learned that the people would no longer bow the neck to the yoke of their pride and their tyranny. Well, he, at any rate, would be taught a lesson that day: he would be made to mourn with tears of blood the deadly wrong, which he had committed. He and his brood! Let them look to themselves! Men and women had gone to the guillotine for less, had watered their marble floors with bitter tears for crimes which were as venial sins compared to this morning's outrage.

Already the crowd had begun to move in the direction of the château; they had all been impatient enough to go. What cared they if the aristo "up there" were guilty or not? They wanted to march, to shout, to threaten, as others had done in Paris and Versailles. In the far distance from over the mountains came, from time to time, the dull rumbling sound of thunder; occasional flashes of lightning lit up the heavy storm clouds with a weird purple light. The air grew hotter and more oppressive every moment, but they all wanted to be up and doing—the storm was finding an echo in their hearts.

"To the château, André!" they said. "We'll help you in your revenge."

Talon made feeble efforts at protest.

"And you come with us, Citizen Talon," André concluded grimly.

Tarbot and Molé took Talon by the elbows. There was a general movement along the road. Men, women, children: they all joined in the procession. The men, earnest and determined; the women, bitterly vindictive; the children, innocently curious. There were fourscore of them at least, fourscore bent on demanding reprisals for an unparalleled wrong.

And André, silent and absorbed, with eyes aglow and mouth set, saw, through a veil of red, a woman's face with large, innocent eyes and soft fair hair—a woman, just a girl, in a rose-coloured silk which made her seem like a flower bud. He hadn't seen her for many years. She must be a woman now.

Bah! What had he to do with women, and visions of women seen through a mist the colour of blood? The one woman in the world he had ever cared for lay stiff and stark now, silent in her ruined home. And all that misery, all this injustice and unbounded sorrow lay at the door of those people "up there"!

Heavens above! How he hated them all.

97

# Chapter XX

The Abbé Rosemonde, having finished his orisons, bethought himself of Marigny and little Aurore up at the château, ignorant, mayhap, as yet of the storm that was about to break with raging fury over their heads. At one moment he had thought of speaking to those poor misguided children who were being led away by disaster into acts of violence, the terrible consequences of which God alone could foresee. He had thought of admonishing André Vallon, who bitter resentment was causing him to whip up the tempers of his sympathizers.

The worthy Curé shook his head dolefully: that poor lad! Led astray on the very threshold of manhood by his obstinacy and wilfulness: full of generous impulses, and such a good son! He would have made a kind and faithful husband if only the times had been different. And now that this awful grief had descended upon him his obstinacy would harden his heart still more against the comfort which religion alone could give. A pity! A sad, sad, pity, that this catastrophe had happened. It was the will of God, of course, and he, poor, humble priest, bowed meekly before it, but, oh! How he wished that it had not happened. He couldn't imagine who had conceived such an inhuman project, for never for a moment would he contemplate the idea that Monseigneur would act so cruelly.

"Mon Dieu! Mon Dieu! Sainte Vierge Marie!" he murmured fervently, "Turn the hearts of those poor, ignorant people of France to a better knowledge of religion and virtue."

Thus the old man prayed while he tramped up the familiar woodland path toward the château. He had been able to reach the slope without being seen by the crowd, who were still standing outside the ruined cottage, talking and murmuring. At one moment the Abbé thought that he heard the voice of Hector Talon. Well, of course, as a priest and a Christian he wished no harm to come to anyone, but if it pleased God to punish Talon, Talon who had the ear of Monseigneur and was such an evil counsellor, he, as a man, would not complain.

Now, as he tramped upward, the good Curé could hear echoing from the valley below the distant clamour of the angry crowd: André's sonorous voice and the hoarse shouts that rang with the promise of mischief.

The atmosphere was terribly oppressive; there seemed to be no air here under the trees; not a leaf stirred, and an evil smell seemed to rise from the dust in the road. The Abbé hurried on. He knew that he could do nothing "up there," but he could warn Monseigneur of what was brewing against him. It might be wise to seek safety in flight while there was time.

There was the width of the terrace and the gardens, with the distant postern gate which gave on a lonely part of the wood, where it might be possible to await quietly a better turn of events.

Indeed, the Abbé had to hurry. Looking down from a point of vantage, into the road below, he could see that the crowd had begun to move. To the priest it seemed as if their number had swelled. But his eyes were short-sighted, and many months ago he had broken his spectacles; he had never had any money since with which to buy new ones, so he couldn't see very well. He hoped that the crowd was not great and that Talon was with them. Surely Talon would act as a restraining power over the others.

Mon Dieu! Mon Dieu! How foolish it all was! If only Mademoiselle Aurore and Jeannette were out of the way, for arguments with noisy crowds were not fit for women's ears.

Fortunately he was well ahead of the misguided lambs. He almost ran up the perron, pushed open the great gate, and hurried across hall and corridor and up the marble staircase to the distant small withdrawing room, where Monseigneur usually spent the best part of the day.

Aurore was there with her father. She was busy sewing, and Monseigneur was reading a paper which seemed highly to incense him, for just as the Curé entered the room he crushed it in his hand and threw it on the floor with an oath. The priest sank, puffing and panting, into a chair:

"Those poor people! Those poor miserable fools!" he began, and mopped his streaming forehead.

Monseigneur looked at him and laughed.

"You need not tell me," he said curtly. "I know."

Aurore looked up from her sewing; she looked first at her father, then at the Abbé; then she put down her work. Something terrible had happened. The strange glitter in her father's eyes, the anxiety and distress in the Curé's face, but, above all, her intuition and a sense of foreboding told her that something terrible had happened.

"What is it?" she demanded.

"Those poor people," the priest murmured, "they are so foolish—so ignorant—"

"Ruffians and devils!" Monseigneur declared, and struck the table with his fist, "they have learned at last that I, for one, am not to be defied."

Aurore took hold of his hand; the one with which he had struck the table.

"What has happened?" she demanded again.

There was a moment's silence. Only a few seconds. But during those seconds she heard. The window was open, and she heard the clamour—the sound of feet tramping up the slope and of a dull murmur that mingled with the rumbling of the distant thunder. She knew what it meant. Without doubt an in a moment, she knew what it meant. Newspapers, pamphlets, rumours had found their way to this lonely corner of France. Aurore de Marigny knew that all over the country demagogues—men like that André Vallon—spent their time in inciting all the ruffians they could get hold of to do acts of violence against persons of property. She knew that. And she knew what the outcome of such provocations had often been. Outrage. Death. Sometimes worse than death.

She questioned her father. She had the right to know. They would all hold their lives in their hands in a few minutes when the crowd reached the château. She had the right to know, she declared. Something had roused the village folk to frenzy: what was it?

Monseigneur shrugged and said nothing. The glitter in his eyes was like that of a madman. The old priest, overcome with emotion and the heat, could do nothing but mop his forehead. And the clamour from the valley grew louder and louder, the dull murmur of voices and the tramp of naked feet in the dust of the road.

And suddenly Pierre came bursting into the room, with Jeannette weeping and trailing behind him. They knew everything. Pierre had heard it all—Heaven knew how—but he had heard so he ran up—like the old Curé had done—to warn Monseigneur and Mademoiselle. He was breathless and inarticulate, but Monseigneur did not interrupt him while he blurted out the whole terrible tale: the six ruffians, the eviction of the women and children, the firing of the cottages, the death of Marianne Vallon.

Charles de Marigny appeared indifferent to the whole thing and entirely disdainful. He did not even wince when Pierre spoke of the death of Marianne. The priest moaned and ejaculated: "Mon Dieu!" and looked to Heaven for guidance, while Aurore listened wide-eyed, horrified. At first she was incredulous and turned to her father with an appealing and mute: "Is it true?" But his glance was obstinately averted. He stared out of the window—listening—listening for the coming of that rabble which he despised so utterly, even though their approach now probably meant death to him and to Aurore.

A few minutes later the crowd had invaded the courtyard. The shuffling of naked feet, mingling with the clatter of sabots and the tramping of shoes, sounded like the breaking of surf on a pebble beach. The voices were subdued, like the distant murmur of an angry sea. There were no shouts, only murmurs and occasionally the whimpering of a child.

Monseigneur rose.

"The gate—" he said curtly to Pierre.

"Barred and bolted, Monseigneur. Oh! Monseigneur didn't think that I would allow..."

Charles de Marigny did not listen. He had opened the drawer of the table against which he now proceeded to examine carefully. Aurore's large troubled eyes watched him as he drew his tall figure to its full height and then turned to the door. With a sudden little cry she ran and stood between him and that door. "You are not going to meet them, Father!" she exclaimed impulsively, and put out her arms to stop him, but he pushed her roughly aside.

"You don't imagine," he retorted coldly, "that I would allow that rabble to come in here?"

"If you go," she protested, "I come with you."

He took hold of her wrist with such violence that she nearly cried out with pain. Who was she, he demanded, to stand in his way? How dare she pit her feeble woman's will against his determination to deal with those ruffians as they deserved?

"I order you to stay here," he commanded; and not heeding the servants' look of horror or the Curé mild protest he dragged her roughly from the door.

"Are you trying to defy me," he thundered, "like that riffraff over there?"

And the look, which he cast on her—on her, the child of his heart, the apple of his eye—was so laden with fury that she shrank from him as if he had struck her in the face.

Then he opened the door. It gave on one of the great reception rooms, used as a ballroom in the olden days. A long vista of parquet flooring, of mirrors and girandoles, of tapestries and consoles, stretched out to the other great doors opposite. Aurore turned a last appealing look to the Curé.

"You must obey your father, my child," he said. "God will protect him, and you can do nothing."

He struggled to his feet and beckoned to Pierre. Charles de Marigny had already gone through the door, and now the Abbé Rosemonde and Pierre went out in his wake.

## Chapter XXI

The great room was empty. Silent and majestic, with its gilded mirrors and chandeliers and rows of chairs ranged round the walls as if ready to receive the ghosts of the grand ladies and gentlemen who had chatted here a few short weeks ago, had flirted and laughed and fluttered their fans and danced the minuet in their high-heeled shoes before they made their way up the steps of the guillotine or sought safety in an obscure corner of some foreign land.

But Charles de Marigny had no mind for sentimental recollections just now. He strode across the room to the great central window and threw it open. Like the sudden bursting of a dam, the sound of the surging crowd rose in a strident cadence. Monseigneur stepped out on the balcony and looked down on them. How ugly they were! Dirty, unkempt, clad for the most part in filthy rags! He loathed them! Oh! How he loathed them! The men! The women! Those half-naked, unwashed children! Were they human at all? In the olden days he would have classed all that rabble as lower and of less consequence than his cattle or his dogs.

He stood there for quite a few moments looking at them, his arms resting on the marble balustrade, the pistol in his hand. They had come to a standstill in the vast forecourt and were evidently debating what to do next. Then a man's figure detached itself from the rest. He wore an old military coat, one of the sleeves of which was empty and fastened to a button on his chest. He wore shoes and stockings, but his head was bare, and his hair was the colour of a horsechestnut when it bursts its green prickly shell.

There was something vaguely familiar in the face, those dark eyes and chiselled features, which recreated in Monseigneur's memory a vision out of the past—a boy half naked, with straight young back and firm limbs standing at the whipping post, while he and Hélène de Beauregard looked on rather amused. Hélène had put up her lorgnette and compared him to a rebel angel. He looked more like a demon now.

He strode across the forecourt and up the perron. Two others, more swinish than the rest, followed him. Charles de Marigny watched them. No one had caught sight of him yet, for the balcony was thirty feet from the ground and twenty from the top of the perron. The three men came to a halt in front of the great wrought-iron and gilded gates.

Pierre whispered to Monseigneur:

"Good thought I had of locking them. They'd want a cannon to break them open."

The men, seeing that the gates were locked, appeared to hesitate, and suddenly the man with the empty sleeve looked up.

"Marigny!" he called out and pointed to the balcony. The crowd at once gazed upward. They saw Monseigneur. They shouted, "Assassin! Open the gates!" The women waved their arms; the men shook menacing fists. But Charles de Marigny remained motionless and detached, with an expression of withering scorn on his pale, aristocratic face.

"Open the gates, Marigny," André Vallon commanded. "The people here want a talk with you."

De Marigny's sole response was a peremptory:

"Get out of there! All of you, get out!"

"Don't be a fool, Marigny!" André retorted loudly. "The people will not stand your arrogance. They have come to speak with you, and speak with you they will, if they have to pull down these stone walls about your ears."

"Get out!" Charles de Marigny called out in reply. "The gates through which you came are open! Get out!"

"Open the gates!" they all shouted.

"Get out!"

The tumult was waxing fast and furious down below. Murmurs had long since turned to raucous shouts, in which the words, "Traitor! Tyrant! Death!" came clearer than the rest. But "Death!" Clearest of all. The Abbé Rosemonde tried in his feeble way to restrain Monseigneur, but Charles de Marigny shook himself free with a loud oath from the kindly hand on his shoulder.

"Open the gates!" André's voice rose above that of the others, and Tarbot and Molé, like a pair of savage dogs on the leash, cried out, "Open the gates or we'll burst them open!" Whereat a boy's voice in the crowd rose shrilly:

"If we burst them open there'll be no talking: only death for the traitor."

"Death! Traitor! Assassin!"

"The guillotine!"

Pierre's teeth were chattering with terror. He kept on murmuring, as if to give himself courage: "They can't burst them open! They can't! They'd want a cannon!"

Charles de Marigny drew himself up. Only his hand now, the one which held the pistol, rested on the marble balustrade. He wanted them to see him better, to see the contempt with which he regarded them and their futile efforts to intimidate him. He turned half away from the balcony as if that rabble down there was not even worth a glance. He shrugged ostentatiously when the words, "Assassin! The guillotine!" rose more and more insistently from below.

"Let us go back, M. l'Abbé," he said calmly, "and see what Aurore is doing. When these muckworms are tired of shouting they'll clear out fast enough."

As far as he was concerned that was all! Rabble! Riffraff! The scum of humanity! That is what they were! And trying to frighten him? Ludicrous, of course! Contemptible! What a fool to have brought his pistol! As if those cravens would ever dare—

A simultaneous cry from the Abbé and Pierre caused him to swing back suddenly.

The man with the empty sleeve had clambered up to the balcony. With the aid of projections in the stonework and the age-old ivy which, untended, had spread over the wall, he had pulled himself up. Tarbot and Molé were following him, but he, André, had got there first. One arm can be as good as two when fury whips up the blood. With the aid of his one arm and a sinewy pair of legs he was soon over the balustrade, even before the cry of alarm spent itself in the old priest's throat.

Monseigneur swung round. The pistol was in his hand, even with André's head.

"Another step and I shoot!" he called.

"Shoot and be damned!" André retorted, and with a bound was on the floor of the balcony. His arm shot out; his fingers, hard as steel, closed round De Marigny's wrist and forced his arm up, up, and back from the shoulder. The pistol went off with a loud report and then dropped from the nerveless hand to the ground.

From the crowd below came an infuriated yell.

"A moi, Pierre!" Charles de Marigny shouted. And then, "Let go my arm, canaille!"

Before Pierre could come to his master's rescue, Tarbot and Molé were over the balustrade, too, and onto him. They took no notice of the Curé, for he had fallen on his knees, poor old man! And was imploring God to protect Monseigneur; but they held Pierre down while André forced De Marigny, step by step, back into the room. Like a vise, that one hand of his was nearly wrenching the upturned arm out of its socket.

"Mon Dieu, ayez pitié!" the priest murmured fervently, whilst Monseigneur, though half swooning with pain, reiterated obstinately, "Canaille! Canaille! Get out!"

The crowd, baulked of the sight of their enemy, had resumed their cry of "Assassin!" A few of them, more vigorous than the others, tried to follow their leader's example by climbing up the ivy-covered wall. The other's shouted, "Open the gate!" whereupon Molé, the wheelwright, seized Pierre by the arm and said curtly:

"You hear them, citizen? Come and open the gate."

"Pierre, I forbid you," Monseigneur attempted to command, but Molé had already marched Pierre out through the door, while André, step by step, pushed De Marigny back into the room.

When he had got him right over to the other end, with his back to the door of the small boudoir, he released his arm. It fell, nerveless and numb. Obviously the man was in great pain, but pride kept him on his feet. Obstinate and arrogant he was; he could be cruel, too, where his dignity was at stake; but he was no coward, either morally or physically. He did not regret the firing of the cottages, that act of madness, which had brought this yelling horde about his ears. He felt faint and giddy, but with a mighty effort he kept himself upright. There was a chair close by, but he would not allow himself to sink into it, and even while André stood towering above him like a statue of wrath and vengeance, his lips continued to murmur mechanically, "Canaille! Get out!"

André gave a contemptuous shrug:

"Canaille we are," he said with a sneer, "that's understood, but we are a canaille who today demand justice. You have committed an outrage which calls to Heaven for vengeance, and we have come here to show you that we mean to get it."

"Murder, I suppose?" De Marigny said coldly.

"Killing is no murder when justice demands it. A few hours ago two defenceless women and a crowd of children were turned out of their homes by your orders. My mother gave up her life to rescue the few belongings of a poor widow and her children. As sure as that I hold your worthless life in my hands, her death is at your door. Killing is no murder, Marigny, when it means justice."

Still De Marigny did not flinch. He made no reply, and for a few seconds they stood facing each other, these two men, each the product of his own upbringing and of his century; each imbued with the passion and cruelty of men when they defend what they hold most dear. Charles de Marigny, unbending and imperious, seemed at this moment to be entrenched within the last outpost of his caste, and to be safeguarding his right of property and the privileges of his birth. Immaculately dressed, his hair carefully powdered, his fine linen scarcely disarranged even after a hand-to-hand struggle with this renegade, his pale face betrayed no emotion, only a withering contempt. And André Vallon, the typical child of this bloody revolution, the son of a people who for generations had suffered and toiled like beasts of burden and looked with patient, submissive eyes on the pomp and luxury that never could be theirs; who had never eaten their fill while others feasted; who had wallowed in poverty and ignorance with hardly the promise of Heaven to save them from despair: André with shabby coat and empty sleeve, with glowing eyes and heart overflowing with resentment for past tyranny and un-avenged wrongs, André stood for those stirrings which men like Rousseau had first infused into their blood. And as De Marigny worshipped privilege, so did these youngsters worship at the shrine of the newly discovered goddess, Liberty. A new dawn had arisen for them, and they fell on their faces and adored. They ate the fruit of the Tree of Knowledge. They learned and they pondered, and from out the depths of their soul they evolved the consciousness of the dignity of man.

"Canaille we are!" he had thrown back the challenge in De Marigny's face: "low, unwashed, and ignorant, but men for all that. For centuries your cast denied us the right to live, as we desired, to share in what goodness the world holds—the right to hold our homes sacred, our wives and daughters inviolate. But now we are your masters at last. We've butchered, we've despoiled, we've killed, but the measure of justice is not yet full. Hundreds of you have mounted the guillotine, and hundreds more shall do the same until we get what we demand—justice!"

All that he said and more, while Charles de Marigny's face expressed nothing but disgust at being in such close contact with this filthy horde.

# Chapter XXII

And now the crowd came pouring into the château. Pierre had been made to open the gate, and they all rushed up the marble staircase. They invaded the hall and the vast reception rooms. Awed at first by so much magnificence of which they had no conception, by the gilding and the crystals and the damask chairs, and by the mirrors, which reflected their dark faces and their rags and made their numbers seem so much greater than they were.

But the awe soon wore off. So much magnificence! And there were the Louvet children homeless; and Marianne Vallon lay dead in her ruined home.

"Well, André!" one of the men asked. "What says the aristo?"

"Not much to say, I imagine," said another.

"I am for slitting his throat at once and have done with him." This from Tarbot, the ex-butcher, who always kept a knife in his belt.

"I prefer the guillotine," declared Molé sententiously. "It's more effective. An example to others, what?"

"Let's hear what he's got to say first, and then we'll see."

De Marigny's fine white hand felt in his pocket and drew out a lace-bordered handkerchief, which he raised to his nose. With a rough gesture André tore it out of his hand.

"Play-acting, Marigny!" he said with a sneer.

"Let me slit his throat, André!" Tarbot demanded.

"Murder, by all means," De Marigny retorted coolly.

"Murder? No," André declared. "I too am for the guillotine. The people want to see you die a dog's death. Murder? Bah! Will one moment's anguish in your miserable life give us back our youth spent in toiling so that you might feast; give us back our health impaired by starvation while you ate and drank your fill? The last drain of your life's blood, Marigny, cannot make good your tyranny. It cannot! It cannot! You cannot make good, for you have nothing now—no power, no riches, none of the claptrap that made you think you were a creature apart while we were just swine."

His words acted like a gust of wind on a smouldering flame. Some were for immediate murder, others like the thought of the more protracted agony of the guillotine, but all wanted this man's death. They hungered for it. They ached for a sight of his blood. There was not a man or a woman there who did not see that pale, proud face through a veil of crimson. But they still help their breath like wild beasts when they have sighted their prey and are ready to spring. Like felines they were, licking their jaws, enjoying to its full the sublime sense of power over the life and death of a fellow man.

"Strike him, André!" one of the men shouted. "I am for instant death."

"Remember your mother, André!" yelled another. "Why wait for the guillotine."

And suddenly the door behind De Marigny flew open, and Aurore rushed in, a vision pale and ethereal, with fair hair loose and eyes as dark as the midnight sky in June. In an instant she was beside her father, her arms were round him, her head was against his breast. Her slender body was a shield between him and his enemies.

André had uttered one loud, savage oath, and then remained dumb, staring at the girl, while the crowd, taken aback for a few seconds, soon began to laugh and jeer. A fresh spectacle this: this fine lady with her laces and her frills. The wolves in expectation of the slaughtered sheep rejoiced at sight of the lamb.

"For God's sake, Aurore, go back!" Monseigneur exclaimed. At first he had been half dazed, hardly believed his eyes when he saw Aurore. He was like a man in a trance, not fully wakened from a dream. "Monsieur l'Abbé, take her away!" he added, vainly trying to perceive the

Curé's face in the midst of the crowd. He himself did what he could to drag Aurore's arms away from his shoulders, whilst the old priest made a vain effort to reach her. But all this was of no avail. It was Molé, the wheel-wright, who seized hold of Aurore by the waist and dragged her away from her father. In a moment she was surrounded. The women in the forefront pulled at her gown and tore at the lace of her sleeve.

"How much did your gown cost, my cabbage?" one of them jeered.

"As much as would keep a family in food for a year," declared another.

"Strip it off," suggested one of the men with a coarse laugh.

One of the women grabbed at her fichu; another tugged at the ribbon in her hair; the older ones lifted her dress and pulled at the lace petticoats, the dainty stockings and silk garters. Obscene jests went round:

"Strip off her clothes!" called Legendre, the young imp with the game leg.

"Pigs! Curs! Let her go!" De Marigny cried at the top of his voice, and tried to reach his daughter, but the whole crowd was in the way, laughing and jeering, pressing round the girl with shouts of derision and of glee. They elbowed De Marigny out of the way. One of the men struck him on the face with his fist, and he fell bleeding to the ground. He tried to drag himself up again until another man kicked him and he lost consciousness.

Aurore gave an agonized cry of horror, the first she had uttered since she had faced the crowd. Wildly, like a young animal at bay, she looked about her, and her eyes met those of André Vallon.

He as outside the crowd, had stood there ever since she first came into the room, vaguely retracing in his mind the childish features of ten years ago in that lovely face, contorted with fear. With a mechanical movement his hand went up to his breast, where all those years ago her head had rested for one brief moment, on the very spot where they empty sleeve was now attached. Her soft fair hair had tickled his cheeks; the scent of violets and roses had risen to his nostrils. He had been in a dream until the rough blow on his face from the hand of an insolent fop had awakened him and kept him awake all those years with the memory of a crowning insult.

He had been in a dream then; he was in a dream now, until her eyes met his. Then suddenly he pushed his way through the crowd. With his one arm he seized Aurore round the waist and lifted her off her feet.

"The wench is mine!" he called aloud.

Holding her closely to him, he pushed his way back as far as the door of the boudoir to the accompaniment of vociferous shouts and laughter from the astonished crowd. Here was a novel spectacle, forsooth!

"He was always a madcap, that André!" the women declared, while laughter brought tears to their eyes. Laughter, perhaps, or something a little softer, more gentle: a vague sense of romance never quite absent from the hearts of a Latin race.

André had allowed the girl to slide out of the shelter of his arm. She collapsed on the floor right against the door like a pathetic bundle of laces and frills. She was not quite conscious. Terror and horror combined had obscured her senses. With her small trembling hands she grasped the corner of a console as she slid down on her knees, and through her bloodless lips came pitiful moans and whispered murmurs, "Father! My father!"

André stood guard over her like a desert beast over its prey. He stood, tall and erect, with head thrown back and legs wide apart, a vivid presentment of the conquering male. The crowd was certainly amused. Some of them tried to push forward to peer once again closely at the aristo, her silks and her laces, but André with his stentorian voice kept them all at bay.

"Hands off! The wench is mine!"

"What will you do with her, André?" a voice called laughing out of the crowd.

"Take her for wife, pardi," André retorted. "I must have someone to wash and cook for me. The wench pleases me. She's mine!"

This sally was greeted with a wealth of coarse jests from the men, but the women were all on the side of André. They liked his looks, his flashing eyes, darker than ever in his pale, determined face. They liked his full red lips, which showed a glimmer of white teeth like those of a young cat.

"Let him be, he was always a madcap!"

"If he wants the wench, why shouldn't he have her?"

And whisperings went the round: stories of André Vallon's pranks before he left the village to seek fortune in Paris. Not a boy for leagues around he had not licked, not a pretty girl whom he had not kissed.

"Let him have her if he wants her."

The men agreed. Even Tarbot, whose lust for killing had a few moments ago turned him into a savage brute, shrugged his wide shoulders and said coolly with a coarse jest:

"Better than the guillotine, anyway!"

One of the men who had worked at the maire in Nevers added sententiously:

"If he likes to take her for wife there would be no guillotine for her."

"Is that so?" the others asked.

"The new law," the man from Nevers declared curtly. "A patriot may save an aristo from the guillotine if he chooses to marry her."

They discussed this matter from several points of view. Those bigwigs up in Paris were always framing new laws, but this was not a bad one. France was in need of children. The men, at any rate, were all in its favour because, forsooth, they were well-favoured, those aristos— soft skins, fluffy hair, better nourished than the poor village wenches. The women, on the other hand, liked the romance of it, especially if the patriot was young and handsome, like André Vallon.

André himself listened to all the comments and the murmurings with a vague smile on his lips. Perhaps he only half heard what was said. His glance more often than not wandered round to that motionless figure, crouching against the door, and when a pitiful moan came to his ears, a look almost of ferocity flashed out of his eyes.

The priest had contrived to get near to Aurore. He stooped and put his hand on her shoulder. He whispered comforting words to her, but the only response she gave was a pathetic murmur: "My father? Where is he?"

André, at sight of the priest, had become more and more impatient, and suddenly, like a man who has come to the end of his tether, he turned and kicked open the door. The small withdrawing room beyond was in semidarkness. Jeannette was in there, squatting on a low stool, weeping into her apron, which covered her face. There was a book on the floor, an open workbox, a piece of embroidery on the table with a thimble and scissors beside it. The room looked cosy in the half light with all these little intimacies. André glanced into it, then down on the crouching figure at his feet. God in heaven! How he hated it all! The beauty, the cosiness, and the perfume as of a bouquet of flowers that seemed to dull his senses!

"Stop your mumblings," he said roughly to the priest, "and take her in there."

Aurore wouldn't move, though she looked up for a moment when she heard the door open behind her. Not seeing her father, she turned on André.

"My father!" she demanded.

He took her by the wrist and dragged her roughly into the boudoir.

"I'll look after your father," he said curtly. "He's safe enough for the moment."

The Abbé Rosemonde slipped in after them and closed the door. Strangely enough, the crowd did not attempt to follow. They stood outside jeering and sniggering, vastly amused at the turn of events. So unexpected this romance of the aristo and that mad-cap André! It might turn to tragedy, some of them thought, but even so, it was better than the guillotine.

Some of the men gazed down on De Marigny lying unconscious in a corner of the room with a bleeding wound on his face: Bah! He was hardly worth a kick now. A miserable rag of humanity, trampled in the dust, as he had been wont to trample those whom he despised. His very life he owed to one of the despised rabble, and his daughter, who was his pride and joy, would be the property of a man whom in the past he would have looked on as lower than his dog. She would have to cook and wash for him as Marianne Vallon had cooked and washed up at the château. It was that, or the guillotine for the lot of them. Ah! This revolution was indeed a great thing. It had turned the tables on those proud aristos with a vengeance. More power to it's elbow, and long life to Georges Danton and all its makers.

Long life, above all, to the child of the Revolution, André Vallon.

# Chapter XXIII

At first Aurore had made futile efforts to free herself from André's grasp. Then, feeling helpless, she gave up the struggle, whereupon he immediately released her wrist. She turned at once to the door.

"Open, M. l'Abbé!" she called. "I must find Monseigneur."

The priest would have obeyed, but André barred the way.

"I said that I would look after Marigny," he said curtly. "You stay here with her."

Aurore's hand was on the doorknob.

"Wait here, M. l'Abbé," she said, "while I speak with Monseigneur."

André was quite close to her, looking down on her half quizzically, yet wholly in scorn. She threw back her head and returned his mocking glance with defiance and cold contempt, and when he put his hand over hers she withdrew it quickly, as if she had been touched by some noisome animal. A grim smile curled round André's set lips.

"If you go out through this door," he said coolly, "it means death to your father, to this priest, to your servants and to you."

Defiance in her eyes gave way to horror. She did not know what had become of her father. The turmoil in the next room had subsided to such an extent that she had not realized there was still danger there from the crowd. This male ruffian here, with his brute strength and mocking ways, seemed to be the only living creature that she need fear. Apparently he had divined her thoughts, for without another word he turned the knob and gently opened the door. A murmur of many voices came to Aurore's ears. There were no longer any shouts, no imprecations or threats—only that steady murmur, and now and then a laugh. Just as the moment a man's voice rose above the rest, and a phrase, coarse and hideously offensive, accompanied by a cruel laugh, brought a blush of indignation and of shame to the girl's face. It suffused her cheeks, her forehead to the roots of her hair; only her lips remained bloodless. The glance, which she cast up at André was almost one of appeal.

Miserable and helpless, she gazed round the room, longing to find something—weapon, anything wherewith to end this terrible situation. Again he seemed to divine her thoughts, gave a light laugh and a shrug, then pointed to one of the chairs across which lay Monseigneur's elegant sword, with its jewelled hilt and chiselled scabbard. As she made no movement—indeed, she could not have moved a limb just then—he went over to the chair and picked up the sword. He made pretense to examine it; with his one hand he worked the blade out of the scabbard, and with that irritating, quizzical glance of his held the hilt out to her.

"Will this answer your purpose?" he asked.

Strangely fascinated by that blade from which, at the moment, the evening light drew dull fantastic rays, she raised her hand and took hold of the hilt. Here was the weapon to her hand: what should she do with it? The brute stood there, waiting and mocking: oh, for the strength to plunge this blade into his cruel, callous heart!

"Aurore, my child!" the priest exclaimed, for, acting on blind impulse, Aurore had stretched out her arm and was holding the point of the blade to her throat.

"Let her be, Citizen Curé," André said coolly. "Reason has already told her that with her death my wish to save her father—and you—will vanish. Look, what did I tell you? Even proud ladies listen to reason sometimes. And, anyhow, that sword was both futile and ridiculous."

The sword fell out of Aurore's hand. Futile and ridiculous! How true and how humiliating! Helpless, hopeless, and ashamed, she buried her face in her hands.

"André, my son!" the priest entreated, "you must have pity on us all."

"Pity?" André retorted lightly. "Pardi! Am I not showing you all pity of which any man is capable? Have I not snatched her and her miserable father, and you, my good friend, out of the jaws of death? Has not my pity for her stayed the murderous hand of our friend Tarbot and saved her from outrage?"

"Yes, my son," the Curé admitted, "and of a certainty God will reward you; but surely you do not intend to carry your cruel intention to its end?"

"What cruel intention? I have no other intention with regard to this wench save to take her for wife."

"But, André, my son, that is impossible."

"Impossible? Why?"

"Look at her, my child. Does she look like the wife of—"

"—of a rapscallion?" André broke in with a sneer. "That is as may be and for her to decide. If the prospect is so very displeasing, all she need do is to open this door and let the rest of the canaille have its way with her, with her father, her servants, and with you."

Then, as neither Aurore nor the Curé spoke another word, he went on, with an impatient shrug:

"Perhaps you are right, Citizen Curé: the scheme will not work. It is impossible, as you say, and I'd better let our friend Tarbot have his way with you all."

Once more he turned to the door; but it was Aurore this time who barred the way. A dull, half-choked cry came involuntarily from her throat:

"No! no!"

She put out her hand, and he seized it.

"Ah!" he said with a sigh of satisfaction, "reason has spoke more loudly this time. Well! Which is it to be, my fine lady? Death at the hand of Tarbot or marriage with the canaille?"

The grip on her waist was like a tentacle of steel, but she welcomed the physical pain almost as a solace to the mental agony of the moment. She would not look at him, but turned appealing eyes to the old priest, who, of a truth, could offer neither advice nor consolation. It was for her to decide and he, for one, was content to leave it all in the hands of his Maker. He clasped his hands and prayed as he had never prayed before.

"Look at me, Aurore," André commanded. "The decision rests with you and not with the priest."

With what seemed like a refinement of cruelty, he once more gently opened the door. They were still laughing and jeering out there.

"My father!" she murmured.

And then added under her breath:

"For his sake, if you'll sear—"

She could say no more, for she was on the point of swooning. André's powerful arm encircled her drooping body, while an immense sigh of satisfaction rose from his breast.

"Par Dieu!" he said lightly. "I had no idea you were so beautiful, ma mie!"

And of a truth she was exquisitely beautiful, with those deep, unfathomable eyes of hers filled with terror and with hate, her red lips parted in a final appeal for mercy. She had been on the point of swooning, but now that he raised her to him—that she saw his face, his dark eyes, his cruel, sneering mouth closer and ever closer, a moment's consciousness returned to her with the horror of it all.

"Let me go!" she gasped. "I hate you!"

"Of course you do, my dear," he retorted. "We hate each other—that is understood. But Fate has decided to link us together until, like two wildcats, we shall have torn one another's soul to shreds. In the meanwhile, in the presence of our friend, the Citizen Curé, we will seal our mutual promise to one another with a kiss."

She felt helpless and stifled as his arm held her closer and closer; with her two hands she tried to push against him—his face, his breast. But her struggles only seemed to amuse him; his eyes flashed mockery instead of passion, while they seemed to search the very depths of her soul.

"You are beautiful!" he reiterated slowly—very slowly—while those mocking eyes of his drank in every detail of her loveliness: her blue-veined lids, her perfect mouth, the exquisite contour of throat and chin. "You are beautiful, but, on second thoughts, ma mie, I'll not kiss you yet. Not today. I'll wait," he added with a light laugh, "till those perfect lips ask mine for a kiss."

And suddenly he slackened his hold on her, lifted her off the ground, and carried her to the sofa. He called peremptorily to Jeannette, who was whimpering under cover of her apron, and ordered her to look after her mistress.

Then, without another word, he strode out of the room.

## Chapter XXIV

The crowd in the meantime had worked its will in the old château. With the exit of the hero and heroine of a brief romance, reaction had set in. The fury of reprisal, merged for a moment in laughter and coarse jests, reasserted its domination. The aristos were ashamed and punished; the cidevant Marigny lay half dead on the floor; but this seemed hardly compensation enough for two smouldering cottages and the death of a valiant woman. Not enough, of a truth, with all this magnificence flaunted in these gorgeous halls, with tapestries and sconces and mirrors, all accessible to eager, needy hands. Not much notice was taken of Marigny. Once kicked conveniently aside, he was allowed to remain lying there. Dead or alive? Who cared, when there were damask curtains to be had for the taking?—useful things to replace shawls and blankets long since worn to rags. Down came the curtains, one after the other, torn down by vigorous hands. In the vast banqueting halls there was not much that was useful, but there were chairs and tables to replace humble ones that had been used for fuel when other wood was so dear. And in the bedrooms there were beds and mattresses and pillows and blankets; there was china and there were carpets. The crowd wandered from room to room, from stately hall down to pantries and kitchens and bakehouses. The cellars were empty, and so were the larders, but there were pots and pans galore. Where silver and gold were hidden they knew not. Perhaps they never even thought of such things. It was the chairs and the tables, the curtains and the pots and pans that they needed and that they took.

Who shall judge them? Who condemn? They had nothing, and they took. For generations successive governments had taken from them all that they had. Human nature will always try and hit back when it has the chance. They were not evil, these people here; they were not really cruel and rapacious by nature: hunger and want had made them so, and the sense of oppression and injustice. Who, of a truth, shall condemn them?

When they were tired of looking and had their arms full, when they were wearied with the day's work and emotion, they wandered homeward. The evening was drawing in, and squalid homes called to them, and the longing to gloat over stolen treasure and find use for it all. One by one, or in groups of twos and threes, they trudged back through the vast halls, shorn now of much glory, down marble stairs, and across the forecourt. Their naked feet were sore with tramping; they wanted to get home.

André stood for a long time by the door, listening and watching. The great reception room was deserted by now, but he could hear the crowd wandering about the château; he could hear cries of delight and laughter and guessed what was going on. He made his way across the room to the window, staggering in the darkness like a man drunk. Leaning against the window frame, he gazed out into the fast-gathering gloom. From the distance, now and then, there still came the dull rumbling of faraway thunder, and from time to time the treetops were lit up with the reflex of distant lightning, but the storm never broke over Marigny on that never-to-be-forgotten day in July.

André watched the crowd, as, one by one, they came through the gate, bearing their loot—furniture, tapestries, clothes. The women staggered under their loads; the men looked like beasts of burden, dragging their shoeless feet over the paved forecourt. Slowly, wearily, they made their way down the wooded slope. André, through the darkness, could still distinguish some of them: the women in their faded kirtles; the naked bodies of little children; Tarbot and his red cap, Molé and his ragged shirt. He thought of his mother, lying on the old paillasse, with a ragged shawl to cover her body, and all around her the ruins of her home. And with thoughts of her there came into his soul an immense wave of shame.

The large empty room with its torn tapestries and gilded chairs lying topsy-turvy about the floor became filled all at once with imps and demons who hopped all around him and cried, "Shame!" in his ears. They called him a fool and coward. Why not have allowed the mob to have its way with the aristos? Were they not his friends? Riffraff, like himself? Then why have interfered? There might have been some satisfaction in seeing justice done. A life for a life! Those miserable aristos for the saintly woman who lay silent and stark in her devastated home.

With a rough gesture he brushed those imaginary demons away. Shame had brought the blood beating in his temples. "Coward!" and "Traitor!" he called himself, and then signed with a great unexplainable longing. "Justice! Truth! My God! Where are they now?"

The room was so still! So still! André strained his ears to hear any sound that might come from the boudoir. After a moment or two he heard a soft grating; the door was opened very gently, a narrow shaft of light pierced the gloom, and the old priest tip-toed stealthily into the room. André listened without stirring: the old man had left the door slightly ajar and now groped his way cautiously about in the darkness. A moment or two later soft murmurings came to André's ears; then a sigh—a struggle. And the priest's kindly words:

"Lean on my arm, Monseigneur..."

And then another sigh. A whisper: "Aurore!"

"She is safe, Monseigneur. Shall we go to her?"

"Has that canaille gone?"

"There is no one here now, Monseigneur..."

"My head! My head! May God punish those ruffians!"

"Do lean on me, Monseigneur.... I am quite strong.... Don't be afraid."

André's eyes, accustomed to the gloom, could now perceive the two old men moving slowly towards the door. Instinctively he stepped back from the window farther into the shadows, and thus, hidden from view, he waited until the priest had piloted De Marigny back into the boudoir.

As the Curé was about to follow, André called to him:

"Citizen Rosemonde!" The priest paused with his hand still on the doorknob, and André called again: "Close that door. I want to speak with you."

The voice was low, scarcely above a whisper, but so peremptory that the priest, after a few seconds' hesitation, closed the door and came across the room. With the passing of immediate danger to Monseigneur and Aurore he seemed to have recovered something of his natural dignity. He approached André not as a servant beckoned to by his master, but as a minister of God, with a mission to mediate between warring souls.

"What is it you wish, my son?" he asked.

"Only to give you a word of warning, citizen," André replied curtly. "You must understand once and for all that my mind is made up. I have decided to take that woman in there for my wife. As you have taken the oath of allegiance to the Republic, you are bound in law to perform the marriage ceremony. You know that, do you not?"

"I know it, my son, but—"

"There is no 'but' about it. If you refuse you forfeit every privilege, which your oath of allegiance has conferred upon you. Your church will be closed, and you may or may not escape with your life. But even that is beside the question, for if the marriage is not solemnized in your church it will be done in the maire, which, as you also know, is all that the law requires."

"André, my child," the priest protested, "I implore you to think over what you propose doing. I beg it of you in your mother's name—"

"Do not speak of my mother, Citizen Curé," André broke in harshly, "or I swear to you that I will call the worst of that rabble back and hand over that damned assassin to them to be dealt with as they choose."

"But such a marriage is an outrage, André!"

"Was not the eviction of two defenceless women and a pack of starving children an outrage? Was not the ruin of their homes an outrage? My mother's death—was that not a murder most foul?"

"Ah!" the priest exclaimed, "then you admit it, André?"

"Admit what?"

"That your whole purpose is one of revenge."

"Call it justice, Citizen Curé. You'll be nearer the mark."

"And you, my son, will be the first to suffer."

André shrugged with cynical indifference.

"Bah!" he said. "Your friend Marigny would tell you that muck-worms such as I are made to suffer."

The priest was silent for a moment or two. His heart ached for this man whom he had seen grow up in this village—a merry, carefree lad whom the cruelty of fate, and perhaps of men, had rendered bitter and cynical. But it ached also for the exquisite girl whose every instinct of pride and aloofness, would be outraged by this monstrous union.

"You will kill her, André," he sighed, "if you persist."

"Bah!" André retorted drily. "She's young. She will get used to being the wife of a caitiff. And anyhow, her life and that of her father will be safe. I can see to that."

"Alas!"

"Why alas?"

"They would sooner be dead."

André gave a scornful laugh.

"The aristo's sword," he said, "is still handy."

"I forbid you to mock, André," the priest retorted with energy. "Religion which you choose to ignore still holds sway in the hearts of many, and religion forbids—"

"Suicide," André broke in. "Yes, I know! Well, the rabble only needs recalling—"

"André, in Heaven's name, don't talk like that! I am appealing to your pity—"

"Pity? Would you call it pity to let a pack of snarling hyenas loose once again on this house, to stand by and see that arrogant old madman in there massacred before his daughter's eyes, to see her brutalized and outraged as a prelude to death? Is that what you would choose for her, Citizen Rosemonde?"

The old priest's head fell upon his breast. He felt utterly helpless and ashamed of his helplessness. A little while ago he believed in his mission of conciliation, but that mission had failed. His simple faith in divine interference had received a rude shock, as did his earnest belief in the justice of the Royalist cause. For here was a rebel who gloried in his rebellion, who demanded justice from God and man with as much right as the most earnest adherent to the old régime. Like André himself a while ago, the Abbé Rosemonde could have signed with unutterable longing, "Truth? Justice? Where are they now?"

"I suppose," he said with a doleful shake of the head, "that you've said your last word, and that nothing which I can say—"

"No, citizen," André broke in impatiently, "nothing. I have said my last word. Go down into the village, if you have a mind, and talk to the men there. Tell them that religion bids them forego revenge, and that if a man smite you on the cheek, to hold out the other so that he might smite you again. Tell that to men who have toiled and starved and sweated and seen their wives and children die for want of food, while the tax collector stood at the door and seized the few sous that would have bought them bread. Tell it to men who have seen their brides dragged from their arms to satisfy the caprice of their seigneur. Talk to them of forgiveness, Citizen Curé, now that they are the masters of France and have the power to give back blow for blow and outrage for outrage."

Again the priest was silent. There was so little that he could say. Never before had he been made to feel that there was something after all to be said for those terrorists who had earned for themselves the obloquy of half the world, but who had, of a truth, been the first to instil into a downtrodden people a sense of their power, both as men and as guardians of their families' welfare and of their family honour. Demagogues they were, and stirrers up of infinite trouble. They had let loose on the sacred soil of France a horde of savage brutes bent on ruin and persecution. All that was true enough, but there had been such an infinity of wrong to put right that nothing short of this immense upheaval could possibly have done it all. But dominating all other thoughts and fears in the old man's heart were those for Aurore.

"You will be kind to her, André," he implored, "if she consents."

"I care not if she consents or no," André retorted. "Either she is mine or I let loose the floodgates of the people's wrath on this house till there remains nothing of it but a few blackened stones like those of my mother's cottage, nothing but a memory of all the arrogance and the cruelty which have tuned us all into the wild beasts that we are."

André had spoken all along in a kind of hoarse murmur and without making a single gesture. Now his voice broke into a sob. He stood there in the darkness by the open window with the last glimmer of the western light outlining his clear-cut profile, the firm jaw and noble forehead with its crown of chestnut hair. And while he spoke he looked out into the distance, where far away in the peaceful valley below a puff of smoke still hung in the heavy storm-laden air. Just a puff of smoke there where the cottage once stood, where he, André, had spent the thoughtless years of childhood, where he had first learned the bitter lesson of manhood, where he had dreamed and planned and waited for this hour which had struck at last.

"You have not yet told me, André" the Curé said at last, "what you wish me to do."

"I want you to be prepared to give my bride and me the nuptial blessing in your church tomorrow."

"Blessing!" the priest exclaimed with the nearest approach to sarcasm he had ever in his life expressed.

"As you please, of course—or as she pleases, for the matter of that. I am satisfied with the maire, as the law directs."

"I will do as God wills," the priest concluded with gentle dignity. "But let me tell you this, my son: your union with Aurore de Marigny is on the understanding that her life and that of her father and servants will be safe. God is long-suffering, remember, but believe me that He will know how to punish you if you should break your word."

He turned and slowly groped his way across the room. André watched him till the door of the boudoir finally closed upon him.

Then he, too, went his way.

# Chapter XXV

In an angle of the staircase André came across Pierre, concealed behind a marble column, crouching there in the dark like a frightened rabbit.

"Come and lock the gate after me, citizen," he said, and with scant ceremony dragged the man out of his hiding place.

Pierre, trembling but obedient, followed him. When the great gates fell to with a clang behind him, André stood for a moment on the perron, breathing in the heavy air of this summer's night. It seemed as if he longed to be rid of the scent of perfume and of flowers which clung to his nostrils and made his head ache with its cloying fragrance. Once or twice he passed his hand across his brow and through the thick mop of his hair. His talk with the priest, which had resolved itself into a kind of profession of faith had left him in a state of bewilderment. He felt that he had become a puzzle to himself.

"Am I a brute?" he murmured. "A wild beast—a pitiless savage beast? Or just a man who has lost the being dearest to him in all the world and has nothing left in his heart but the very human desire for some measure of revenge?"

He wondered what his dead mother would have said had her precious life been spared and she had been a witness to this afternoon's tragedy. She, with her quiet philosophy and sober common sense, what would she have said in face of the homeless Louvet children and her own ruined home? Would she still have preached her favourite doctrine that evil cannot be cured with more evil? And would she still be hugging the fond belief that those aristos "up there" had learned something from the terrible events which had precipitated their king from his throne and left him and their kindred to the guillotine? If he had eyes to see and ears to hear, would that arrogant madman "up there" have infuriated the people to the point of seeing his daughter insulted before his eyes?

"They have learned nothing," André murmured to himself. "The lesson has, it seems, not yet been driven home."

He cast a look back on the stately pile, majestic still, in spite of approaching decay. All the windows were dark save one at the end, and here a feeble light glimmered behind a drawn curtain. They were in there. All of them. The aristo, the priest, and the girl. The priest had told him by now of the ultimatum, which meant life and safety in exchange for union with one of the canaille. And André then pictured to himself what they would all say: imagine Marigny's vituperations, the priest's exhortations, and the girl's tears. She would weep, of course, and protest; beat her wings like a bird caught in a trap; and André wondered how she looked when she wept. Women were usually ugly when tears trickled down their cheeks and their noses became red. Did those great unfathomable eyes become red and swollen, he wondered, or did the tears make their depths more mysterious still?

"Bah!" he exclaimed impatiently, "as if I cared!"

He strode down the steps and across the flagged forecourt. He was on the point of turning into the bridle path, which led down to the valley through the woods when he spied a dark figure which slipped quickly past him and then through the gates into the forecourt. André watched the figure as, presently, it mounted the perron and, in a moment, disappeared through the great gates into the château.

Now, the gates had been locked by Pierre when André left the château a few minutes ago. Pierre must have opened them again almost directly, which meant that the nocturnal visitor was a familiar of the house and was apparently expected.

"Talon, of course," André thought. "Now I wonder what the rascal is up to. He gave us the slip this afternoon. Then why has he come now?"

The result of his cogitation was that he retraced his steps and turned back into the forecourt just at the moment when a dim light travelled past the row of windows on the front of the château and stopped short at the door of the boudoir, where it was suddenly extinguished.

# Chapter XXVI

André was wrong in his supposition. Talon was not expected at the château: it was by chance that Pierre had stood for a time by the gate, busy with lighting a couple of lanterns which he usually carried with him about the house. He had spied Hector Talon and opened the gate for him. He gave him a lantern, and Talon made his way across the hall and up the stairs with a catlike tread. He was one of those men who have carried the trick of walking noiselessly to a fine art: he made no sound as he went across the great reception room and came to a halt outside the boudoir door. Here he extinguished the lantern, then waited. Stooping, he glued first an eye and then an ear to the keyhole. What he heard seemed to please him, for his hatchet face broadened into a leer.

He knocked softly at the door, heard Monseigneur's voice and Jeannette's shuffling tread. The door was opened, and with a timid: "May I enter?" he stepped into the room.

Monseigneur was half sitting, half lying across the sofa: his cravat was undone. Aurore was behind him, intent on placing a white linen bandage over his forehead. M. l'Abbé de Rosemonde was sitting at the table in the window with his breviary open before him. No one said a word to Talon as he entered, but after a moment or two Jeannette, still at the door, turned to Aurore and asked: "Can I see about supper now, mademoiselle?" Aurore nodded, and Jeannette went away.

Talon ventured a step or two farther into the room.

"Monseigneur..." he began in his most obsequious tone.

De Marigny raised his head slightly; half opened his eyes, and looked Talon up and down as if he did not know who he was.

"Why are you here?" he asked at last. "Get out!"

"Monseigneur," Talon reiterated in a gentle, persuasive voice, "you know you can command my devotion. I am here to offer you my services."

"There is nothing you can do," Charles de Marigny said wearily. "Go away."

Talon glanced from one face to the other. The Abbé appeared absorbed in his breviary. Aurore had not once glanced at him. Talon thought the Abbé's attitude looked the least uncompromising.

"M. l'Abbé," he pleaded, "do, I entreat you, persuade Monseigneur that it is in his best interests and those of Mademoiselle Aurore to listen to me. I have come with the best and most loyal intentions."

Thus directly appealed to, the Abbé said, not unkindly: "Even so, my good Talon, I don't see what you can do. I don't suppose you know all that happened here this afternoon. You were so very safely out of the way."

"I do know, M. l'Abbé," Talon rejoined. "Everything."

At which Aurore's tired, swollen eyes shot a quick, suspicious glance at him.

"I met that blackguard André Vallon just now," Talon went on glibly, "coming away from here... alone. He chose to jeer at me for my loyalty to Monseigneur, and to threaten me with denunciation as a traitor if I did aught to cross his villainous schemes." He paused a moment, measuring the effect of his outrageous lies, and then went on, dropping his voice almost to a whisper: "He openly boasted before me of—of his coming marriage with Mademoiselle Aurore."

Again he paused, waiting for a word, a sign, either from Monseigneur or from the girl. He felt sick with apprehension and found it terribly difficult to keep up this appearance of obsequiousness, the habit of which he had lost in these past few years. He also felt very tired. He had had a very trying day, both physically and emotionally. His head ached, and his feet were sore; his knees scarcely bore him. He wanted to sit down, to fall back into the easy familiarity to which he had accustomed himself of late, but he had too much at stake to dare risk offending Monseigneur or Mademoiselle. He had garnered scraps of information from the crowd as he met them wending their way homeward, but had scarcely believed his ears when, with much jeering and laughing and obvious satisfaction, they told him of Citizen Vallon's extraordinary project to marry the daughter of the aristo.

The last thing in the world Talon could have foreseen! The last thing in the world he would have wished. De Marigny's daughter married to a man like Vallon—well known in influential places as a friend of Danton—and "goodbye" to his beloved scheme of obtaining possession of the estates. There would no longer be the slightest need to emigrate or to transfer the property for worthless bonds to him. The situation was perilous because it was imminent. The women in the crowd had talked of the legal marriage taking place on the morrow. Talon had hurried up to the château. He wanted to clear up this dangerous situation. If Aurore de Marigny had indeed agreed to the marriage in order to save her father's life and her own, she must as quickly as possible be made to realize that such a sacrifice was unnecessary while there was a faithful and loyal bailiff at hand to show an easier and more dignified way out.

It was a little disconcerting to see her so calm and silent, and Monseigneur more disdainful than ever, when he had thought to find them both distraught and verging on despair. In spite of his aching feet and tired back Talon did not sit down, and as the Abbé appeared to be more approachable than the others, Talon kept his attention fixed on him:

"Monsieur l'Abbé," he began, "you are a holy man; your loyalty to Monseigneur is as great as my own. Surely you will not allow this monstrous union to take place."

"You know as well as I do," the Abbé replied simply, "that I am powerless to prevent it."

"I know nothing of the sort, M. l'Abbé," Talon retorted with well-feigned vehemence. "Anyone who, like yourself, has Monseigneur's complete confidence can prevent it. You especially."

"My ministration," the Abbé said, "is not imperative. André Vallon is a lawyer, and he knows that. If I refuse—"

"I did not mean that, M. l'Abbé!" Talon broke in impatiently. "We are none of us lawyers here, and yet we all know that by the new marriage laws a declaration before the maire is all that is necessary. I did not mean anything so futile."

"Then what did you mean, my good Talon?" the Curé asked, naïvely.

"That Monseigneur and Mademoiselle must get away while there is still time."

"Get away?" The old man was puzzled, for he had never heard of Monseigneur's half-formed project to emigrate. "Get away? How? Where?" He closed his breviary and leaned forward, listening eagerly, while even Monseigneur seemed to forget his pain and weariness and sat up to gaze inquiringly on Talon, and Aurore's great tired eyes seemed indeed to probe to the very depths of the man's soul.

Talon glanced round, satisfied. He thought the time had come when he might sit down, and he sank into a chair with a great sigh of satisfaction. He beamed on Monseigneur, with arms outspread, like a kind and benevolent father talking to weeping children: "Voyons, Monseigneur," he said, "Mademoiselle! Did you really think that Talon would abandon you in the hour of your greatest need? Why, ever since that awful rabble set out to intimidate you up here, I have been scheming and planning to encompass your safety."

"Don't talk so much drivel, Talon," Monseigneur put in drily, "but tell us what you want."

"To get you away from here as soon as possible."

"Too late," Monseigneur sighed involuntarily.

"Why too late? It wants three more hours before midnight and eight before the dawn."

"What do you mean, Talon?"

"That I will have a covered cart here at your door about three o'clock of the morning. One of my farm hands will drive you to Nevers. There you can get the diligence to Bourges. It starts soon after dawn. At

Bourges you can easily get a further conveyance as far as Tours....
You have money, I suppose?"

"Yes, some—but no papers, no passports—nothing!"

"I have both," Talon continued eagerly. "I have papers and passports
which were made out six months ago for my brother-in-law, who was
a widower, and his daughter. He died before he could undertake the
journey, and she has gone to live with relatives somewhere in the
South. I found the papers among his effects without ever thinking that
they would be of use. They are yours, if you like to use them. You can
easily make up to look like the owner of the passport, Achille Vérand:
he was about your age and build; and young ladies," he concluded jocosely, "can always be made up to look like one another."

The whole thing was a lie, of course. It was more than six months
since Hector Talon had nursed hopes that Charles de Marigny would
one day decide to emigrate. He had forged or stolen the papers, or
mayhap just acquired them from some influential friend. Men like
Talon always contrive to get what official documents they want. Anyway, there they were, the blessed, blessed passports! Talon laid them
on the table, and the table was then dragged across to the sofa so that
Monseigneur could look at them at his ease. Monseigneur, Mademoiselle, and M. l'Abbé all pored over them. Those blessed, blessed
passports!

They were made out in the name of Achille Vérand, doctor of philosophy, aged sixty, native of Vanzy in Nièvre, and of Mariguérite Vérand
his daughter, spinster, aged twenty-two. The descriptions? Well, they
certainly did tally in a wonderful—an unexplainable manner. And all
the papers had the official seal of the maire of Vanzy and the counter-
sign of the local member of the Committee of Public Safety, which sits
at Nevers. Everything was in perfect, in absolute order. It was a most
marvellous, a most heaven-sent coincidence that Monseigneur and
Mademoiselle could make up so easily to resemble Achille and Mar-
guérite Vérand.

Aurore, even Aurore, in her eagerness forgot all her prejudices against
Talon. He was no longer to be suspected of evil intentions. He was the
harbinger of hope. Captives, they were being shown the way to deliv-
erance; drowning, they felt a hand stretched out to drag them to the
shore. M. l'Abbé was once more getting convinced that God was on

the side of the Royalist cause. And Talon was entirely in his element. Easy, familiar, jocose, he propounded his plan, satisfied that at last, not only was he in sight of the life's desire, but actually held the prize in his hand.

"You could go too, M. l'Abbé," he said, "if you wish. I can arrange papers for you also."

He had friends in Paris, he explained. Certain services which he had rendered the country had forced men in high places to recognize his worth, so if M. l'Abbé desired... But M. l'Abbé gently shook his head.

"While the altar of God stands in Val-le-Roi," he said, "I shall be there to administer the Holy Sacraments. But, Monseigneur," he exclaimed in no ecstasy of hope, "my dear Aurore, to think that freedom can, with the will of God, be yours!"

She talked of not going without him, but he said earnestly: "Your father is your first consideration, my child. It is his life and your honour that are in peril. Your father must be your first and, indeed, your only thought."

And frankly, Monseigneur agreed with him. Probably he did not think that the Abbé would be in any danger, once he and Aurore were out of the way. It was against them that the fury of the mob and of that brutish ruffian Vallon was directed. And to his proud spirit any human life was worth the sacrifice to save the daughter of De Marigny from the outrage of a union with an André Vallon.

Presently some of the excitement subsided, and Talon's plan was soberly discussed. Aurore went out of the room to put a few necessities together for herself and her father. The cart, Talon explained, would be at the gate one hour before the break of dawn. Two hours' drive, and they would be in Nevers. At six o'clock the diligence started for Bourges. Talon had thought of everything, and the farm hand, who would drive the cart, was loyal and reliable.

Only one more matter had to be settled: the assignment of the Marigny estates to Hector Talon, bailiff, native of Val-le-Roi in Nièvre, for the sum of two million livres, payable in State assignats, receipt of which was hereby acknowledged by the vendor Charles Henri Marigny, cidevant Duc de Marigny. Monseigneur hardly did more than glance at the papers. The horrors which he had gone through that afternoon had somewhat sobered that arrogant sense of possession and prerogative which theoretically he would have guarded with his life. But when it came to Aurore's future—her future with that brutish ruffian—by God! Charles de Marigny would have assigned all his worldly belongings, without counting the cost, to any man who saved her from such a fate.

He signed the papers, and Talon solemnly laid on the table assignats with the face value of two million livres. He had sufficient self-control not to show too plainly how intense was his satisfaction. He folded up the papers most carefully and tucked them inside his coat.

"This is a step which you will never regret, my friend," he said.

"Perhaps not," De Marigny retorted drily, "but let me assure you of one thing, my man, and that is that you will regret it—bitterly—if in any way you play me false."

"My dear sir," Talon protested. "How can you think—"

"Oh! I know more about the laws of this hellish government than you suppose. I know, for instance, that these assignments are not valid if the assignor dies within the year. The State in that case takes possession of the property. So it is not in your interest, you rascal, to play the traitor, and you know it."

"My good friend—"

"Enough! Mademoiselle and I are safe from your double-dealings for one year. Long before then, please God, we shall be in Belgium. And when sanity once more reigns in this demented land, and the King— God save him!—comes back into his own, your rule over my property will automatically cease."

"I know that, my good sir!"

"A sound-minded government will soon make you disgorge."

"I am taking that risk."

"Well, so long as you know that you are taking it... I only wanted you to understand that I am not the fool you fondly imagine. I am taking a risk, I know—but I am banking on the not far distant future when rascals such as you and ruffians like that Vallon will get their deserts."

"In the meantime," Talon concluded with undisguised sarcasm, "you deign to accept the use of my cart and horse, my farm hand, and the passports which I obtained for you at my own risk and peril to help you to flee this country and seek safety in Belgium."

To this Charles de Marigny vouchsafed no reply. The shaft had probably gone home. He despised this man, called him at pleasure a rascal and a thief, but he was at this moment the only being in the whole land who could save him and his daughter from death and worse than death. Talon, having had his say, was now ready to go.

"We meet in happier times, my friend," he said drily, "times happier for you, I mean. When you are safe in Belgium you will, perhaps, remember to whom you owe your safety. I will administer this estate as if it were my own for good and all. The wretched brat whom you call your king may come into his kingdom some day. Personally I doubt it, or I would never have done this deal. The cart will be here at the hour I have named. Goodnight! Pleasant dreams! M. l'Abbé, your servant."

He shuffled out of the room, and for some time his footsteps, gradually dying away in the distance, were the only sound that broke the stillness of the night.

# Chapter XXVII

The Abbé Rosemonde had resumed his orisons. Monseigneur was lost in a brown reverie from which the creaking of the massive gate as it was opened and then shut again roused him after awhile. He lent an ear to Talon's footsteps as they echoed faintly along the flagstones of the forecourt.

A moment or two later Aurore came back.

"That awful Talon gone?" she asked with a sigh of satisfaction.

"Yes, thank God!" De Marigny replied. "I hate the sight of the rogue."

"He has saved us—"

"I know that," De Marigny was ready to admit, "but he has done it for his own ends. He has saved us, as you say, my dear. And for this I suppose we should be grateful."

"There is no possibility," Aurore queried anxiously, "of his playing us false?"

"It would be entirely against his own interests if he did," De Marigny replied drily.

"And at three o'clock we go!" she said with a long-drawn-out sigh. And then added under her breath: "I am glad that it will still be dark. I hope it will be very dark."

"It will make it safer, of course."

"Not because of that," she murmured.

"Then why...?"

"I would rather not see Marigny when I go."

"You will see it when you return, my child," the Abbé put in cheerily. "This state of things cannot last. It will not last. I believe in God, and He will soon be avenged."

Aurore smiled on the kindly old man and quickly wiped her eyes. She loved Marigny and dreaded the long farewell—dreaded, even now, going into the unknown. The priest had risen and was looking for his hat.

"I don't think you had one, M. l'Abbé," Aurore said, smiling at him through her tears.

But suddenly both tears and smile vanished. She looked frightened. Her eyes dilated, her cheeks became the colour of ashes.

"What was that?" she murmured hoarsely.

"What, my dear?"

"What is it, Aurore?" Monseigneur asked frowning.

She seemed to be listening and put up her hand with her finger pointed towards the window.

"Didn't you hear?" she whispered.

Both the men shook their heads. She tiptoed to the window and softly pushed aside the curtain. Again she listened. The two men remained silent, for she had put her finger to her lips. But no sound came from outside, and after a little while Aurore allowed the curtain to fall back in its place. She still looked very white, and her knees appeared to be shaking under her, for she sank into a chair.

"But what was it, Aurore?" her father asked.

"I thought I heard a sound," she murmured, "just outside the window, as if—"

"As if what?"

"I don't know. As if someone had been there—listening."

"It was Talon's footsteps you heard going across the forecourt."

"Perhaps," she admitted reluctantly, and once more tried to smile.

The Abbé had finally turned to go.

"You are going, M. l'Abbé?" she asked, trying to speak calmly, though her lips were still quivering and bloodless.

"Yes, yes, my child. I'll go home now and prepare everything."

"Prepare what, M. l'Abbé?"

"To celebrate for you both," the old priest replied with fervent earnestness. "The church will be quite ready for you directly you pull up. You will tell the driver to stop at the churchyard gate. I will say Mass and give you both Holy Communion. After that, you can go on your long journey fortified by God's blessing. Now, if there's anything else I can do..."

Monseigneur also had risen. In spite of his vaunted self-possession, he, too, was feeling keenly the separation from his ancestral home. He felt that in going away from Marigny, in joining the large crowd of émigrés who had turned their backs on their country and found refuge in foreign lands, he would leave behind him something of his pride of caste, something of his dignity, something subtle and indefinable which, even if he came back one day, he would never again recapture. The old priest no doubt knew what went on in the heart and mind of his old friend. He took his leave in silence, grasping the hand, which, perhaps, he would never touch again. Aurore continued to smile as she bade him farewell.

"Soon after three o'clock," she said, "we'll be outside the church door."

The hand, which she gave him felt cold, and her eyes still looked dark and filled with terror. The priest patted her hand reassuringly.

"There was no one, I am sure," he said, nodding in the direction of the window. "But I'll have a good look as I go out and shoo the malefactor away. Don't be frightened, my child. I have the feeling that you are under the special protection of the holy angels this night."

He looked so serene and so reassuring that Aurore felt comforted. She found a candle and lighted it.

"I'll see you to the gate," she said.

Together they went out of the room, Aurore holding the candle high above her head. As she crossed the threshold, she could not repress a shudder: all that she had gone through that afternoon in this great gilded room came back to her with a rush of memory. Pierre had closed the window, but the night was no longer dark outside. The storm clouds had drifted away, and the waning moon had risen and tipped the treetops with her silvery light.

"It won't be so dark, after all," the priest remarked.

They had gone down the stairs and crossed the hall. The priest opened the gate.

"Go back, my little Aurore," he said as he once more bade her good-night. "You must have lots to do, and your father will be getting anxious."

After he had gone she stood for a moment at the gate, watching while the priest walked briskly across the forecourt. A soft breeze fanned the flame of the candle, and she shielded it with her hand so that the light fell on her face and the loose golden strands of her hair. And suddenly she had the feeling that a pair of eyes was watching her out of the gloom. Hastily she blew out the candle. She was ashamed of her nervousness, for, in very truth, she was shaking with terror, while her reason told her there was nothing to fear. The Abbé's serenity put her to shame, as did her father's coolness; she tried to steel herself against this humiliating weakness, but her teeth chattered persistently, while her head felt heavy and hot. At last she heard Pierre's voice behind her; he came shuffling across the hall, carrying a lantern. Aurore left him to close the gate and ran back as fast as she could across the hall.

## Chapter XXVIII

Aurore had considerable difficulty in getting together the few necessities, which she and her father would need for their long journey. With aching heart and burning indignation she beheld the havoc which vandal hands had wrought in the château. Her bed had been stripped, her clothes stolen, her father's belongings had all been looted. Fortunately, there were attics and hidden recesses in the old mansion where, in the days of plenty, many things had been stowed away. With the help of Jeannette, Aurore searched for and found dark travelling clothes for herself and her father, also some changes of linen; and together they dragged down a couple of old valises in which they packed the travellers' most pressing future needs.

Aurore and her father did, after this, contrive to snatch a few hours' sleep—he on the sofa, she in an armchair. At three o'clock they were both up; washed and dressed. Half an hour later the covered cart was at the gate.

Pierre and Jeannette were going as far as Val-le-Roi to assist at the service of Holy Communion which M. le Curé had promised to hold in his little church. They wept copious tears while they hoisted the valises into the cart and then climbed in, in the wake of Monseigneur and Mademoiselle Aurore.

Precisely at half-past three Monseigneur le Duc de Marigny and his daughter looked their last upon their stately home. Slowly the cart lumbered down the wooden slope. A quarter of an hour later the driver pulled up at the gate of the churchyard of Val-le-Roi.

The waning moon was low in the western sky, and over in the east the first faint streak of dawn tinged the horizon with silver. The little church was dimly lighted from within. Aurore jumped down lightly from the cart, and Charles de Marigny followed. After them came Pierre and Jeannette. The little procession thus formed went through the gate and across the flagged path through the churchyard.

They were within a few metres of the porch when a dark figure came out of the shadow and then stood still, as if waiting for them. Aurore gave a quickly smothered cry of alarm and clung, trembling, to her father.

"Who is there?" she called in a hoarse whisper.

"Only the bridegroom, citizeness," came a mocking voice in reply, "waiting for his bride."

Aurore and De Marigny, numbed with terror, had come to a halt. Neither of them felt able to move. André Vallon emerged fully out of the shadow and came a step or two nearer to them.

"Come, ma mie!" he said coolly. "The church is ready. The Curé waits. Shall we proceed?"

He put out his hand to take hers. De Marigny, shaking himself free of his torpor, tried to interpose.

"Do not touch her!" he cried peremptorily.

But André seemed not to notice him. He glanced over his shoulder, called aloud: "Citizen Tarbot!" and calmly took Aurore's cold, limp hand in his.

Then only did she perceive that there were other people here, moving in the shadows. A man came forward. It was that awful Tarbot.

"My witnesses for our wedding, ma mie," André said coolly. "You're servants will do for yours. Come!"

A small group of people had emerged from under the porch. Aurore felt like a dumb animal, helpless in a poacher's trap. She couldn't see her father, for those awful men were all around him, but she heard his voice, peremptory at first, then hoarse and smothered. She felt herself lifted off her feet and carried into the church. The flickering tallow candles on the altar showed her the Abbé Rosemonde on his knees with his head buried in his hands. Behind her there was the sound of feet shuffling along the flagstones. The voice she dreaded most in all the world whispered in her ear:

"You didn't think, ma mie, that I should be such a fool as to let you run away?"

She realized then how futile had been this attempt to flee, how she had never really believed in its possibility. Even during those few moments of sleep she had been conscious of Fate that was both inevitable and relentless. It was no use praying to God: God was cruel and meant her to go through with this sacrifice. She had thought to escape, and the trap had closed on her once more, more firmly, more inexorably than before. All she could long for now was her father's safety—the certainty that this awful sacrifice would not be in vain.

As once before, André seemed to divine her thoughts.

"There are friends here," he said coolly, "looking after your father's safety. And," he added, "once the knot is tied between us, you need have no fear whatever for him."

She glanced up into the face of this man whom she hated with the intensity of a suffering martyr for a ruthless tormentor. She saw nothing in his eyes but cruelty and mockery. She had the feeling that, try how she might, she could not combat his will; that, like a ferocious brute, he had marked her for his prey, and that she was his thing, his property, the trophy of his victory not only over her but over her kindred and her caste. Nothing but death could ever set her free again. Were it not for her father, how gladly would she have welcomed death, if death could have been swift and sudden, an act of God without the agency of that brutish crowd, whose gibes and snarls and insults still rang in her ears.

Through the stillness she heard a distant rumble of wheels and a driver's call to his horses, and then her father's voice once more, uttering that awful word "Canaille!"

In a moment she would have turned, ready to run back to him, but André had her by the wrist, and she could not move.

"They are taking him back to Marigny," he said drily. "He was doing no good here and might have come to harm. When Pierre and

Jeannette have done their duty as witnesses, they can go and join him there and serve him as they did before."

"Let me go with him," she pleaded involuntarily. "Give me one more day, and I'll swear—"

"You are going to swear loyalty to me at the altar first, ma mie," he rejoined lightly. "After that, we shall see."

He led her to the altar rails, where a couple of chairs had been placed ready for them. Aurore followed as if she were in a trance, hypnotized by this powerful will, which dominated her and broke her spirit. She despised herself for a coward, and yet knew that she was, in fact, utterly helpless, caught in toils which no power on earth could now sever until this monstrous sacrifice had been offered up on the altar of filial devotion.

The Abbé Rosemonde was already waiting for them at the rails. He had his breviary in his hand. He had prayed to God for guidance, and God had remained dumb. Half an hour ago André Vallon had come to him and demanded his services for his marriage with Aurore de Marigny as the law ordained, and the priest, as a citizen of the new Republic, was forced to obey this law, which his heart condemned.

Prayers and admonitions were all in vain. Even the old man could not fail to realize that the sacrifice of Aurore was the only means to save her life and that of her father. With heart half broken with pity he began to read the Latin prayers, which his church prescribes for the blessing of those who desire its ministrations when entering the bonds of matrimony.

"Deus Israel conjugat vos...."—"May the God of Israel unite you...."

It would be impossible to say what went on in Aurore's heart. She stood at the altar, mute and passive. Her lips murmured no prayer, nor did she glance in the direction of the tall, motionless figure by her side. She was only conscious of that intense fear of him which at moments caused her teeth to chatter and her hair to cling matted to her moist forehead. Close beside her Jeannette and Pierre were weeping and mumbling, while a small crowd of village folk—women and men—clustered around the bridegroom.

Surely a more strange pair never stood before God's altar for such a purpose. Victim and tormentor, with hearts overflowing with resentment and bitterness. To André the Latin words, the Gospel, the Creed, the Offertory prayers seemed like sounds out of dreamland, phrases belonging to the land of memory, to a land which he had not visited since boyhood and which seemed divided from the present by an ocean of injustice and wrong.

Anon the Abbé Rosemonde came down the altar steps. He had a small plate in his hand, which, as he arrived at the rails, he held out to the bridegroom. André sought in the pocket of his coat for the two gold circlets, which in the midnight hour he had taken off his dead mother's fingers. Her wedding ring and that of his father, dead when he, André, was still a baby. She was lying so still, so still in her ruined cottage, with a peaceful smile around her lips. What André had thought and felt when he knelt down beside her and forced those stark fingers to yield up those tiny gold emblems of a happy union he himself scarcely knew. All that he remembered afterwards was that bitterness seemed for the moment to give way in his heart to the immense sorrow in which he had not yet been able to indulge. Just for those few moments he felt free to give rein to tears. There was no one there to see him, no one to pity him or, perchance, to mock. And now, when he took the rings out of his pocket and put them on the plate, it was only by the greatest effort of will that he choked back those tears, which again rose insistent to his eyes.

A sound like a long sigh came to Aurore's ears. She heeded it not, did not know whence it came. She was staring—staring at those two gold circlets, the material presentment of what her self-immolation would mean for the rest of her life. Jeannette and Pierre were sobbing audibly; the crowd of village folk were down on their knees, trying to recollect forgotten orisons.

Abbé Rosemonde took the small, cold white hand and the other, strong and rough, and placed one within the other. Aurore felt a shudder pass through her body; every drop of blood fled from her cheeks and gushed back to her head, and André felt her hand in his, fluttering like the wings of a captive bird.

With a steady hand he slipped the ring upon Aurore's finger and in the clear voice echoed the Latin words murmured by the old Curé. They were the old familiar words, heard so often at the weddings of friends, a good deal about love, something about sickness and death. Then came Aurore's turn. The crowd of village folk craned their necks to see what she would do. Would she recoil at the last moment in the face of the magnitude of the sacrifice? There were women there who vaguely understood what went on in her soul and who marvelled if at the last she would rebel. But with a mighty effort of will Aurore held herself erect and did not flinch. Something had occurred during the past quarter of an hour while she knelt at the alter rails which gave her the strength to go through with this holocaust of herself until the end. Perhaps it was a retrospective vision of what she had endured yesterday, of the outrage from which she had been rescued by the man beside her, of her father's arrogance and madness, which had brought all those horrors about. Certain it is that she did not flinch, not even when she in turn echoed the words murmured by the Curé. She murmured the Latin words not understanding them altogether, and the Abbé Rosemonde in the simplicity of his heart barely mumbled those wherein she should have sworn to cherish her tyrant, the cruel wrecker of her happiness.

Soon it was all over. André Vallon, the demagogue, the child of this bloody revolution, was the lawful lord and master of Aurore de Marigny, the descendant of kings. The village folk gave a sigh of satisfaction. They felt that now they were the equals of those great people up in Paris whose will was law, whose voice was the voice of God. Abbé Rosemonde whispered a few last words in Aurore's ears. He placed his hand in reverent benediction upon her head. André stood by, obviously impatient. His friends pressed round him and tried to grasp his hand. The women wept, why they knew not. Through the coloured window glass the dawn was creeping in, and the tallow candles on the altar flickered more and more dimly.

"You will be kind to her, André," were the last words the good priest spoke before he left the sanctuary.

André gave an impatient shrug.

"Come, ma mie," he said Curtly, and with his habitual peremptory gesture he put his arm round Aurore's waist and led her out of the church.

The waning moon was nothing now but a half circle of filmy white vapour. Out in the east a July dawn had already set the fires of heaven alight. The horizon was aglow with crimson and gold, with emerald and chrysoprase, and tiny fleecy clouds, blood red and splendent, lay like streaks of flame across the sky.

# Book III

## Chapter XXIX

When Aurore awakened from a long dreamless sleep it was evening. She was lying in a bed, the soft whit sheets of which smelt of dried roses and lavender. Facing her were two tall windows masked by delicate lace curtains through which the light of a street lamp came dimly peeping.

For a long time she lay here, with aching head buried in the sweet-smelling downy pillow, while, one by one, the events of this fateful day came back to her mind on the wings of memory.

The market cart. The last glimpse of the old home. The little church of Val-le-Roi. The figure that came out of the shadows. The bridegroom awaiting his bride. After that there was something of a bank, a veil through which floated the figure of Abbé Rosemonde, the altar, the flickering tallow candles, and a dark face with compelling eyes and cruel, mocking mouth. Spirit voices echoed words, which her ears at the time had only vaguely heard.

"Deus Israel conjugat vos...."

"You are going to swear loyalty to me first, ma mie...."

"Wilt thou take this man to be thy lawful husband?..."

"Once the knot is tied between us you need no longer fear...."

Then the ring upon her finger. Jeannette's weeping farewells. The murmurings of the village folk. The carriole outside the churchyard gate. The long drive in silence, with her eyes fixed on the strong brown hand close to her, which handled the reins and the whip—the hand of André Vallon, her husband!

Yes, it all came back now! She had slept for a while and had mercifully forgotten, but now it all came back. After the interminable drive in the carriole over the jolting roads they had reached Nevers when the sun was already high in the heavens. In the fields just outside the town there was a stretch of ripening corn, from which a lark suddenly rose with joyful song up to the sky.

The carriole came to a halt in a nice broad street outside a house, the door of which bore on a metal plate the names JULES MIGNET and below it DOCTEUR EN MEDÉCIN. André put up his whip, threw the reins over the horses' backs, and jumped lightly down from the carriole.

"Come, ma mie," he said, and held out his arm to help her descend.

In answer to the clanging of a bell, a neatly dressed maid opened the door and greeted André with a smile.

"The Citizen Doctor?" André asked. "Is he in?"

"He is busy at the hospital just now," the girl replied, "but the Citizeness is upstairs."

The small paved hall and stone staircase smelt of ripe apples and of soap. André ran up the stairs. This time he didn't say, "Come!" but Aurore nevertheless followed. She had no longer any will of her own. It seemed as if that strong brown hand was driving her with whip and reins as it had done the two horses in the carriole.

Double doors on the first landing were wide open, as André's firm footsteps rang out on the tiled floor an elderly woman came out of the room beyond. She was small and frail looking and had slender white hands which she held out to André with the friendliest of greetings.

"Had a good journey?" she asked.

André kissed her hand and then stood aside, disclosing Aurore.

"And that is your young wife!" the old woman exclaimed, and this time her two arms extended towards Aurore, and a sweet smile lit up her pale wrinkled face. "You are right welcome, citizeness," she said. And Aurore felt two kindly arms encircling her shoulders and a friendly kiss pressed on both her cheeks.

"This is the Citizeness Mignet, ma mie," André said. "A dear, kind friend who has offered us hospitality until we can continue our journey to Paris."

"For as long as you will stay in my house, my dear," the old lady said, fondling Aurore's hand but gazing on André with eyes full of deep affection. "I don't suppose he ever told you, but your husband saved my son's life at Valmy. He lost his arm while he carried him to safety under the fire of Prussian cannon. Not only my house, but all I possess in the world is his and yours for the asking."

But while she spoke André had made good his escape. Aurore heard him clattering down the stairs.

"He is always like that," the old lady said, with her gentle smile. "He can't bear me to say a word about what we owe him, Jules and I. But one day when André is not there my son shall tell you about it, and you will be prouder of your handsome husband than you ever were before."

"But you are tired, my dear," she went on, "and here I am chattering away instead of looking after you. Come and sit down here in the sun-shine while I get you a nice cup of hot coffee, or would you rather have some nice sweet chocolate?"

She led Aurore to an armchair placed by the window, through which the warm July sun came in smiling. Aurore thanked her with a wan smile, and she was not really tired and that she would prefer coffee, whereupon the old lady tripped out of the room.

And Aurore had remained sitting there with the sunshine caressing her hair and cheek, looking about her as in a dream. The room had not a great deal of furniture in it, but the few pieces that were there revealed a fastidious taste. Fine work of the Louis XIV period was displayed in a splendid bureau and a fine Boulle table, in the Aubusson carpet and tapestried chairs. There were two or three pictures on the wall, which suggested the fantastic brush of Lancret, and above the fireplace a delicate mirror which must have hailed from Venice.

Aurore had the feeling that this could not be reality; that this was some kind of dreamland out of which she would presently emerge fully awake. Did people who were country doctors and bourgeois possess Boulle furniture and Lancret pictures? Of course not. At least, Aurore had never supposed that they did. Louis XIV bureaus and Aubusson carpets were to be found in ancestral châteaux and not in the plebeian houses of small provincial towns. And this old lady, who now came tripping back in her dress of soft gray silk with the exquisite lace fichu round her shoulders and beautiful cap covering her gray hair, she of a certainty was not the mother of an obscure country leech, the sort of man who, if he had been called in to attend a sick person at Marigny in the olden days, would not have been admitted to eat at Monseigneur's table. "Citizeness Mignet!" That awful word "citizeness," which had the power to arouse the most bitter resentment in the heart of every aristocrat, could surely not be applied to her.

She held in her fine white hands a cup of exquisite Sèvres china from which arose the delicious scent of steaming Mocha. Aurore took the cup with a grateful if pale little smile. She drank the coffee eagerly and felt a little better after it. Only with half an ear did she listen to the old lady's pleasant chatter, out of which only a few disjointed sentences penetrated to her inner consciousness.

"Your room is quite ready, my dear.... I shall take an old woman's privilege and call you Aurore.... When you wake up in the morning... How proud you must be of your husband.... Prodigies of valour at Valmy... My son says..."

Surely, surely, none of that could be real! The old lady was just one of those fairies of which Aurore had read when she was a child in the books of M. Perrault—the fairy godmother in "Cinderella" or "The Sleeping Beauty." She would vanish presently, and she, Aurore, would wake to find herself back in her bed with the blue damask curtains in her room at Marigny. Dear, dear Maringy!

Nor was the gold ring on her finger real. There was no such person as André Vallon, who had dared to call her "ma mie" and looked down on her with such a cruel, mocking glance. She gazed down on her own hands, her left hand with that narrow gold circlet round the fourth finger; and oddly, with her right hand, she toyed with the ring, twisting it round and round.

"And now I shall take you to your room," the old lady said in her smooth, gentle voice. "Come with me, my dear."

She smiled, and her old eyes twinkled as she gave Aurore's cheeks a little pat. "You will want to be alone with your husband," she said.

And now, after all those hours, and lying on this sweet-scented bed, Aurore supposed that she did then follow the old lady out of the room and up some stairs. But of that she remember nothing. She did not even recall her first impression of this room with the tall windows veiled behind delicate lace curtains and hangings of rose Du Barry damask. Here again memory registered a blank until the moment when André Vallon came into the room.

# Chapter XXX

Memory can be terribly cruel!

Aurore, lying numb and tired after a few hours' heavy sleep, felt the full force of this cruelty.

One by one, pictures, which she would long all her life to blot out from her mind rose before her aching senses. Visions of shame and of cowardice, which she felt would forever after, leave a stain upon her soul. Even now memory most cruel brought the blush of humbled pride to her cheeks.

She, Aurore de Marigny, daughter of one of the proudest houses in France, claiming kinship with Royalty, the apple of her father's eyes, the worshipped mistress of a regal ancestral home, she had grovelled at a plebeian's feet; on her knees she had begged him to set her free, entreated him with words that in the past she would only have spoken to her King.

She had begged him, on her knees, with hands clinging to his rough clothes, to let her go back to Marigny and to her father; begged him to look on his vengeance as complete, since he had broken her spirit and humiliated her so that she would never dare look one of her own caste in the face again.

And memory mocked her with that picture of herself, lying like a crumpled heap of silk and laces at the feet of the man whom she hated and loathed and despised beyond what she would have thought herself capable of feeling. And through it all he had remained cool, sarcastic, indifferent.

"Do not cry, ma mie," he had said once: "you will make your eyes red."

And another time: "In Heaven's name, do not raise your voice. You don't want our friends down below to know that we have already embarked on matrimonial quarrels."

But the words that memory recalled more insistently were more fateful than all:

"While you are my submissive wife no one dare touch your father or you; but if you choose to leave me, no power on earth will save either of you from the guillotine. I care naught," he added presently, "about that arrogant father of yours: let him die a dog's death, for aught I care, but I do not choose to see my wife's pretty head roll into the same basket as those of the enemies of France."

"I hate you," she had murmured once. "I shall always hate you."

"I have no love for you, either," he had retorted coolly, "but we shall get used to each other."

And when in her agony of mind she had cried out, "Why—why have you done this? You hate me, you say—then why not let me go?"

"Because..." The word had escaped him, vehement and fierce; the cruel expression she had learned to fear had flashed for a few seconds out of his eyes. But the next moment he pulled himself together, seemed, indeed, to shed his fury like a mantle. A mocking smile chased away the ferocious glance, and he said lightly:

"Because you are beautiful, ma mie; you are my wife and I wish to keep you. That is all."

In the olden days Aurore de Marigny, even when she was little more than a child, had been wont to despise the airs and graces, the megrims and mild hysterics in which her elegant friends so often indulged. She had always been a fearless child: at games, on horseback, nothing frightened her. In an age when women affected the weaknesses of their sex as a sign of aristocratic birth, she would find joy in breaking in an untamed colt or accompanying her father in his shooting expeditions after wolf or wild boar in the forests of Ardennes. She had never known fear until now, when a beggarly caitiff held her like a slave in thrall. But with memory's cruel insistence there came back to her the knowledge that she was afraid; that there was one man in the world the sight of whom caused a quiver of abject fear to go right through her body, the sound of whose footfall caused every drop of blood to flow back to her heart. Why, she couldn't say.

It was that despicable fear which at this fateful hour had taken such hold of her that, even while his formidable arm encircled her waist and raised her from the ground where she had been cowering like a frightened beast, her senses suddenly forsook her, her head fell back, her teeth chattered as if in ague, her limbs felt as cold as ice. Broken and bruised by the terrible mental and physical struggle, she was numb and limp, had not one spark of fight left in her, or the strength of a kitten. She felt herself lifted off the ground and laid down somewhere, where it was soft and warm and sweet smelling. She heard the dreaded footfall receding from her, the opening of a door, and then a call.

There were other people in the room presently—a man and a woman. Aurore couldn't see them; she had not the energy to raise her eyelids; but gentle kindly hands undressed her, took off her shoes and stockings, combed her hair and moistened her face with sweet-smelling water. She felt herself being tucked up in a soft downy bed, and soft murmurs that sounded pitiful and motherly soothed her throbbing senses.

A man's voice, persuasive and authoritative, said, "Try and drink this, citizeness, it will make you sleep." She obeyed and drank the slightly bitter liquid that was held to her lips. After that she lay placid and quiet and, presently, must have dropped off to sleep.

# Chapter XXXI

The stay in Nevers was made endurable for Aurore through the absence of her husband.

Her husband!

The Mignets explained to her that André had left for Paris on the very day of their arrival, while she was lying asleep. He wouldn't have her disturbed. He had gone in order to make arrangements for their new home, and he had gone full of joy and hope, because Citizen Danton had sent a courier over from Paris confirming the happy tidings already sent to Val-le-Roi a few days ago, that he would be overjoyed to see his old friend and colleague André Vallon again. There was work and to spare for young hands and young brains who had the welfare of the people at heart. The education of the young and the reclaiming of the unfit were the two questions that occupied the minds of the committees at the present moment, and Danton held out hopes of an important post for André in connection with these questions.

"It is the sort of work that will appeal to your clever husband, citizeness," the Doctor said, "now that the loss of his arm has compelled him to leave the army. The illiterates in France have been reckoned by the million in the past. Whatever else the present great upheaval may do, it will certainly remedy that crying evil."

"They are opening schools all over France," the old lady continued, "not only for the young, but also for the afflicted: the deaf and dumb and the blind."

"Schools?" Aurore remarked with a slight lifting of the eyebrows. "To teach what?"

"The elements of education," Madame Mignet replied quietly. "These must no longer remain the privilege of the few."

"And is my—my husband taking a hand in this scheme of education for the million?"

"Indeed, yes," the Doctor said. "I understand that Citizen Danton has obtained an important post for him in connection with the schools for the blind."

"Citizen Danton is the most influential man in France," Madame Mignet went on to explain to the somewhat bewildered Aurore. "He has a charming young wife. Madame Roland is one of their intimate friends. You and your husband will move among the most brilliant and most intellectual society in Paris."

Aurore was indeed bewildered. She gazed on this fastidious-looking old lady with the aristocratic features and delicate hands, who talked so calmly of Danton, the hideous master butcher of this awful slaughterhouse, the man whose large plebeian hands were stained with the blood of hundreds of his fellow men. Madame Mignet, or Citizeness Mignet as she preferred to be called, could talk of that man and his circle as "intellectual" and "brilliant," and took it for granted that she, Aurore, daughter of Monseigneur le Duc de Marigny, would find pleasure in their society. Pleasure? Aurore could only marvel whether she would have sufficient courage to show her horror and loathing should the hands of those butchers be extended in friendly welcome to her.

It seemed impossible that people like the Mignets should look complacently on the wholesale butcheries which were turning the fair city of Paris into a shambles; that they could condone the hideous crime of regicide about to culminate in the still more deadly sin of the execution of the Queen; that they could utter such names as Danton or Robespierre, Carrier or Desmoulins without a shudder. And when, after a few days of quiet intimacy, Aurore ventured to put the question to Madame Mignet, the old lady replied with strange earnestness:

"My dear, since the beginning of all times men have perpetrated horrors against one another. It is the devil in them, but the devil would have no power over men if God did not allow it. Could He not, if He so willed, quell this revolution with His Word? Must we not rather bow to His will and try to realize that something great, something good, something, at any rate, that is in accordance with the great scheme of the universe must in the end come out of all this sorrow?"

"But, surely," Aurore protested, "you must look with horror on these wholesale murders."

"I look with horror on every act of violence committed by man against his fellow creatures. I look with horror on every war where men are trained and encouraged to kill or maim one another. I look with horror upon the slave owners in our colonies, where men drive their fellow creatures with whip lash  and torture to toil so that they themselves may reap. All these, my dear child, are horrors, which we women condemn and shudder at. But wars there will always be, because man will always defend his property against aggression, and there will be revolutions in this world so long as men use their power in order to enslave others."

Aurore hotly defended her caste. On her father's estate the people were content and prosperous.

"I am sure they were," Madame Mignet admitted, with an indulgent smile, "but throughout the history of the world, the innocent have suffered together with the guilty. Great evils need desperate remedies. The children of France, egged on by centuries of misery and spurred by starvation, have struck blindly about them in their scramble for food. In the mêlée noble heads have fallen along with some that were heavy with guilt. But it is God's will, and we must have patience. France is a great and glorious country. This is the period of her travail. From it she will bring forth liberty and progress which, as the years roll on, will cause her children to forget what they have endured in the cause."

It was amazing to hear a woman of refinement talk so placidly about it all. In fact, Aurore could not help remarking to herself how strangely like this old lady's philosophy of life was that of Abbé Rosemonde. Resignation to the will of God. Contentment in leaving everything in His hands. She felt a kind of mild contempt for this placidity, and yet, what right had she to scorn anyone? She, the miserable coward who shrank from the hurt that her father's death would cause her, and to save herself and him had grovelled at the feet of one whom she despised?

But it was only toward the end of her stay at Nevers that she spoke of all this to Madame Mignet. She wondered how much of her history the old lady and the Doctor knew; if they realized that as far as she was concerned the greatest horror she had ever experienced was when she found herself the wife of one whom her father had so justly dubbed "Canaille!" They, of course, would not understand how her entire being was in revolt against this slavery. André Vallon was admittedly a poor man, which would mean that she, Aurore de Marigny, would be little better than a servant to a despicable knave. Ignorant of the commonest elements of household work, she would be a constant suffering victim to his gibes and his tyranny. But it was not the work that she feared, it was the mental, the moral, the physical contact with one whom she hated.

And all the while that she was at Nevers, her ears were constantly filled with his name. Though absent, he seemed always to be there in this home of culture and refinement, as he was ever present apparently in the hearts of his friends. From beginning to end, Aurore was forced to listen to the story of André's heroism when he carried Doctor Mignet on his back out of range of the Prussian cannon; how a chance musket shot had shattered his arm and he had dragged himself and his swooning comrade back to the French lines, only to return to the scene of danger and bring to safety half a dozen more of his wounded comrades until, stricken with a raging fever, more dead than alive, he in his turn had completely lost consciousness.

With a wealth of detail and a plethora of exciting incidents did Doctor Mignet recount not only this story, but others in which André Vallon was the hero and had accomplished prodigies of valour.

"Four citations, citizeness," he said with undisguised enthusiasm. "Dumouriez, before his abominable treachery, always spoke of Vallon as the bravest soldier he had ever had under his command; and when the crash came, when Dumouriez, whom the whole of France trusted as an able general and a loyal patriot, when he sold his sword to the enemies of his country, Vallon was one of those who put heart into the troops, who revived their courage and led them to a series of victories which culminated in that glorious day of Valmy."

And the old lady would then conclude with a happy little sigh:

"Indeed, citizeness, André is a man to be proud of as a husband and as a friend."

And Aurore wondered if all those stories could possibly be true. Valour, loyalty, selflessness, these were the attributes of her caste. Caitiffs like André Vallon surely were not capable of such noble impulses. They had no educations to guide them, no tradition, none of the examples, which formed the glorious history of a noble race such as hers. It couldn't be true. The whole thing was an exaggeration on the Doctor's part. He was blinded by his affection for a comrade in arms, by dangers passed together, by suffering endured for the sake of France, when the whole of Europe raised its hand against her, and the Prussian hordes invaded her sacred soil.

"I look with horror on every war," the old lady had said. And for the first time in all these miserable years Aurore was conscious of a vague feeling of shame that so many of her kindred had turned their sword against their country in the hour of her greatest peril, or sought refuge and safety on foreign soil.

"France, my country!" an unconscious poet had once sung. "She may have erred, she may have sinned, but still she is my country!"

# Chapter XXXII

Indeed, these few days in Nevers in the company of two charming and intellectual people were both pleasant and peaceful. It was years since Aurore had the opportunity of listening to conversation other than the somewhat naïve philosophy of Abbé Rosemonde and her father's somewhat monotonous if fully justified diatribes against the new régime; and though she felt that she could never agree with the opinions and ideals expounded so eloquently by the Mignets, yet she could not help feeling interested, taken out of herself, made to feel that at any rate the original makers of this terrible revolution were men of high ideals actuated by the purest of motives.

The day of departure came, alas! all too soon. André came to Nevers to fetch his wife. The sight of him revived in Aurore's memory all the terrible times she had lived through. All the quietude of the past few days seemed to fly from her soul At once she felt irritated, with her nerves all tingling and on edge. She watched the carriage drive up to the door and saw him jump down and take his valise from the driver. She thought he looked ill, but supposed that perhaps the journey had been trying. It was only later that she heard that he had actually come from Val-le-Roi, whither he had gone first from Paris in order to see after his mother's grave in the churchyard there.

It was not till late afternoon that Aurore found herself along in her room with her husband. She certainly thought that he looked different, somehow: older perhaps, but certainly different. He had been to Marigny and spoke to her about his visit there.

"Your father refused to see me," he told her, "which I suppose was natural. But I questioned Pierre and Jeannette and also the Citizen Curé. They all told me that physically he was well, but not quite normal in his mind."

"Mon Dieu!..."

"It is nothing to be alarmed about. I spoke to the leech—Citizen Journet—whom you know. They used to call him in the olden days if any of the servants were sick. Your father, it seems, condescended to let him feel his pulse and to take the potion which he prescribed."

"If I could only see him..."

"You wouldn't do him any good. On the contrary, if you were there he would let loose the floodgates of his resentment and work himself up into a delirium of fury. I put the question to the Citizen Doctor and Abbé Rosemonde: they both thought it best that he should be kept very quiet for a time, under the care of Pierre and Jeannette."

"You seem to have been very kind," she said, feeling grateful yet loath to acknowledge her gratitude.

"Only seemingly," he replied lightly, in that flippant, mocking tone of his which still had the power to irritate her. However, she kept sufficient control over herself for the moment to swallow the sharp retort which hovered on her lips.

There was a moment's silence between them, and then he mentioned Talon.

"I have got the deeds of sale out of that thief, at any rate," he said.

"The deeds?"

"Why, yes! The deeds of sale of Marigny and of all the estates registered in your father's name to Hector Talon."

"I had forgotten," she murmured.

"He hadn't," André replied drily, "not your father's."

"What does that mean?"

"That I had the title deeds registered in your name, under the plea that your father was non compos mentis."

"But I couldn't allow—"

"What?"

"I should be defrauding my father."

"Would you rather Talon had possession?"

"Rather he than you," she retorted coldly.

At the moment she hoped, rather than thought, that a slight shadow passed over his face. They had both been standing during this brief conversation, carried on with a kind of casual indifference on his side and with thinly veiled animosity on hers. She had intended to wound him with the sharpness of her tongue, and having, as she hoped, succeeded, she turned coolly away from him and sat down in the winged armchair by the window. With ostentatious care she disposed the folds of her gown about her, fiddled at her fichu, allowed her daintily shod foot to peep from beneath her skirt. Then she took up a piece of embroidery and started to ply her needle with the appearance of being deeply engrossed in her work.

André watched her in silence for a moment or two. Had she looked up she would have seen the mocking smile which curled round his lips.

"I suppose," he said after a while, "that my wits are specially dull this afternoon. Would you be so gracious as to explain just what you mean by 'rather he than you'? It sounds enigmatic to me."

Aurore kept her eyes fixed on her embroidery frame, drawing the thread in and out as if the destinies of France rested on the success of her work. With her head slightly tilted to one side, her fair hair free from powder, like a golden halo above her smooth forehead, a look of concentration in her deep blue eyes, she looked perfectly adorable. She knew it, and felt a great measure of strength in the knowledge. A woman is soon conscious of victory when she knows that she is beautiful, and Aurore, young and inexperienced as she was, was no exception to this rule. What worried her was that she could not keep her hands entirely steady or still the beatings of her heart. She knew that if she spoke her voice would betray the fact that she was vaguely frightened. She had hit out rather blindly and thoughtlessly because his cool indifference had exasperated her, but now she was afraid of what he might do. He was cruel and vengeful, she knew that, and she felt frightened, like a child who has been naughty and knows that it is going to be punished.

But she would not for worlds let him see that she was anything but indifferent, and so she remained silent and went on drawing her embroidery thread in and out with cool ostentation. But, suddenly, and without any warning, he came up close to her and, with an impatient oath, snatched the work out of her hand and threw it on the ground.

"Please answer my question," he said coldly.

The needle, it seemed, had slightly grazed her finger, drawing a drop of blood. She put the finger to her mouth. Then she rose from her chair and stooped to pick up her work. He put his foot on it. As she straightened again she found herself quite close to him, looking up into his face.

"I meant just what I said," she said, as coolly as she could, though she felt that her nerves were beginning to give way; "that I would sooner any man in the whole of France had Marigny rather than you."

"A very natural sentiment on your part, no doubt," he rejoined calmly, "seeing that you honour me with such active hatred. But had you equally honoured me by listening to me just now you would have heard me say that the title deeds of Marigny are not inscribed in my name but in yours."

She broke into a harsh, derisive laugh.

"A pretty bit of sophistry, forsooth," she retorted. "You must think me a food, indeed, if you imagine I do not see through your tricks. A marriage with the aristo, pardi! To humiliate her, what? And to avenge wrongs in which she had no share? Your precious friends believe that tale, do they not? But they are the fools, not I. I know enough of the laws of your murdering government. A wife's property belongs to her husband, and that is the reason why you forced this monstrous union upon me. It was in order to feather your nest, to obtain possession of the lands and château, which if my dear father and I had perished on the guillotine would have become the property of the State. Marry the aristocrat, forsooth, to avenge a mother's death! Par Dieu! 'Twas a pretty story to cover the grasping avarice of an upstart out for loot!"

She had succeeded in working herself up into a state of uncontrolled fury. Fear had given way to a kind of nervous exultation at her own power to wound. All unknowing, he had put the flail in her hand wherewith to chastise him. And chastise she did. Whether she believed in what she said or no didn't seem to matter: all she knew was that her words must hurt him. They must, even though he stood there close to her, entirely motionless, looking down into her glowing face with eyes the expression of which she could not entirely fathom. But that was because she was excited, unable to reason and to think, only to strike with words that must hit at what pride he possessed, as a whip lash would have struck at his face. It was only when she was forced to pause in order to draw breath that that awful mocking smile which she hated worse than his cruelty curled once more around his lips.

This goaded her beyond endurance. Her nerves were completely unstrung. She couldn't have controlled them even if she would. She was just longing for an actual whip wherewith to strike, longing with all her soul to make him cringe and suffer at last as he had so often made her suffer.

With a strange cry, as much of pain as of triumph, she suddenly raised her hand and struck him in the face....

"You little fool!"

That was what she heard. The voice did not sound quite like his. Perhaps she had expected a roar, a cry of rage, a savage oath—he was a beast, and beasts usually bellowed when they were hurt; but all she did hear was a low, contemptuous laugh and those three words, "You little fool!"

But what happened was quite another matter. His formidable arm shot out, and in an instant both her wrists were tightly held together as in a manacle of steel. She felt as if her arms were wrenched out of their sockets, and in the agony of it her knees gave way under her. She felt herself sinking to the ground, and through a mist of semi-consciousness she saw his face quite close to hers—a cruel, mocking face with a gleam of ferocity in the eyes.

"On your knees, you little fool!"

What a harsh voice it had become! And then that laugh! Mockery! Contempt! Mild amusement! The whole gamut of what was most humiliating and most riling.

"Let go my wrists," she said as steadily as she could, though she was ready to cry with pain. "Let go! You hurt me!"

"Hurt you?" he went on coolly. "By God! I mean to hurt you, you infuriating little vixen! I am going to keep you here on your knees until those red lips of yours have begged for pardon."

"Let me go!" she cried aloud. "Brute! Brute! Let me go!"

"As soon as you have begged for pardon!" he retorted grimly.

"Never!"

"We shall see!"

He sat down in the winged chair and still held her by the wrists. She was on her knees, crouching at his feet, for there he held her pinioned with one foot on the edge of her gown. She could not move.

"Coward! Let me go!"

"Not I! Coward," he continued coolly, "is an attribute of mud-larks such as I, but so is obstinacy you'll find, ma mie. Anyway, you are going to stay here on your knees until your sweet lips have claimed and received a kiss of forgiveness."

Just for a few seconds she had an uncontrollable desire to scream at the top of her voice in the hope that some member of the Mignet household would come to her rescue. But her pride revolted at the idea of being found in this humiliating position, and with all their adoration for this brutish husband of hers they might even take his part against her, and ridicule might then be piled on humiliation—a thing too awful to contemplate. She thought that he would tire; those fingers of his, which felt more and more like iron clamps around her wrists, were bound, she thought, to loosen their hold a little after a time. Manlike, he would grow weary of sitting still. The slightest movement on his part, and the tension would relax. That would be her opportunity for escape, and, of course, she would not be caught unawares again. If only she could have closed her ears to his voice, to his gibes and his sneers and, worse still, to this scornful admiration.

"So you thought out that pretty story for yourself," he said at one time: "that I schemed to marry you in order to obtain possession of your impoverished estates. Name of a name! You have imagination as well as beauty, ma mie"; and then he added irrelevantly:

"When you sue for pardon I shall kiss you, Aurore, for your lips just now look as luscious as two cherries."

Involuntarily a sob rose to her throat, her pretty head fell forward, and great hot tears fell from her eyes.

"Don't cry, ma mie," he said gaily. "I didn't cry when that charming cousin of yours struck me in the face just because you happened to fall into my arms one day. I was only a boy, and you were a child. Do you remember that day, ma mie?"

His voice seemed to die away somewhere in space. The shades of evening were drawing in. It was quite dark in the remote corners of the room. Aurore felt faint and sick, dreading, yet longing for, unconsciousness. At one moment hope revived. There was a knock at the door, and she heard André's voice calling:

"What is it?"

"Supper is ready, citizen," came the servant girl's voice in reply. "Will you be coming down?"

"Not tonight, Marie," André replied. "My wife is fatigued, and I will stay with her. Pray the Citizen Doctor and the Citizeness to excuse us."

After that Aurore sobbed like a child. She was tired and hungry and in pain. She sobbed, and through her sobs she heard the hated voice saying quite lightly:

"Give in, ma mie. You won't regret it. If I had a hand to spare I would put a finger under your pretty chin and try and teach you that it is quite good to kiss."

She did give in, in the end. She felt ashamed, abjected, cowardly. A brief while ago she would have scorned the idea of any woman giving in under such humiliating conditions. But it was not only physical pain that compelled her. It was something more than that, and she knew it. It was the enforcement of a will greater than her own, the absolutism of physical, moral, and mental strength, which seemed to rob her surrender of its most galling sting. She raised her head and almost with an air of defiance she threw out the word, "Pardon!" At once her wrists were released, but her whole body was imprisoned instead. Weak and broken, with head thrown back and eyes closed, she remained motionless in the crook of his arm. For a long, long time she remained thus, expecting and dreading that kiss. She felt that his eyes were on her, revelling—she had no doubt of that—in her beauty. And for this she hated and despised him as much as she hated and despised herself. For one instant she opened her eyes and looked into his. What had compelled her to open them she didn't know. It was still that immense power which appeared to be in the very air about her, bending her will and breaking her spirit. Had she read fury, passion, or hatred in his eyes she might, she felt, have forgiven him in her turn, have felt less ashamed of her cowardice; but all she encountered was a kind of gentle, indulgent mockery, mild amusement at what to her meant the uprooting of all that she had held inviolate, the surrender of what she held far deeper than life.

He was amused at her humiliation and could laugh at her distress. She gave him one look and then said loudly and quite steadily:

"I never knew what hatred meant until now."

"We'll call it that if you like," he retorted lightly, "but isn't it good?"

And then he kissed her.

# Chapter XXXIII

Since that day many months had gone by, and Aurore, sitting once more in the large winged chair by the window in that pretty room at Nevers and watching the snowflakes slowly fluttering down from the leaden sky thought of the long, long time that separated her from the past, and of the interminable days that still lay, wearisome and monotonous, before her, until she was an old woman, too old to recollect and too old to feel.

She had been very sorry at the time to leave the quietude of the house at Nevers, not thinking that she would ever see it again. The Mignets had been so kind! So king! She marvelled often just how much they knew. She had dreaded the journey to Paris in the company of her husband, had dreaded the life that lay before her—the great unknown! The leap into a future which she pictured to herself as dark and lonely and laden with sorrow.

But things in life have a way of not being either quite so pleasant or so unpleasant as one anticipates; and Aurore's first impression of the apartment in Paris, which was destined to be her home was certainly not so unpleasant as she had imagined. It certainly was spacious and sunny. Situated on the Quai de la Ferraille, high above the noises of the street below, it had a fine view over the river and the towers of Notre Dame. She wondered whom it was who had presided over the furnishing of it, but didn't like to ask. She thought that she detected a feminine hand and a woman's taste in her bedroom, with its muslin curtains and flowered chintz hangings. All very simple, even Spartan, but with nothing to jar on her fastidiousness. In an adjacent small boudoir she found a comfortable armchair, a worktable, many appurtenances necessary for needlework. These only a woman could have selected, so Aurore thought, and wondered who it could have been.

There were also a number of books ranged on shelves on one side of the room. As soon as she had an opportunity Aurore looked to see what they were. Rousseau, of course, and Diderot, and also Voltaire and D'Alembert; the speeches of Mirabeau and reprints of the early numbers of L'Ami du Peuple. But there were others too: the poets and essayists of the Grand Siècle, Molière, Coidorcet, Bossuet, and many more. Somehow she felt that each one had been chosen specially for the moulding of her mind. Herein she suspected her husband, and wondered how any man could be so dense or so arrogant as to suppose that she would swerve one iota from the principles and the faith, which she had been taught to believe were the only possible rules of life.

But apart from such rebellious thoughts and during those early days of August, Aurore set out resolutely to live the life, which she believed was to be hers to the end of time. She wondered how she was ever going to live and to endure. And yet other people did it; other women in this awful city of Paris had learned how to live and how to suffer. How amazing that was! Amazing and un-understandable! The Reign of Terror was at its height. The glorious revolution, which was going to regenerate the world and bring about the millennium with unbroken happiness for all, could now be best described as a conjugation of the verb "to fear": I fear, thou fearest, he fears, we fear, you fear, they fear! Men and women in Paris went daily, hourly, in fear of their lives; in fear of the lives of those near and dear to them. Every day accusations, trials, condemnations, and the procession of victims to the guillotine. Terror, indeed, was the order of the day, the darlings of the crowd today were the execration of the mob on the morrow.

And yet, life went on just the same.

People walked about the streets, met each other and talked over the events of the day—the death of this man, imminent arrest of that other; Robespierre's latest speech; the news from the front. They went to the theatre and the opera; they dined at restaurants. Young people made love; old people died; babies were born. Life went on just the same.

Aurore saw very little of the outside world. She went daily to market with the pleasant middle-aged woman who helped her with her ménage; she stood in the queues, waiting her turn to purchase the few ounces of bread which the law allowed, and spent the money which André had given her for the purchase of such food as was obtainable. Her life was Spartan in the extreme, but she had no rough task to perform. There was no question of washing and scrubbing—the nice middle-aged woman did all that; but Aurore soon found herself strangely interested in keeping her new home dainty and comfortable and her table as free from monotony as possible. The feeling gradually came to her that this was more of a real home to her than stately Marigny had ever been. There, during its days of splendour, everything was ordained and arranged by an army of servants without any reference to her own special wishes. Probably she had no special wishes in those days, as everything went on in its own perfect routine. There was never any hitch: housekeepers and majordomos saw to it that Mademoiselle was not troubled with such trifles as the arrangement of flowers in her room or the composition of a menu.

But here, in the sunny rooms of the Quai de la Ferraille, everything depended on her, and the thrill was very real when there were a few asters to be bought in the market, or there was a possibility of obtaining a thin old fowl that made excellent soup.

Aurore heard vague rumours from time to time that men in high places kept rich tables in their homes while the people starved; that certain restaurants in the Rue St. Honoré, patronized by Robespierre, the Incorruptible, and his friends on the influential committees, served their customers with the richest of food and choice wines bought for a song from the cellars of dispossessed aristocrats. She heard that in the country there was no shortage of luxury; that Danton's house at Arcis was noted for its good cheer.

All that she heard and more, but she had soon schooled herself to know nothing, to listen to nothing, to comment on nothing. She never went to a theatre; she had never set foot inside a restaurant. She only walked for exercise, and then only in the fields round about St. Martin and Passy. It was the only way to endure life. Strangely enough, quite apart from the interest in her home, she was not really unhappy. What sorrow and anxiety she felt was purely outside herself. The fate of the unfortunate Queen caused her immense grief, but she never spoke of it; through gossip gleaned in the streets, or through the placards at street corners which she could not fail to see, she learned of the condemnation and death of many whose names had been familiar to her since childhood: relatives, friends, acquaintances. Many she knew had found shelter abroad, and more than once she half broke her heart with regret that her father had always set his face so obstinately against emigration. They would be together now—she and he—secure in England or Belgium, with only the echo of all these horrors to disturb their peace, instead of this daily agonizing contact with it all.

She remembered that a year or less before this she had heard rumours of an organization of English gentlemen, headed by a mysterious chief who was known as "The Scarlet Pimpernel," who risked their lives in order to help those who were in danger of death, who were unhappy and innocent, and who longed to flee from this terror-stricken land. She remembered that her father had obstinately refused to get in touch with these gallant Englishmen. He hated the English, he said, and would not owe his life to any of them. Aurore, at the time, thought no more about it. She did not hate the English, but she didn't want to leave Marigny, and in that remote country district the danger to her father and herself did not appear imminent.

Until that awful day in July, which seemed now like a nightmare, she had no realized how hated she and her father were in the villages, and how intense was the enmity of the people against her caste. But here, in Paris, her eyes were soon opened to much that she had never fully understood before: she soon realized how miserable and ignorant the people were, and how easy it was to arouse in them passions of hatred, of resentment and cruelty. She also realized how helpless now were those men who, with the highest possible ideals to spur them, and an infinite understanding of the injustice under which the poor had groaned for centuries, had let loose the floodgates of this titanic revolution. They were helpless now, and, one by one, paid toll with their lives for all those dreams of liberty and justice which were going to make this word regenerate and happy, and only succeeded in making it more miserable and more foul.

Her husband, André Vallon, was one of these. He had come back from the war full of enthusiasm and of hope. Since he could no longer fight the enemies of his country abroad, he would fight them within its borders: traitors, who would sell France to her foes, who would allow the Prussian heel to tread her sacred soil; upstarts, who filled their pockets and their bellies while others groaned and starved. They were the enemies whom men like André Vallon were ready to denounce to an outraged people. The people were ready enough to have those traitors thrown to them as bait for their revenge, but, having tasted the sweets of retaliation, they soon cried for more. And Aurore watched clouds of anxiety gather over her husband's brow. Day by day he became more absorbed, more silent.

When first they had settled down in Paris he had often talked to her of the great upheaval which was convulsing the country: he spoke with great moderation, careful not to outrage her principles or her belief. He brought her books to read, pamphlets that interested her even though they could never convince. André could talk well when he liked; he knew his Rousseau and discussed him with Aurore in a manner, which opened up her mind to social questions of which she had never dreamed before. She was intelligent and responsive. She had a great desire to learn, and, in spite of herself, she caught herself more than once looking forward to a quiet evening in the Quai de la Ferraille, tête-à-tetê with her husband, listening to his talk while she worked. He would speak very freely of the social ideals that had brought about the Revolution, of men like Lafayette and Mirabeau, of the original Legislative Assembly, the Constitution of '89, and the Declaration of the Rights of Man. But it was always of the past that he spoke. Of the present and the future he never uttered a word, and Aurore, through innate delicacy of feeling, never mentioned the names of those demagogues who had been André's colleagues and friends at one time, and who had since been hurled down the steep path of enormity and of crime by the avalanche which they had let loose and no longer could control. She never once uttered the name of Danton, the master butcher who had been André's friend.

From time to time she had news of her father, and André held out hopes to her that she would see him soon; but he never spoke again of Marigny, though she had a strong suspicion that he was administering the estate through an agent whom he had placed there for the purpose.

Soon she had the conviction that he was taking her presence in his home absolutely for granted. She was his wife and looked after his comfort. Sometimes she was also a pleasant companion with whom he could talk of extraneous subjects. He had never once set foot inside her room.

He taught her to play chess, and now and then they would have a game in the evening. The lamp, set on a tall stand behind Aurore's chair, lit up the tender gold of her hair, the curve of her shoulder peeping through the folds of her lace fichu, her delicate hand supporting her chin. She was beautiful, and she knew it. But whenever she looked up from her game she invariably saw his head bent, intent upon the next move, and his eyes fixed upon the board.

He had never once kissed her since that evening at Nevers.

177

# Chapter XXXIV

Towards the end of September André announced to Aurore his intention to take her to Nevers.

"The Mignets," he said, "will be very happy to have you with them, and there will be a chance for you of seeing your father."

A quick cry of protest came involuntarily to her lips.

"I would rather stay here!" she said, and then could have cried with vexation, for at once that mocking smile which she hated came curling around his mouth.

"I would not wish to burden Madame Mignet with my presence," she went on, as coolly as she could. "I know from experience how difficult housekeeping has become, and a visitor must be a burden in any house."

"The Citizeness has been longing to see you again, she tells me, and Paris is not the place for you just now."

It was not often that he assumed this air of authority over her, but Aurore was sensible enough to know that when he did any kind of resistance would be useless. In this great era of liberty a married woman was still entirely dependent on her husband. She had no money or property apart from him, and he had complete control over her affairs and over her movements. Aurore, who had a great regard for her own personal dignity, would never have demeaned herself by argument or resistance, which could only result in defeat.

As a matter of fact, she knew quite well why she was being sent out of Paris, and in her innermost heart could not help feeling thankful that there were some kind friends with whom she could stay, away in a quiet provincial town, until the terrible events which were looming

ahead had come about and vanished into the past. The trial of the unfortunate Queen had been decreed by the Convention. This, of course,
would be nothing but hideous mockery and would inevitably end in
her condemnation and her death. André did not wish his wife to be in
Paris when that occurred.

He took her over to Nevers on one of the last days in September.

The drive in the diligence through the beautiful valleys of the Nièvre
and the Allier, where the trees that bordered the road were already
clothed in the gorgeous russet and gold mantle of autumn was
strangely soothing. More than once Aurore fell asleep in spite of the
roughness of the road, the heat inside the diligence, the querulous
murmur of conversation of her fellow passengers. When a sudden jerk
aroused her from these fitful slumbers she usually found that in her
sleep her head had fallen sideways and come to rest on her husband's
shoulder. She would look up at him, half dazed and with a beating
heart, only to find that he was sitting bolt upright, staring straight out
in front of him, and had not apparently as much as noticed her.

The Mignets were, as usual, more than kind, and did all they could to
make their guest happy. But a strange restlessness now had possession
of Aurore, and the peaceful atmosphere of this refined household
seemed to irritate rather than soothe her nerves. Very little news from
Paris penetrated as far as this sleepy cathedral town. The diligence to
and from the capital only plied once a month now, and the meagre
sheets, which it brought, were at once snapped up by a privileged few.
As Aurore never spoke with anyone outside the household she could
only learn what the Mignets chose to tell her. She more than suspected
that news was being kept from her when it was more than usually horrible or alarming. She did hear of the condemnation and death of the
Queen, and this caused her unmitigated grief. She also heard of the
wholesale execution of the Girondists, the brilliant party whose members were the first to try and cry halt to the holocaust, which they
themselves had set in motion. The élite of intellectual Paris perished
on the guillotine on that awful last day of October, and with them perished the last of the moderatists who might have stemmed the tide of
butchery nine months before the surfeit of carnage put an end to it at
last.

Aurore could not help wondering at times how her husband would fare
though all the turmoil that followed the execution of the Girondists. It

was obvious, even to her who knew so little, that no man's head was safe upon his shoulders if he expressed the slightest desire to see the end of all the slaughter, or showed anything but satisfaction at the orgy of blood that went on day after day. And Aurore, with all her hatred and dread of André, knew him to be entirely fearless and disdainful of his life where his ideals and his beliefs were at stake. As in the days of his youth, when he had boldly expressed his views on the Rights of Man and the iniquity of the old social system that allowed two thirds of humanity to starve so that the remaining third might feast, as later on he had joined Danton in the denunciation of those tyrants who had learned nothing from the lesson taught them by an outraged people, so now he would with equal boldness tilt against the assassins, who through sheer fear for their own lives were vying with one another in atrocities and had turned the beautiful land of France into a gigantic shambles.

Sooner or later, thought Aurore, he would fall a victim to his moderatism. It would be a pity, she thought, because there must be so few men of sane fews and true patriotism left in the country now. Once or twice she spoke about André to the Mignets and showed an anxiety on his behalf, which she hoped would please them. It did. And as usual the Doctor and the old lady at once embarked on their wonted eulogy of their friend.

"They daren't touch him," the Doctor said decisively.

"Why not?" Aurore retorted. And then added: "It seems to me that, as they dared raise their guilty hand against the Queen, they would dare anything."

"That was different," the Doctor asserted.

"Why different?" she demanded.

"André's life is consecrated to the service of the poor and the afflicted. One could hardly say that of the unfortunate Marie Antoinette."

"She never had the opportunity," Aurore protested hotly.

"Perhaps not. But, anyway, while she lived she was a constant inducement to a handful of hotheaded traitors to betray their country for her sake. You would be surprised, citizeness, if you knew the number of conspiracies, of intrigues, of treacheries that were daily hatches in order to overthrow the Republic and replace the Austrian woman or her son on the throne."

"Then do you mean to tell me that you—" Aurore retorted vehemently.

"Don't ask me that question, citizeness," the Doctor broke in with earnestness. "I am no politician, nor am I the guardian of my country's laws. I only wanted to point out to you that the execution of Marie Antoinette in no way suggest danger to your husband."

"Unless things chance very much for the worse," the old lady put in, "the country cannot afford to lose its André Vallon."

"Why not?"

It seemed a strange question for a wife to ask. Madame Mignet, for the first time since the beginning of their friendship, cast a disapproving eye on Aurore.

"My dear," she said coldly, "you know better than we do that your husband is the only man in France at this present moment who has thoroughly mastered the system of teaching the deaf and dumb. By means of signs, which he does with his one hand, he has taught scores of such poor afflicted souls how to exchange and assimilate ideas. And the same with the blind. Surely you knew all that."

Aurore's silence was her reply. She felt ashamed. How could she own to these dear, kind friends that she had not yet been on such terms of intimacy with her husband that he could speak to her about himself or his work? She had only been a pleasant acquaintance in the sunny home of the Quai de la Ferraille, one with whom a busy man could discuss the abstract theories of Rousseau or the speeches of Mirabeau. To her husband she had only been an intelligent opponent at chess or piquet, but never a confidant. Not hers the sympathetic ear into which a man could pour the tale of his struggles, his strivings, his disappointments. Not hers the loved voice whose gentle tones could soothe the nerves jaded by fatigue.

Much against her will, a few hot tears rose to Aurore's eyes. She rose quickly and turned away lest those kind friends should see them.

But after that she no longer tried to disguise from the Mignets the fact that she and André were two beings apart. They had guessed it, of course, but out of delicacy had never given her a hint that they knew. The full circumstances of her marriage were, of course, unknown to them, but it was very clear that the ideals of a Royalist and those of a child of the Revolution were as far apart as the poles. Love alone might in time have bridged over the distance, but alas! As Madame Mignet remarked to her son one day when they talked the matter over together, there is no love between them on either side. Womanlike, she put the blame for this on Aurore.

"She is beautiful," was her comment on the situation, "but I am afraid that she has no temperament; and André ought to have had either a clinging, affectionate little wife, who would have mothered him, or else..."

The old lady paused and put on a demure expression. She knew what she meant, and so did her son, and between them they decided that Aurore of the wonderful eyes and the cherry-red mouth did not possess any of the attributes, which would have made André happy.

"Unless..." Madame Mignet added, who was nothing if not enigmatic. And then she said with a hopeful little sigh, "One never knows."

And Aurore, sitting in the large-winged chair by the window in the pretty room at Nevers, watched the snowflakes slowly fluttering down from the leaden sky. She also watched other things from that pleasant point of vantage—people hurrying by with heads bent against the cold wind, the poor little half-frozen children hurrying home from school, the gossips at the street corner, and the itinerant menders of tin pots or earthenware, and, once a month, when the diligence came in from Paris, her husband, André Vallon, with a small valise in his hand, pausing a moment at the door to ring the bell.

# Chapter XXXV

It was on one of the first days of March that Aurore had the surprise of her life. André, in the course of his visit, announced to her the early arrival of her father at Nevers.

"He will be safer here," he explained, in response to Aurore's little cry, half of joy and half of alarm. "The people in the villages suffered terrible privations during the protracted winter, and tempers over there are none too placid in consequence. Some few hotheads might engineer a regrettable coup."

"But—"

"But what?"

"This will not entail any unpleasantness?" she suggested tentatively.

"Unpleasantness?"

"For you, I mean, or—"

"No, why should it?"

"Or danger?"

"Danger? For him? Certainly not. He will be much safer here."

"I didn't mean for him."

"For you, then?"

"Of course not!" she retorted, and then added with a shrug, "As if I mattered."

"Then I don't understand what you do mean by danger. Danger to whom?"

"To you."

He said nothing for a moment or two, but she felt that those searching eyes of his were seeking to find some hidden thought, some unexplainable motive in those two words which she had murmured below her breath. After a few seconds' silence he gave a light shrug and said drily:

"I can but echo your own words—as if I mattered!"

He turned to go out of the room. Involuntarily she called out:

"André!"

The first time, the very first time that she had called to him by name. He paused at the door with his hand already on the knob and half turned to her:

"At your service, citizeness."

His voice was quite harsh and his tone cold, so cold that the impulse, which had made her call to him seemed frozen suddenly into a kind of miserable shyness. He was not the sort of man to whom one could offer sympathy or comfort. Nevertheless, Aurore was conscious of an intense pity for her husband. All of a sudden he appeared to her so lonely! Introspective, too, probably through being so very much alone. And young, scarcely older than herself, and with all his hours spent amid the afflicted, the blind, the deaf and dumb, the miserable poor! In constant contact with everything that was most wretched and most squalid!

And with all his ideals of a regenerated world lying shattered around him! Lonely and disappointed! And she, his wife, could do nothing to comfort or cheer him. When she tried to find the right words with which to touch his heart, she was stupid and tongue-tied. Even now, when she felt so desperately sorry and so deeply grateful, she could not find those words, which perhaps might have brought a faint gleam of pleasure to his eyes.

All she could do now was to murmur a few words that were quite un-intelligible and apparently failed to reach him. She made a great effort to control herself and her voice and finally contrived to say fairly steadily:

"I only wished to ask you about the arrangements for my father. When does he come?"

"Tomorrow," he replied equally steadily, "by carriole. I have secured a nice apartment for him close by here in the Rue de la Monnaie. Pierre will drive him over, and he and Jeannette will look after him as they have done all along at Marigny."

"You are very kind," Aurore murmured. "I wish—" she paused and then went on more glibly "—I wish I could show you in some way that I—that I am not ungrateful."

"There is no question of gratitude," he said drily. "I made you a promise that while you are my wife your father's safety would be my care. I am trying to keep my promise, that is all."

"You are ungracious," she rejoined. "Does not the English poet say that 'Rich gifts wax poor when givers prove unkind'?"

"I would not for the worlds have you think me unkind."

"Then tell me."

"What?"

"How I can best repay you for the trouble my father has been to you."

"I assure you—"

"André," she insisted, "please!"

Again his name on her lips. Once upon a time she had hit at him with a moral whip lash and she had also struck him in the face. Neither mor-ally nor physically had she hurt him then, and he had not even winced at the time. Then why, at sound of his name on her lips, did that frown appear upon his brow as if he were trying to keep back something, to control some movement—or was it words?—while an unmistakable look of pain crept into his eyes? Only for an instant, though. Within the space of a second the look of pain as well as the frown had vanished, and there was that mocking smile—that hateful, hateful mocking smile which she so dreaded, curling again around his lips.

"Since you desire it, citizeness," he said drily, "I will tell you that you would earn my deep gratitude if you refrained from listening too patiently to your father's diatribes on the present political situation. Believe me, we all know it to be terrible. But words won't mend it, not just yet. Your father very naturally hates me, he will—"

"I shouldn't allow him—" she broke in hotly, and then paused, her impulse once more checked by that miserable, unexplainable shyness. He put up his hand as if to deprecate anything else that she might say.

"And now," he said, "I am more than repaid."

He went out of the room, and she was left standing there with a big, big ache in her heart, an ache that she could not very well account for, but it forced tears up to her eyes. Tears of anxiety? Of pity? Of regret? She did not know. She only knew that she was desperately miserable and that not even the prospect of seeing her father again so soon had the power to console her.

But had her eyes been gifted with the power to see through material objects she would have made her own heartache seem light and easy to bear. She would have seen a man, strong of will and of iron purpose, broken down by the force of a passion he could no longer control. Gone were resentment and bitterness, pride was torn to shreds. Here was just a man madly—passionately in love. Slowly he fell on his knees; his arm rested against the door; his face was buried in the crook of his arm; and a mighty sigh came from the overburdened heart and broke in a convulsive sob.

# Chapter XXXVI

Charles de Marigny arrived the following afternoon. Aurore had been full of eager joy to see him. All morning she had been busy in the apartment of the Rue de la Monnaie, putting it to rights, making it look as comfortable and as gay as she could. The house was at the end of the street, and the windows of the parlour commanded a beautiful view over the Grande Place, the Ducal Palace, and the river beyond. The room was flooded with sunshine.

After an exceptionally severe winter the spring had come in early, with warm days and an absence of cold winds. The shrubs in the gardens of the Palace were covered with tender green. Lilac, syringa, and jasmine were in bud. Aurore went about her task humming the old chansons:

"Il était une Bergère, et ron—et ron, petit Pataplon!"

and

"Nuage, beau Nuage, qui passe Triomphant!"

She couldn't sit still. At every sound of wheels or clatter of hoofs she ran to the window to see if the carriole was in sight.

But at sight of her father her high spirits quickly sank. Looking down on him from the window, as he got out of the carriole, he appeared to her to be years older. She ran down, and he embraced her with passionate effusion, but the very next moment he pushed her away from him as if the sight of her horrified him. He followed her upstairs, however, leaving Pierre and Jeannette to deal with the carriole and luggage. He did not so much as give a glance round the sunlit room, but threw himself into a chair like a man wearied to death. He had not yet uttered a single word.

Aurore came and knelt down beside him. She would not admit to herself how appalled and disappointed she was. She, who had been the apple of her father's eye, felt as if he were a stranger to her, a stranger whom she almost feared. Her anxious glance searched the face that she had loved so dearly, vainly seeking for that expression of almost passionate tenderness wherewith he had been wont to regard her. But now there was a kind of fierce glitter in his eyes, which would suddenly die down and give place to a dull, vacant stare. Aurore felt intensely sorry for him, for his face betrayed the suffering which he must have endured throughout this long autumn and winter, brooding over his wrongs, all alone up at Marigny, and seeing the horrors and the outrage of this terrible revolution pass like a nightmare before his eyes.

He said very little that first afternoon, and never once touched upon his daughter's marriage or asked either after her husband or the kind friends in whose house she was staying.

But the next day he appeared more loquacious, was apparently happy at the thought that he would no longer be parted from his darling little Aurore, and fell in with all her plans for spending as much time together as possible. They would drive out into the country, or go up the river, and they would spend long evenings together, talking over old times.

He spoke quite rationally, but Aurore could not help noticing that his movements were jerky and that while he talked his hands kept on shaking and his fingers fidgeting with anything that was handy. And suddenly he mentioned André Vallon by name, quite dispassionately at first. Aurore was at her favourite place on a low stool beside his chair, with one arm over his knees. He took hold of her hand, and she noticed that his was burning hot. Carefully, insidiously, he invited her confidence.

"Tell me, my little Aurore," he said, and his tone was gentle and soothing. "Don't be afraid to tell me how unhappy you are. I know you are unhappy, my beloved child, but our troubles always seem less, you know, when we tell of them to a sympathetic ear."

"When you were little," he went on, as Aurore made some evasive reply, "I was your mother as well as your father. You used to tell me everything—all your childish troubles. Tell me your troubles now, my darling. Tell me everything. That cruel, inhuman beast! I'd like to know to what lengths his brutality could go."

And as Aurore still continued to parry his direct questions he put down her reticence to the desire to spare him pain. His tone became more insinuating still, and a look of deep cunning came into his eyes. He leaned forward in his chair till his mouth nearly touched her ear.

"I'll rid you of him, my little Aurore," he whispered. "I have thought it all out. That's why I consented to come to this miserable hole. You trust me. I know! I know just what to do. You needn't tell me anything. I can guess. The brute! The beggarly knave! I know! But I'll rid you of him. Never fear!"

Aurore did all she could to soothe him, but, in spite of herself, her heart was filled with a great and nameless dread. There was something dangerous in the fanaticism of her father's hatred, and although the Mignets and André himself did all they could to reassure her, she had the growing conviction that there was method in her father's apparent madness. He took to roaming about the streets for hours at a time, and Jeannette told Aurore that when he returned he usually brought back with him a lot of news sheets over which he pored and pondered for the rest of the day. Jeannette and Pierre both said that Monseigneur slept very little; they heard him pacing up and down the room half the night through and muttering to himself. Aurore questioned the two faithful souls as to what Monseigneur said when he muttered like that, but it seemed that those mutterings were mostly unintelligible; the only words they ever heard clearly were: "Quite simple—quite easy! That is what I must do," which certainly did not tend to reassure Aurore.

One day, when she came to see the old man, Jeannette told her that he had just gone out, but had spent all morning poring over some news sheets. One in particular he had been intent on for more than an hour, Jeannette said; it was still lying on the table beside his chair. Aurore went into the parlour and had a look at the news sheet. It was an old number of the Moniteur, bearing a date in September of last year. It contained the full text of Merlin's abominable "Loi Relatif aux Gens Suspects." The Law of the Suspect! Obviously, De Marigny had been perusing it; the page with the text lay uppermost; there were notes in the margin in his handwriting. Certain passages were underlined; for instance:

Art I: Immediately after the publication of this Decree, all suspected persons on the territory of the Republic who are still at large will be arrested.

And below that there was:

Are reputed suspect I: Those who, either by their conduct or by their relations with former tyrants or aristos.

And the last half dozen words were underlined.

# Chapter XXXVII

At what precise moment the first dart of a horrible suspicion entered her heart Aurore did not know. All she realized was that an awful danger threatened her husband at the hands of her father.

The horror of such a thing!

She knew, as did everyone these days, that one denunciation, even if it came from an irresponsible person, was often sufficient to bring about the arrest of a fellow creature—arrest which almost invariably was the precursor of death! And with her mind fixed upon this fact she recalled her father's wild rambling words: "I'll rid you of him.... I know what to do.... Quite simple.... That is what I must do...."

Quite simple!

Now Aurore's mind worked more quickly. Something had to be done, and done at once. But what? Firstly, where was the unfortunate madman now? Had he already set out on his proposed trail of treachery and crime? Aurore called to Jeannette and to Pierre. She questioned them and questioned them. Where was Monseigneur? They did not know. Where did he go when he went out aimlessly like this? Just about the streets, sometimes in one direction, sometimes in another. He was fond of the river-bank. The river! Great God in heaven! For one moment Aurore caught herself almost hoping that he had courted the river in a mad desire to put an end to all his misery. Almost hoping! Heavens above! Was she going mad, too? She was, unless she could get a more definite idea of whither her father had gone. But for the moment, since they knew nothing, Pierre and Jeannette must go back to their work. She, Aurore, wished to be left alone to think, to find out something—something!

She looked about her in the small sunlit parlour, feeling helpless and her soul in darkness. She beat her hands together in a wild longing for inspiration. What about money? Had he taken any with him? Aurore knew where he kept it—in the drawer of the small escritoire. She had often seen him take out a livre or two to give to Jeannette. Now she went to look. The pocketbook that was usually in the drawer was no longer there. There were two packets instead. One was addressed to Pierre and obviously contained money, paper and coins. The other was addressed "To my little Aurore." She opened it. There was a letter written in his familiar careful hand.

My Darling Little One [it said]:

I promised you that I would rid you of the inhuman monster who has blighted your young life, and I am going to do it. By the time you get this I shall be on my way to Paris. That archrogue Talon, who is as useful fortunately as he is servile, has made all necessary arrangements. His wife has relatives in Paris, and I shall stay with them. For the first time in my life I shall accept hospitality in a plebeian house, but I have no alternative. What I want to do can only be done in Paris, but there it can be done quickly. Do not try and find out what I am about to do or how. Wait patiently for a further letter from me. Talon will bring it you. I may be caught in my own toils, but I care not so long as I have made you happy and free.

Your devoted Father.

Aurore read the terrible lucubration until the end. Then she refolded the letter and slipped it in the bosom of her gown. She had no doubt now as to what she meant to do, but she wouldn't leave anything to chance. So she hunted through the drawer again and through the whole of the escritoire for some written trace of Hector Talon, that awful, miserable, obsequious Talon! So it was he who was at the bottom of this abominable treachery! Aurore hunted for a letter, a sign of him, as a careful gardener would hunt for the trail of the slug that had impaired his plants. But she found nothing. Talon was a man—no, a worm— who worked underground in the darkness and left no trace of his slimy way.

Then Aurore once more questioned Jeannette and Pierre. Had they seen—did they know anything of Hector Talon? And she wrung the truth out of them, poor miserable wretches! Talon had been in Nevers two days. He had visited Monseigneur. He had bribed them to say nothing to Mademoiselle of these visits. He had been here early this morning, and he and Monseigneur then went out together, Talon carrying a small valise, which Pierre had packed with a few necessities at Monseigneur's orders.

And then Aurore saw red. She felt like a tigress in a fury, would gladly with her two feeble hands have seized those two fools by the throat. They had taken money, money to hold their tongue, while Monseigneur le Duc de Marigny, who bore one of the greatest names in France, and was own cousin to her martyred king, accomplished the vilest act of treachery that had ever disgraced a canaille.

But what was the good of fury, what the good of vituperations, now that the crime was on the point of accomplishment? One fact she did wring out of the trembling lips of Pierre. Lucile Talon's relatives lived in No. 67 of the Rue St. Honoré. Well, that, at any rate, was something. Aurore knew now where she could find her father.

She was half-dazed when she reached the Mignets' house. Without circumlocution, straight to the point, she told them what had happened.

"I must go to Paris," she concluded calmly, "at once. How can I do it?"

"My dear child," the old lady protested, "you cannot go to Paris like this, all in a moment."

"I have my papers, money, everything," she said. "Help me to find a conveyance, as the diligence does not leave till next week."

"But what can you do, child?"

"Warn my husband before it is too late."

To every protest, every objection she gave the same reply: "I must go to my husband before it is too late."

And then she said at last, "If you will not help me I will find a way somehow, but I am going before the day is out."

Help her? Of course they would help her! Were they not the kindest people on God's earth, and was not André Vallon the beloved friend of their heart? Doctor Mignet would, of course, accompany Aurore as far as Paris, and while she went to put a few things together he set out to find coach and horses which would take them as far as Auxerre, where they could pick up another conveyance to take them on to Melun and to Paris. That was probably the route chosen by Talon for Monseigneur, and Aurore would be close on her father's heels.

# Chapter XXXVIII

To anyone returning to Paris in this awful year 1794, after an absence of several months, the aspect of the once gay and lovely city must have been appalling. Streets half deserted; furtive, ill clad figures slouching about the open places; aspects of dire poverty in a blatant contrast with brilliantly lighted restaurants or theatre porticoes; sounds of strident laughter alternating with heart-rending moans. Laughter and tears, and words scarcely whispered lest they be overheard.

This great, this sublime revolution, which was to bring universal freedom and universal happiness, how immense has been its toll of misery and of crime! Penury is terrible; certain necessities like soap and sugar are hardly obtainable. Bread is more and more scarce; the queues outside the bakeries line up during the small hours of the morning and last all day.

The wolves of the Revolution are busy tearing one another to pieces. After the Girondins, the Dantonists. Danton, the great Georges Danton, the lion of the Revolution, who for five years has held the snarling, screaming pack on the leash, has atoned for his weaknesses as well as for his crimes, on the insatiable guillotine. Too weak to stem the flood, which he himself had let loose, he perished as he had allowed others to perish—his king, his queen, his comrades, his friends. Too weak! The great, the virile Danton, with the resonant voice and tempestuous eloquence, too weak to combat his cunning, slimy adversary, the Sea-green Incorruptible with the ascetic face and the pale eyes! Then what chance had others against the all-powerful dictator who with one word hissed through his thin lips could send any adversary without trial to the scaffold?

It was a month and more since the Dantonists had perished on the guillotine, and Maximilien Robespierre was sovereign master of France.

A Child of the Revolution

Aurore, sitting inside the diligence, which had brought her and the Doctor over from Melun, had no eyes for outward things. Whether Paris was changed or not since last she had been in the city, whether the streets looked dismal and the restaurants lively, she neither knew nor cared. It was a lovely day in May: the chestnut trees in the Tuileries gardens were full of blossom; the sun shone and the sky was blue; but Aurore say nothing of these beauties of nature. Now that the time was so near when she would see her husband her febrile impatience was such that it was only by a mighty effort of will that she was able to sit still in the crowded coach and not allow her fellow passengers to become aware of the state of her nerves. They might have thought her demented. Doctor Mignet sat beside her and now and then gave her hand a slight pressure, which comforted her for the moment.

At last the lumbering coach came to a halt at the Cheval Blanc, the posting inn close to the Pont Neuf. The Quai de la Ferraille was quite close. Aurore elected to walk while Doctor Mignet would look after the luggage. He announced his intention of putting up at the Cheval Blanc, if he could get a room.

"I shall be within five minutes' walk," he said kindly, "so you can call on me, my dear, whenever you want me."

It was then three o'clock in the afternoon. The usual crowd swarmed round the Palace of Justice, waiting to see the prisoners being hustled out after their condemnation, or the well-known advocates or members of the Convention sally forth after the grim work of the day was done.

Aurore paid no heed to anything round her; wrapped in her travelling cape with the hood pulled over her head she walked rapidly, looking neither to right nor left. But suddenly the crowd surged along the bridge, and she found herself hustled and pressed against the parapet: a couple of tumbrils surrounded by men in uniform were forging their way through the throng. They were the prisoners who had just stood the mockery of a trial and were being taken back to La Force or the Temple for their final toilette before their ultimate journey to the guillotine. A few tatterdemalions in the crowd shouted: "A la guillotine!" Others hurled insults at the prisoners, but the bulk of the people looked on with a kind of stolid indifference, showing neither joy nor horror.

Aurore, pressed against the parapet, saw the tumbrils pass along quite close to her; she saw the prisoners standing with hands tied behind their backs; and suddenly the full force of the horror, which she saw reached her consciousness. She searched those faces in the tumbrils, realizing for the first time that perhaps she had come too late and that André might be standing there in the tumbril—standing there on his way to death.

When the tumbrils had passed and the crowd drifted away in their wake she remained for a long time there, leaning against the balustrade with eyes blind to everything save to the vision that had just passed by, and lips parted by the cries of horror which she had been at such pains to repress. André had not been one of those poor wretches that were being dragged through the streets of Paris for the delectation of the mob: but the vision of that ghastly exhibition had conjured up the possibility of another, so awful, so terrible, so infernal that Aurore was left wondering if she was not indeed going the way of her father and losing her reason at the foresight.

After a little while she recovered herself, and without glancing to right or left she hurried along the quay. Soon she reached the house wherein she had spent the first few months of her married life! What peace there seemed to be in it! Aurore felt it almost as soon as she passed under the porte-cochère and made her way up the familiar stone staircase. She rang the bell of the apartment as she had done so often in the past, and the same pleasant middle-aged woman opened the door to her.

The woman's eyes looked ready to fall out of her head at sight of Aurore.

"But, citizeness...!" she exclaimed, and clasped her hand together in amazement.

"Citizen Vallon? Is he in?" Aurore almost gasped, and staggered into the vestibule.

The semi darkness indoors after the dazzling sunshine of the street dazed her and made her feel as if she were blind. The woman ran to her and put her arms round her.

"You are ill, citizeness," she murmured. "What can I get you?"

Aurore shook her head: "Nothing!... I am not ill.... Where is Citizen Vallon?"

"At the Blind School, citizeness. He does not usually come home before evening."

"You expect him home, then?"

"But of course, citizeness."

The woman, with gentle solitude, relieved Aurore of the heavy travelling cape. She was obviously puzzled and not a little frightened, but tried to speak as unconcernedly as she could.

"We were not expecting you, citizeness," she said: "at least the Citizen said nothing to me."

"No," Aurore replied more calmly: "he does not expect me. I came with Doctor Mignet."

The woman opened the parlour door. How inviting it looked! The bright sunny room with the muslin curtains, the armchair and her own work table beside the window; the books, the footstool, the chessmen ranged on the board. Aurore's tired eyes roamed round the room and, in spite of the agony of dread, which was gnawing at her heart, an infinite peace seemed to descend on her soul. With a weary little sigh she sank into the armchair, and a wan smile lit up her face in response to the woman's anxious, puzzled gaze.

"What would you like, citizeness?" the woman asked, a little reassured. "A glass of wine, or some hot coffee?"

"Coffee, please, Marie. Some of that lovely coffee you used to make for my breakfast."

"It won't be quite so nice now, citizeness," Marie said with a sigh; "and we have no milk."

"Whatever it is, Marie, I shall love it," Aurore assured her. The woman went away, and she snuggled down into the big chair. How lovely and peaceful it was! The quay below was half deserted; hardly a sound came to disturb the quietude of this serene abode. Leaning her head against the back of the chair Aurore felt a flood of tears rise to her eyes—tears that were not wholly of sorrow.

She drank eagerly the coffee, which Marie presently brought her. After which the kind woman persuaded her to lie down on the sofa and saw her comfortably settled with a couple of pillows under her head. Poor little Aurore! She was so tired, so infinitely weary! Physically and mentally weary. Her limbs ached, and her head. And she had a great big heartache.

And lying there snugly against the pillows she presently fell asleep.

# Chapter XXXIX

The sound of the door and a murmur of voices roused Aurore from sleep.

The next moment André came into the room. She sat up on the sofa, her hands clasped tightly together, her fair hair slightly tousled, and her cheeks flushed after sleep. The shades of evening were drawing in, and the rosy light of sunset had crept into the room. André, at the door, had not yet moved. He was looking his fill on the exquisite vision, which had transformed this simple room into a mansion of paradise.

At last he asked the obvious questions:

"Why are you here? Has anything happened?"

"Yes, André," she replied, "a very great deal has happened. My father, poor wretch, has completely lost his reason!"

"Heavens above!"

"No," she said, "I don't mean in that way, though I do think Doctor Mignet would actually pronounce him mad."

She paused a moment. Her throat felt so dry that she could hardly speak. There were a carafe and a glass on the side table. André filled the glass with water and brought it to her. While she drank he stood beside her, and when she was about to put the glass down he took it from her, and his hand touched her fingers, which were trembling and cold.

"You are overwrought," he said gently. "Don't try and talk now. I will call Marie and she—”

"No! no!" She broke in quickly. "I don't want anyone. I am only tired from the journey, and I must tell you—"

"Yes? What is it?"

"Spurred by his insane hatred against you, my father has denounced you—"

"How do you know that?"

"Never mind how I know: I know it. I swear to you that it is so. One day I will tell you just how I found out, but not now. There is no time. I came to warn you before—before—"

"You came to warn me?" he asked, frowning, evidently puzzled.

"Yes."

"Why?"

They looked at each other, he uncomprehending, not daring to comprehend, and she, seized with that awful shyness which almost paralyzed her will and her tongue.

"Why?" he insisted, but this time he came nearer her, and his voice was hoarse and broken like that of a man gasping for breath.

"Because," she murmured, "because—"

It was her eyes that answered him. Her lips refused her service.

"Because you cared?"

Was there ever a cry uttered by man more exultant than this which rose like a paean of joy from André Vallon's throat? In a moment he was beside her on one knee, not daring to touch her yet, but with ardent, passionate gaze trying to read the secret of her soul.

"Because you cared?" he insisted. "Tell me."

"André!"

"Because you cared what became of me? Say it! Say it! Say the word, ma mie! Tell me that you came," he entreated, "because you cared."

How could she speak? The whole world, the sordid, ugly world, lay suddenly shattered at her feet, and in the gaze that sought and held her own she had a glimpse of such a vision of Elysian fields as human mind could scarcely conceive. She returned his gaze and her eyes, which had always seemed unfathomable, revealed to him the secret which she had thought would remain forever buried in her heart. It was Love that had spurred her to come. Love that had so often made her heart ache almost to breaking point. Love! And the longing to feel once more that dear strong arm around her, to pillow her head against that loyal breast, to hear that great and simple heart beat only for her. He loved her, and she did not know it! And now that the heavenly knowledge had come to her at last it came hand-in-hand with the agonizing dread for his life.

"André!" she said suddenly, all the joy in her heart smothered in this awful dread, "you must leave Paris at once."

He did not seem to hear. He had had his answer from her eyes, and his soul was no longer on this earth. It had gone a-roaming in paradise.

"You came," he murmured, "because you cared."

But, womanlike, she thought only of him, of the terrible danger, which every minute as it sped by brought nearer and nearer to their door.

"You don't understand, André," she insisted. "My father is in Paris. It was only after he left that I suspected—"

"And then you came because you cared."

"André, at this very hour, perhaps—"

"At this very hour I am adoring you, Aurore—"

"There's time to get away," she entreated feverishly.

"And I want eternity in which to tell you how I worship you—"

"In God's name, André!" she cried. "It may mean death if you stay—"

But his hand was buried in her hair and forced her dear head closer and closer to him.

"My exquisite Aurore!" he whispered in her ear, "you are the most perfect being God ever made. I was a fool not to tell you this before, but I will not die, Dawn of my Soul, before I have taught you how good it is to love, how sweet it is to kiss."

He held her so close that she could no longer struggle. His lips were on hers, and she could no longer warn, and he asked the great, the immortal question which lovers have asked since the beginning of time, and the answer to which will open for them the gates either of paradise or of hell.

"Do you love me, my wife?"

And Aurore's eyes and lips answered softly, "Yes."

# Chapter XL

The hours flew by on the wings of an overwhelming happiness, and Love reigned supreme while evening faded into night. The awakening came when the two lovers scarce had finished dreaming. The tramp of feet on the stairs, the knock on the door, the raucous call: "Open in the name of the Law!"

It was quite dark in the room now—quite dark, only through the chink under the door there came a narrow streak of light from the candle which Marie had put on the table of the vestibule, and through the thin muslin curtains over the window the pale flicker of the street lamp cast the objects in the room into deeper gloom.

"Open, in the name of the Law!"

And Aurore, waking from her dream of happiness and love, was suddenly thrust out of the gates of her paradise and hurled back into the hideous world of grim reality. In a moment she was on her feet and across the room. Like a statue of despair she stood against the door with arms outstretched and head thrown back—a statue of despair but also of fury—a woman in defence of her lover.

"Come and kiss me, Aurore!" came a happy voice, broken with yearning, and in the gloom the arm she loved was stretched out in longing to her.

She babbled hoarsely, incoherently, like one half demented:

"You must fly, André! You must... you must... for my sake... there's time... through the window in the next room. The back yard... no one will see you... André... André... you must!"

"Come to me, Aurore... one more kiss," he said slowly; "ten more if there's time...."

"But they are here," she insisted. "André, can't you hear?"

Just then there was a timid knock at the door, and Marie's trembling voice called aghast: "In the name of God, Citizen Vallon, tell me what to do."

"Why, open the door, Marie," André replied quietly, "else they will break it open."

Then, as Marie's hesitating footsteps were heard shuffling across the vestibule, he murmured softly:

"There's time for one more kiss.... Come to me, Aurore."

Obviously she could not move. Horror, despair, had paralyzed her will and her limbs. The woman defending her lover! How could she move from that door, from that thin, futile barrier, the only thing that stood between her lover and death? The next instant André was beside her; she felt again that dear, strong arm around her, her head once more lay upon his breast, she felt the beating of that heart which she knew now was filled with her image. His lips eagerly devoured her eyes, her throat, her hair, and then in one long, impassioned kiss their lips met once more in enduring, all-conquering immutable love.

Outside in the vestibule there was bustle and noise and tramping of feet; hoarse commands and a murmur of voices, and Marie's wailing sobs. Then a knock at the door. A terrible cry rose to Aurore's throat, but it was smothered before it reached her lips, for André's hand was across her mouth.

"Open, in the name of the Law!"

"Three minutes, Citizen Soldiers," André replied glibly, "while I get a light."

And Aurore, clinging to him with convulsive hands, her face bathed in tears, her voice broken with sobs, whispered hoarsely:

"Kill me, André!... For mercy's sake kill me... I cannot live without your love."

"Look at me, sweet, and listen," he murmured hurriedly; and obediently she opened her eyes and looked up at him.

It was quite dark in the room, quite dark; but the feeble light of the street lamp faintly illuminated his face, and she could see that it was irradiated with a wonderful happiness.

"What you want now, my sweet," he said more slowly, "is courage."

"I have none, André," she murmured feebly.

"You will have when you remember that God in His mercy will give you someone else to care for, perhaps, instead of me."

"Someone else? I don't understand."

He pressed his lips close to her ear and whispered a few words very low, so that she could scarcely hear, but which brought a rush of colour to her pale cheeks. Then he looked once more into her eyes and smiled: the happiest, lightest of smiles.

"And if it is a boy," he said earnestly, but still with that happy smile, "do not teach him to hate all those Frenchmen who were his father's friends, with whom he dreamed dreams of making this old world new and happy, and who died for their ideals because they were men and not gods."

He raised her gently from the ground as he had so often done before, carried her into the next room, and there laid her down on the bed. She had partly lost consciousness, but her arms were twined round his neck, and her fingers so tightly linked together that he had some difficulty in getting them apart. She lay very still, but her eyes were open and her lips parted; her body was shaken with heart-rending sobs. He knelt down beside the bed and kissed her once more on the lips, drank the salt tears that lay upon her cheek; he kissed her ice-cold hands, her throat, her feet above the shoe, then slowly rose and went out of the room, closing and locking the door behind him.

She gave one terrific cry: "André!" and jumped up from the bed, her senses alert; she ran to the door—it was locked; with her hands she beat against the panels, she fell on her knees, clinging to that cruel door which hid him from her view, and calling, calling insistently, piteously, like a bird that has lost its mate. And all the while she heard the murmurs of voices, André's calm response: "Quite ready, Citizen Captain." A loud cry from Marie. The opening and shutting of the front door; the tramp of feet slowly... slowly... slowly dying away down the stairs.

And then—nothing more.

Marie coming in a few moments later found her in a dead swoon across the floor.

# Book IV

## Chapter XLI

She became known as "Our Little Lady of Sorrows"—Notre Petite Dames des Douleurs.

She could be seen daily wending her way from the Quai de la Ferraille to the Palais de Justice in the early morning, waiting in the queue until the gates were opened, and thereafter taking her place in the vast hall, always in the front row of the balcony that faced the prisoners at the bar. At first the other habitués of the grim spectacle looked on her as one of themselves, fond, as they were, of watching the prisoners file in, seeing them take their place on the benches facing the judges, with the chief prisoner in the iron armchair in the immediate centre. Women in ragged shawls and tattered kirtles, with dishevelled hair under soiled lace caps, or scarlet berets, who had brought their knitting with them to while away the waiting hours, would nudge Aurore when a well known name was called out or if they recognized a noted prisoner.

"That's Amisal over there, citizness, the third from the end. He tried to assassinate the patriot Collot in the Rue Favart, you remember? Lucky he missed fire, the brigand! Oh! And if it isn't that young scrub Cécile Renaud! She was for murdering the Incorruptible himself. They found two knives in her market basket, you know. Well, her way to the guillotine is clear enough."

But soon they found that she was not interested in their talk. She didn't listen: she only looked. She had great eyes of a colour impossible to define, and wore a dark travelling cape with a hood over her fair hair. She would look and look while the batch of prisoners filed in, but as soon as they were seated and the Prosecutor Tinville began his indictment, she would lean back in her seat and take no more notice of what went on in the hall below.

Until another batch was called, when she would sit up and again look on each face as the prisoners filed in. She never spoke and she never cried, but she looked so sad that a woman one day, seeing her come in rather later than usual, made a place for her by squeezing her fellow spectators and said at the same time, "Here comes the Little Lady of Sorrows. Come and sit by me, my dear. You'll get a splendid view, better than the one you had yesterday."

And so the name stuck to her. And she came, day after day, to the Palais de Justice to watch the prisoners file into the hall, there to receive their sentence of death. There was no alternative. The very fact of being suspected of treason, of being denounced by an enemy or a fool, of being brought to the bar of this travesty of justice, was tantamount to a sentence of death. And Aurore came, day after day, to watch this grim spectacle, because she could not find out to what prison they had take André and could find no other way of knowing what became of him. The prisons were crowded, the jailers overworked and harassed. Vainly had she tried to get sight of the list of prisoners in every House of Detention in and around Paris.

"We've no orders," was the response she invariably got from the concièrge or the captain in command. "Get an order from the Committee, and you can see the list."

"What Committee?" she would ask insistently. "And how can I get such an order?"

"Bah! Leave me in peace!" the man—whoever it was—would reply with a savage oath. "You don't think you are the only female who comes bothering us in this way, do you? If I had to attend to all of you—"

He would then turn his back on Aurore and have her ejected from the room and the door slammed in her face. The rules governing prison discipline had became very severe of late. The visits from outside, which used to be allowed and were a great feature of prison life in the past, were now strictly forbidden. The government had persuaded itself that plots of all sorts were being hatched in the Houses of Detention, and prisoners, in consequence, were not allowed to see anyone. Thus frustrated at every turn, Aurore took to haunting the Palais de Justice. There, at last, she would be bound to see Andrè when he was brought to trial. She would see him when that awful tumbril took him to his death.

She had no hope. None. Though she held but little communication with anyone except, of course, Marie, she could not help knowing that the fate of every prisoner these days was a foregone conclusion. It was only a question of time. Some languished weeks in prison, others even months, some few were hurried through the ghastly process of arrest, trial, condemnation, and death in a few days. Aurore knew that and watched in the Palais de Justice every day.

She had written him a letter, just a few words in which she had poured out her every soul. They were words, which, she knew, would give happiness to his heart and bring a smile to his dear lips. This precious paper she inserted in a heavy gold locket, which she always held tightly in her hand ready to fling it to him if such a blessed opportunity arose.

May had long since yielded to June. June passed on, serene and warm, with its wealth of blossom in the gardens and a bird song in the summer air. All nature seemed to smile while men hated and destroyed one another and dared to mock God with their horrible Mumbo-Jumbo, the feast of the Supreme Bring, with the arch-murderer, Robespierre, parading in azure-blue coat and white breeches as the arch-priest of the new deity.

That was on the 8th of June, less than a fortnight after Andrè's arrest. Doctor Mignet, who had been with Aurore during the first few days of her misery and had attempted the impossible in trying to find out wither they had taken André, had been obliged to return to his duties in Nevers. She hardly noticed his absence. Her heart was dead to all save to an infinity of grief.

It was in the early days of June that she saw her father again. She was walking across the Pont des Arts when suddenly she found herself face to face with Hector Talon. She thought nothing of the meeting at the moment; indeed, she hoped that he had not recognized her. But what he did was to halt for a minute or two as soon as she had passed by and then to follow her.

The next afternoon, when she came home from her daily pilgrimage, she found Marie bursting with what she thought was gladsome news.

"An elderly gentleman has come to see you, citizeness," she said mysteriously. "He is waiting in the parlour."

"Oh, Marie!" Aurore exclaimed involuntarily. "You shouldn't have—"

"Not admitted him!" Marie retorted with the easy familiarity of her kind. "But it's your father, citizeness, your dear old father!"

Aurore listened no further. With a heavy heart she went through into the parlour and saw her father sitting there on the end of the sofa close to the window, the sofa beside which André had knelt that late afternoon when first he had told her of his love. It seemed like a supreme insult, this old man sitting just there complacently gazing out of the window. When she entered he put out his arms and exclaimed with joy and tenderness:

"My little Aurore! At last! At last!"

She had not moved from the door. At sight of him her gorge rose in horror. What kind of a miscreated daughter was she that she should hate her own father? Would she, at least, have sufficient willpower not to allow the full flood of her loathing to surge out of her overburdened heart? He, on the other hand, did not appear conscious of her enmity. As she did not rush into his arms he let them drop and went on talking in a glib, matter-of-fact way:

"You have no idea, ma chérie," he said, "how anxious I have been. I suppose your letter in answer to mine miscarried. I never received it, you know."

"What letter?" she asked.

"I wrote to tell you the joyful news. You never replied. But it was a good idea to come yourself instead."

"What joyful news?"

"Why, that I have fulfilled my promise, ma chérie, to rid you of the inhuman monster who had blighted your life."

"You mean that you wrote to tell me that you had committed the most loathsome act of treachery that ever called down the vengeance of God on a miscreant's head."

Even now he looked surprised, bewildered at her vehemence, thinking that his beloved daughter, like so many women in these terrible times, had perchance lost her reason.

"Aurore, my child!" he exclaimed soothingly.

"I am not your child!" she retorted coldly, "no longer the child of so vile a worker of iniquity as you. You have brought upon me such immeasurable sorrow as no man has ever brought on woman since the beginning of time. The very sight of you turns my heart to stone, and I can but pray to God that I may never set eyes on you again. And now, I entreat you to go before I quite forget that you are old and that you are my father."

She threw open the door and stood aside, pointing to it. De Marigny tried to speak. He rose and came a step or two towards her.

"Do not come near me," she said hoarsely. "My God! Can't you see that I am at the end of my tether?"

"You are overwrought, Aurore," he rejoined coolly. "Heaven knows what is going on in your poor distracted mind at this moment. You have spoken words that I shall find hard to forgive, but a father's heart is full of indulgence. I cannot, of course, stay now and plead with you, for the devil apparently has possession of your mind. It will take all our good Abbé's piety to exorcize him."

Marie was hovering in the vestibule. She looked scared to death as De Marigny came out of the parlour and took up his hat and stick.

"Has she been long like this?" he asked her, indicating Aurore and then touching his forehead.

Marie was indignant.

"There is nothing wrong with the Citizeness's brain," she said hotly. "It is her heart that is broken because she worshipped her husband, and he is like to perish on that awful guillotine."

De Marigny shrugged. How ignorant, how unobservant were people of that class! He looked back once over his shoulder. Aurore had not moved. The hood had fallen back from her head, and her delicate profile, with the wealth of fair hair above it like a golden aureole, looked like an exquisite cameo against the dark portière. She looked a living statue of high breeding, of blue blood and age-old descent—the perfect aristocrat. De Marigny shrugged again. Worshipped her husband, indeed? What nonsense! What a lie! Her mind was slightly unhinged, he concluded, that was all. Once all these horrible times were over and he had her back at Marigny she would be the first to laugh at this woman's foolish talk. And he went away entirely unperturbed.

# Chapter XLII

It was on the 26th of July that the last blow fell. Aurore sitting at her accustomed place in the Hall of the Palais de Justice saw the prisoners file in, and the first to enter was André.

Our Little Lady of Sorrows! She gave one gasp—a sob that rent her heart and caused even those deadened hearts around her to beat with sudden pity.

"Thou hast seen him, eh, my cabbage?" the woman next to her asked. "Which is he?"

Two or three of them put down their knitting. They were interested. They meant to be kind. Their hearts were dulled by all the miseries and the horrors, which they had witnessed—dulled but not dead. Our Little Lady of Sorrows! They were very, very sorry for her! She was so pretty and so young! And she had been watching here day after day for well-nigh two months to catch a last glimpse of her man.

"Don't try and point him out, my pigeon," the woman went on softly; "only nod 'yes' if I guess right."

The woman on the other side said:

"I believe it is that handsome fellow with the one arm. Well, it is a shame that such a fine soldier—"

"Hush, citizeness," someone at the back broke in, "you are talking treason."

That was so. No one was allowed to express pity for the prisoners at the bar, for such pity was a sign of counter-revolutionary tendencies and, as such, punishable by death. Even so, one woman said pointing to André: "He taught the blind to read and the dumb to speak. My daughter, who is blind—"

"Hush! Silence!" came from the rest of the crowd.

Our Little Lady of Sorrows sat and watched, her whole soul in her eyes. She saw André as the chief prisoner of the batch sitting in the iron chair immediately facing the judges. His face looked perfectly serene. He looked older, of course, and wan; prison life had not suited his vigorous temperament; but his dark eyes shone brightly, and around his mouth there was that mocking smile which Aurore had so dreaded once, but which since she had learned to love. Unlike his fellow prisoners André had obviously taken great pains with his appearance. He wore his old military tunic, which, though very worn and shabby, had been carefully brushed. He was neatly shaved, and his chestnut hair was tied back with a bow at the nape of his neck.

Our Little Lady of Sorrows watched him and marvelled that God in His mercy did not allow her heart to break. She listened to the indictment read by Prosecutor Tinville. She heard every lying word, every monstrous accusation. She listened and watched, drawing his soul to hers with the magnetism of her eyes. She threw back her hood so that he should see her better. And suddenly he looked up and saw her. Such a look of joy and happiness and love came into his face, as surely only shines on the faces of the blessed. Thereafter he looked neither to right nor left. Only at her. The Prosecutor finished his indictment, the advocate began to plead. Obviously André heard neither. Yet the advocate pleaded with fervour, even with passion. Even the crowd murmured approval at the defence, but what was the good? Prisoners were condemned long before they faced their judges. The advocate was silenced even in the very middle of his peroration, cut short when he was halfway through an eloquent sentence; and the prisoners were not allowed one word in their own defence.

They were all condemned in a body. Traitors all to the Republic! Conspirators against the State! The sentence was that they be guillotined. And that was all! The mock trial was at an end. They were ordered to rise and make way for others. Some of them screamed and wrung their hands; some called loudly to the people and to the Supreme Being to witness their innocence, some took the blow in sullen silence. But André took it with a gently mocking smile. It had to come, and he was prepared. Death these days was stalking every man: it was bound to be his turn one day, and he was prepared. From the hour when Robespierre and his horde of jackals had attacked Danton the Lion and brought him down, from that hour André, the child of this revolution, knew that he, too, would be its victim. For two months he had languished in prison waiting his turn for the only possible release and dreaming of that wonderful afternoon when first he knew that the woman he worshipped, worshipped him too. So happy, so entrancing had been those hours of supreme joy and love that he felt that Fate and he were quits. God had given him everything, every joy, every happiness, supreme contentment when He gave him this perfect mutual love. So what did anything else matter? Death would only mean a union more perfect—more enduring than anything that Life could give.

All this he tried to convey to Aurore with the last glance, which he was able to cast on her. "Do not grieve, my beloved! The happiness which you gave me was too perfect for this earth, too perfect to last."

Aurore watched him until he too disappeared down the stairs that led to the guardroom. Then quickly she rose. There was one more hope of seeing him, when that awful cart took him back to prison. She could follow the cart, she could see him again, she could throw him her last message of love in the gold locket, which she always carried—perhaps, even, she could touch his hand. Hastily drawing the hood back over her head, she rose to go. The others made way for her, helped her all they could. They murmured sympathetic words as she stepped over the tribunes to find her way out:

"Our Little Lady of Sorrows! So young! So pretty!"

"And that handsome husband!"

"Ah, me!"

"Where will it all end?"

There was a great crowd outside the gates, greater than usual, Aurore thought, as feverishly she forged her way down the great staircase and into the courtyard. The carts were there, ranged in a file to the left of the gates which were wide open. The crowd was dense round the carts. One had just gone with its batch of condemned: the other was waiting by the postern gate. It was round this one that the crowd was thickest. Aurore, with the determination and courage of despair, pushed and struggled to get near. But it was impossible: she was jostled and elbowed out of the way until she found herself pressed against the iron railing, on the stone base of which some of the throng had scrambled to get a better view. The open gates were close by. From such a point of vantage it would be possible to get a view of the prisoners in the cart over the heads of the crown, and then, when the cart moved away, to slip out by the gate in its wake. Some kindly person helped Aurore to hoist herself up on the stone parapet.

There she stood and waited, all eyes, and with the locket grasped tightly in her hand. She heard the people about her talking.

"Those are the ones from the Blind Institution."

"And those from the School for the Deaf and Dumb."

They were pointing to a small group of men and women, two or three score of them, who were gathered close around the cart.

"One of the prisoners taught in those institutions."

"Citizen Vallon. I knew him. A nephew of mine is blind. Vallon did wonders with him."

"He taught the blind to see."

"And the deaf to hear."

"I suppose they have come to see the last of him."

"Poor creatures! What will become of them now?"

"Hush! Here they come!"

The prisoners were filing out of the building and were being hustled into the cart. There were eight of them, five men, three women. The men's coats were tied by the sleeves round their necks. All had their arms tied with cord behind their backs. André was the last to step into the cart: at sight of him one part of the crowd set up a cry, weird and inarticulate, the cry peculiar to the tongue-tied and the dumb: it was taken up by the blind, who had not seen but could guess. The blind called out piteously: "Do not leave us in darkness, Citizen Vallon!" but the dumb could only utter their hideous, inarticulate shrieks.

André stood up in the cart with his old military tunic tied round his neck; his one arm was tied behind his back to the empty sleeve of his shirt. His glance swept the crowd in search of his beloved, and like a magnet her eyes drew his and held them for an instant. Only a few seconds, though, for the next moment he saw those poor afflicted wretches about him, and for the first time his aching heart drew tears to his eyes.

"Vallon!" they moaned and cried. "Vallon!" like children calling in distress to their mother.

The soldiers jostled them, tried to silence them by threats, but they would not be moved, nor would they be silenced, until suddenly out of the crowd behind them there rose a louder cry:

"You scurvy knave! You abominable hypocrite! At last, at last you get your deserts! Scoundrel! Hellhound! Take that in remembrance of those whom you have outraged!"

Aurore saw it all! It was her father, and Hector Talon was with him. Charles de Marigny seemed to have cast all weakness aside, to have suddenly found the vigour of youth through the power of his hatred. It was amazing how he pushed his way through the crowd, right up to the tumbril, and then, with a sudden spring, he put on foot on the hub of the nearest wheel. He was brandishing a stick with the obvious purpose of hitting at André, when the crowd, taken aback for the moment, seized him and dragged him down.

Aurore put her hand up to her mouth to smother a cry. Her father had fallen backward, dragging Hector Talon down with him in his fall. She could see nothing more than that, for the crowd was all over him, and everything seemed confusion—confusion made hideous by weird cries and imprecations. The people in the rear of the crowd declared: "C'est bien fait!" It served the miscreant right for trying to hit at a brave soldier who had lost one arm in the defence of his country. The soldiers tried to restore order and only succeeded in keeping back the crowd— the poor afflicted—at the point of the bayonet.

Aurore's eyes wandered back to the tumbril in search of André. She clutched the gold locket with her last message of love, ready to fling it to him. But she couldn't see him; be must have been struck by the old maniac and fallen down, perhaps, on the floor of the cart. She fingered the thing in her hand feverishly—and suddenly was aware that the thing she fingered as unfamiliar in shape and in weight. She looked down upon it. The gold locket was not there; she had instead a crumpled, soiled piece of paper in her hand; it was wrapped around something hard and rough, possibly a stone. She couldn't think what it meant. What abandoned thief had dared to filch her locket? And then a swift recollection went though her mind like a flash. When she saw her father spring up on the hub of the cart-wheel she had tried to smother a cry of horror and had felt a firm, kindly hand grasping hers.

She had thought nothing of it at the moment, merely thought that some gentle soul was trying to express mute sympathy. Instead of this mysterious substitution! What could it mean? Was it? Could it be from André? Oh! If she could only see him. But there was the crowd, the poor, miserable, afflicted crowd, trying in a futile way to avenge an insult done to the man they revered. The soldiers, reinforced by comrades, had pushed them well away. Aurore could not see what had become of her father. Had he been trampled underfoot by the infuriated mob? Had punishment overtaken him at the very culmination of his treachery?

Just then there was another commotion. A wild, terrified shriek, and Hector Talon was hoisted aloft by half-a-dozen strong arms and then flung, still yelling, into the cart. Some people laughed. The deaf and dumb who had seen gave a weird cry of content. The sergeant in command cast a final glance on the tumbril.

"Allons!" he called with stolid indifference. "The batch is complete! Eight sheep for Citizen Samson tomorrow."

Then he gave the word of command: "En avant," and the cart-wheels creaked on their axles as the horses began to move.

And André! Aurore could not see André! Not even now when the tumbril turned out of the gates so close to her. The crowd surged in its wake, mostly in silence, though the poor blind who were nearest to the cart continued to call on Vallon, while the tongue-tied, uttering unintelligible sounds, hung on to them and tried hard to explain that

Vallon, Vallon, their father and their mother and their friend, was no longer there.

Aurore, more dead than alive, had scrambled down from the parapet. The crowd was perceptibly thinner. A few soldiers were rounding up the poor afflicted. The others, for the most part, hung about waiting to see the next batch of prisoners file out. Only a few followed the tumbril, from which could still be heard the agonized yells of Hector Talon. In a few more minutes the vast courtyard seemed almost peaceful. Just a few people waiting about in small groups here and there. The spectacle of the day was not yet over. There would be at least another five tumbrils to watch. The blind and the deaf and dumb, the wretched and the poor, had drifted away. Wither? No doubt this fraternal government knew. Was this not the millennium so confidently foretold?

The soldiers had restored order. They had done it at the point of the bayonet, driving the afflicted away like useless sheep unfit even for the knacker. They had also apparently dragged away the inaniment and lifeless bodies of those who had been unfortunately or luckily succumbed in the mêlée. Among these was the body of a man who had once been styled Monseigneur le Duc de Marigny, one of the proudest names in France, who once had power of life and death over his fellow men and could toy with the honour of any poor wench who happened to please his eye. His mangled body lay now in the guardroom of the Palace, so-called of Justice; the naked feet of a score of unwashed rabble had trampled the life out of him. Not even decently covered with a sheet, the illustrious remains of a descendant of kinds was destined for a pauper's grave.

But all this Aurore only found out later. Her thoughts, for the moment, were far enough away from her father who had done her such a great—such an irreparable injury. She had found a deserted corner in an angle of the building, and here, unseen by prying eyes, she unfolded the paper which had so mysteriously been thrust into her hand. And this is what was written thereon:

André is safe! Go home and wait for him. Silence and discretion above all.

And below there was the device of a small five-petalled flower roughly tinted scarlet.

And that was all. Aurore, dazed and puzzled, marvelled if she were dreaming now or if the rest of this day had been a hideous nightmare. If, when she woke anon, she would find herself inside the gates of an earthly paradise or of an unendurable hell? André's safe! Where? When? How? BY whose agency had he been snatched from out the jaws of death? How and why had God interfered to prevent the monstrous holocaust?

André safe? Could it be true? Did such heavenly things happen in these days of darkness, of doubt and misery?

And all the while that these doubts, fears, conjectures, alternated in Aurore's mind, with the wildest, most unbelievable hope, she was running home, running like one urged by hope or driven by despair.

André safe! And Paris looked just the same! The quays, the river, the pavements, the people passing by as if nothing had happened. Was life going on just the same, then? If so, surely it could not be true that André was safe.

Marie wondered what had happened to the Citizeness. Her habitual sadness had given place to a febrile restlessness. She seemed unable to sit still. For hours she wandered from room to room, up and down, taking no rest. She tried to eat, but food, apparently, choked her.

Marie asked questions but received no answer. She feared, indeed, that the Citizeness was sick with the fever. She suggestion bed, and toward ten o'clock Aurore agreed to lie down, but only on condition that Marie herself went to bed. She certainly was in a fever then, with cheeks aflame and hands cold as ice. But she did make pretence to go to bed, drank the orange-flower water, which Marie had prepared, and promised to go to sleep.

She waited, quiet as a mouse, until no sound save a comfortable snore came from Marie's room. The good soul had taken to snoring of late, and many a time had the sound set Aurore's nerves on edge. But tonight she welcomed it. Half-past ten. She crept noiselessly out of bed and put on her clothes again. She lit a candle and with it tiptoed out to the vestibule. She set the candle on the table, and she drew the bolt of the front door, leaving it ajar. She pulled a chair close to the door, sat down and waited.... Waited, wide-eyed and expectant, as she had waited, day after day, these two months past in the Hall of the Palais de Justice.

A few minutes after midnight she heard a footstep on the stairs. No need to make a guess as to whose it was: she would have known it among hundreds of thousands. She left the door ajar and went back into the parlour. She sat down in the big armchair. The room was all dark save for the dim light cast in by the flickering candle in the vestibule.

And thus he found her, waiting for him and ready, with arms held out so that he could pillow his tired head against her warm bosom. She gathered him in her arms with that loving tenderness which is the essence of a good woman's passionate love. Her first kiss was on his hair; then only did her lips find his.

Of danger and death, of rescue or safety, there was no talk. All that he said was, "Ma mie!" as, cheek, to cheek, they sat there in the big armchair, forgetful of the world, forgetful of everything save of their love.

# Chapter XLIII

Two days later Maximilien Robespierre and his satellites perished in their turn on the guillotine; that 26th day of July, which had meant life or death to Aurore and André had also meant life or death to the most bloodthirsty tyrant the civilized world has ever known. It was the first eclipse of his power and of his popularity. Swift as had been his rise, his fall from the giddy heights of dictatorship was swifter still. The same throats, which less than a couple of months ago had yelled themselves hoarse with praise of Robespierre as second only to the Supreme Being, now shouted execrations on the fallen tyrant.

Terrified for their own lives his enemies had made a superhuman effort to drag him down. It was he or they, his head or theirs. In the pocket of his coat taken off at the club because the night was very hot had been found a list of names to be indicted on the morrow, names of men to be accused, tried, and condemned. They were the names of the most influential men in the National Convention, Tallien's at the head. It was their life or his, and they put forth all their strength, all their terror, and all their eloquence to bring him down. And they succeeded. On the 26th of July the tyrant was indicted for treason against the Republic; on the 27th, he was dragged, wounded and almost dying, to the bar of the accused; on the 28th, at even, he died on the guillotine.

His death was inglorious and sordid, but it marked an epoch. As if by a magic wand the whole aspect of France was changed. Terrorism died in as many days as it had taken years to maintain itself. Within twenty-four hours the Convention, free from tyranny and from fear of death, passed a law that every man or woman indicted for treason and conspiracy must be served with a Writ of Accusation so that they might know of what they were accused. Prisoners were liberated by the hundred. Houses of Detention were emptied. Justice once more put on the semblance of a bandage over the eyes and held the scales with a steady hand.

And while André and Aurore dreamed their dream of love in the sunny apartment of the Quai de la Ferraille, the aspect of France was

changed. Life went on, but no longer the same, for there was hope in every heart, even though hope was often linked with incurable sorrow.

And that is the end of the story which Sir Percy Blakeney, Bart., told to His Royal Highness that evening in the Assembly Rooms at Bath.

"A fine fellow, your André Vallon," His Royal Highness remarked. "What became of him?"

"He was duly served with a Writ of Accusation, brought to the bar, and acquitted. He has taken up his work again with the blind and the deaf and dumb."

"And he and your lovely Aurore spin the thread of perfect love in their apartment on the Quai de la Ferraille, is that it?"

"I should say as perfect as I have ever seen, sir," Blakeney remarked with a smile.

"Outside your own, you lucky dog!" His Royal Highness rejoined with a sigh. "But what happened to that rascal, Hector Talon?"

"He was indicted for false accusations against a patriot. His name appeared below that of Charles de Marigny on the letter, which denounced Vallon to the Committee of Public Safety, which has now ceased to exist. He died a very inglorious death just a week after he had hoped to see his old enemy go up the steps of the guillotine."

"Did the daughter ever recover her father's body for decent burial?"

"I believe so."

"Ah, well!" His Royal Highness concluded. "I'll grant you, Blakeney, that for a child of that awful revolution, your friend Vallon has come out of the flames unscathed."

# THE END

*Also from Benediction Books ...*
**Wandering Between Two Worlds: Essays on Faith and Art**
**Anita Mathias**
Benediction Books, 2007
152 pages
ISBN: 0955373700

Available from www.amazon.com, www.amazon.co.uk

In these wide-ranging lyrical essays, Anita Mathias writes, in lush, lovely prose, of her naughty Catholic childhood in Jamshedpur, India; her large, eccentric family in Mangalore, a sea-coast town converted by the Portuguese in the sixteenth century; her rebellion and atheism as a teenager in her Himalayan boarding school, run by German missionary nuns, St. Mary's Convent, Nainital; and her abrupt religious conversion after which she entered Mother Teresa's convent in Calcutta as a novice. Later rich, elegant essays explore the dualities of her life as a writer, mother, and Christian in the United States-- Domesticity and Art, Writing and Prayer, and the experience of being "an alien and stranger" as an immigrant in America, sensing the need for roots.

**About the Author**

Anita Mathias was born in India, has a B.A. and M.A. in English from Somerville College, Oxford University and an M.A. in Creative Writing from the Ohio State University. Her essays have been published in The Washington Post, The London Magazine, The Virginia Quarterly Review, Commonweal, Notre Dame Magazine, America, The Christian Century, Religion Online, The Southwest Review, Contemporary Literary Criticism, New Letters, The Journal, and two of HarperSanFrancisco's The Best Spiritual Writing anthologies. Her non-fiction has won fellowships from The National Endowment for the Arts; The Minnesota State Arts Board; The Jerome Foundation, The Vermont Studio Center; The Virginia Centre for the Creative Arts, and the First Prize for the Best General Interest Article from the Catholic Press Association of the United States and Canada. Anita has taught Creative Writing at the College of William and Mary, and now lives and writes in Oxford, England.

www.anitamathias.com,
christiancogitations.blogspot.com
wanderingbetweentwoworlds.blogspot.com